Barcelona-
Borinquen

John David Ferrer

ISBN Number: 0692957383

ISBN 13: 9780692957387

Copyright 2017 John David Ferrer

Printed by CreateSpace. a division of Amazon.com

John David Publishing, All Rights Reserved

Ericka

You were my
inspiration to
never give up!
Best,
John Frind
12/11/17

For Ana Luz, my love and lifelong partner

Barcelona-Borinquén

Part One

Chapter One

Barcelona 1871

Antonio Roche woke up with a jolt when the prison guard came to his straw bed, shook him twice and pulled on him.

"Get up you rich bastard, you are free to go," the guard said.

Antonio thought it was part of a dream. "What?"

"The Magistrate signed an order releasing you, get out and bring all your trash."

"Why?"

The man didn't answer and just pushed the cell door wide open.

"The judge was presented with new evidence regarding your conviction and has freed you. Here are your papers. Read the order; it includes some conditions that are part of your release."

Antonio still couldn't believe it. *After all he had gone through, now he was free?*

It had been two years since the wrought iron gate of the Cataluña maximum security prison, Castell de Montjuic, had clanged shut behind him, beginning his ten-year sentence for a crime he hadn't committed. Antonio knew perfectly well why he had been incarcerated.

He came from a wealthy family; he was an anarchist, an anti-Catholic agnostic, and a proud *Catalán* separatist. Even though a descendant of Spanish nobility, he had earned the enmity of a rival family, the Solers, enough for the family patriarch to frame him for the murder of a mounted policeman. The false accusation had ruined his life.

His father, Agustín Roche, always critical of his son's views, had supported the Soler family in this matter, and Antonio had originally been left to rot in Montjuic. During the past two years, his mother was his only visitor, sometimes bringing a note from Penélope, his beloved sister. Antonio cocked his head at the bulky, bald guard, one of his least favorites. *How can this be? My father wouldn't have interceded in my favor; there's no doubt about that. It could only mean that Soler had the sole eyewitness change his testimony.*

"Are you aware of who I am and why I was put here?" Antonio asked. "Did Teodoro Soler intervene with the judge?"

His voice was louder than usual, but he didn't care. The guard's attitude and this unexpected surprise unnerved him.

"Well, yes, *Señor* Roche Rivera," the guard said in a sarcastic tone, "I am aware of who you are. You should be thankful. Just leave before anyone changes their mind."

After going through all the trouble of finding a false eyewitness for a crime I didn't commit, has Soler simply changed his mind? What has provoked this change of heart? It was not an act of pure generosity, someone intervened, but who could it be? Don Teodoro Soler was anything but a truthful man or a Good Samaritan. This must all be a lie.

"The judge decided you were wrongfully convicted. That's all I know." The guard reached into his jacket and retrieved a document. "Your papers. Leave now!" The man raised his voice at the last two words. Antonio's pulse quickened and he started walking to the exit.

Once past the inner gate of the prison, Antonio was uncertain as to his next step. A breeze enveloped him as he walked to the outside wall, and he smelled the freshly cut grass. A glorious scent. *Ah, freedom at last, but for how long?* He looked at the sun and let it bask over his face. He smiled and opened his eyes. *Yes, I'm still in the courtyard, not in my cell.*

At the outer gate, he asked the sentry, "Where can I find a wagon that will take me to the city?"

"Where is your pass, or release document?"

"I don't need a pass; I'm a free man now."

"*Bien*, then show me your documents."

"Here they are," Antonio said. He was nervous; it still might be a bad joke.

"I don't see a magistrate's signature where it would say, 'Release Approved.' "

Antonio's heart sank. "That's not possible, look again."

The sentry was contemptuous of him. "No, *nada*, you are not going anywhere."

Antonio's voice took on a high pitch. "I was informed that I was released upon proper authority this morning. Please ask Hugo, the bald guard, he's inside."

The sentry put his hand on his pistol.

Antonio's left hand fumbled inside his pants pocket.

"*Espera*, I just found this piece of paper, it must have come loose."

Antonio was desperate. His next move would be critical. He couldn't go back inside the prison. Once there, his release would be delayed by prison bureaucrats. He noticed that the sentry wasn't listening, and was about to blow the emergency whistle hanging around his neck.

"Then shoot me right here. I'm not going anywhere," Antonio surprised at his own bravado. He stared at the road beyond the gates.

"That won't be a problem. Give me that sheet." After a pause the sentry said, "I see the signature, you idiot. I almost shot you for being an ass."

"*Gracias a Dios*." Antonio's blood drained to his knees and he almost fainted.

"Now go down that dirt road to the base of this mountain. Here you won't find any wagons. *Saco de mierda!*"

"*Y tu familía tambíen*," Antonio muttered, just out of the sentry's hearing.

Antonio Roche sighed, trying to shake off the weight of his broken spirit, but he knew that couldn't be so easily done. Prison had a way of aging a person's soul. Even though he was only 21, Antonio felt much older. His body hadn't exactly aged, but as he looked down under the bright sunlight- which he had missed for so long- he saw his bony arms and legs, and what was left of his large frame, weak from lack of exercise. On his arms he sported dried red sores and blotches from sleeping on a crude straw mattress.

He looked back at Montjuic Castle, trying to reassure himself that all this was real, not a dream. Verdant trees flanked the light brown fortress walls, which were covered with bright green moss. That had been his prison. Now the walls just stood there, as if he had never been inside them. Forcing himself to look away, Antonio began his trek down the mountain with multiple thoughts. The first one was his immediate future and what might lie beyond. *Will I be treated differently at home? What will my friends think? How could I possibly find work? Going back to the University is unthinkable. Should I leave Barcelona for good?*

If he had felt out of place in Barcelona society before his imprisonment, how would it be now? He really hated no one, except the Solers. His strongest contempt was reserved for those that feigned fidelity to all that was considered proper and appropriate in society. He despised the Catholic Church. He remembered passing churches in the different parts of his former neighborhood that seemed to mock him, and block his access to a better, a more fulfilling life. Educated in their schools, he had grown to hate the priests, the nuns, and their pious morality. They were all hypocrites. His rebelliousness was born in those schools and had only increased with time.

His next thoughts were about the day he had entered Montjuic prison in 1869, and he fingered the gold chain around his neck, the one that fellow prisoners had looked at jealously, but would not dream of stealing, at least not from him. On that chain hung a small gold cross, a gift from his mother. In spite of his feelings, he would not remove it. Antonio regarded it as a family heirloom, more than a symbol of Christ. No one understood that, except Antonio's mother, Manuela Rivera de Roche. He remembered how much his mother had cried the night he was arrested, and nothing he said would comfort her.

As he continued to walk down the mountain road, a horse drawn wagon, carrying trash from the prison warehouse passed him just as he reached the base. He asked the driver for a ride and was told to sit in the back. The stench of the trash almost sickened him.

As the wagon approached the outskirts of the city, Antonio didn't recognize the new buildings that he passed; the older simple structures gradually had given way to more imposing ones as they neared the *Plaza de España,* a centerpiece of Barcelona.

The closer he came to the city center, the more worried he became about his future. The court order he was given said he must leave Barcelona by the beginning of the New Year, but it didn't mention a specific destination. *Should I leave Barcelona and hide in a small village, hoping that no one will recognize me, or should I move south and disappear? I could change my name and melt into the general population of a large city, like Madrid.*

The authorities had previously suggested he leave for the colonies if he was ever released. Going to America might have its possibilities. Some of his father's friends had left Barcelona for the "Indies" and had made their fortune in sugarcane and rum. They had returned to Cataluña very rich.

Antonio had once spoken to a few of them known as *"Indianos"*, and they'd told him of the profits to be had from their investments in Cuba and Puerto Rico. Life was good there.

He could choose that path. Maybe after a prolonged absence, he could return home and his past might be forgotten. With money, he could redeem himself and fight to have his file expunged of his conviction. Of course, being an anarchist and convicted felon narrowed his field of options. Staying in Spain wouldn't be easy. But traveling alone to an unknown land would be daunting. *How could I survive? What work would I do? I have never earned a living before nor did I ever acquire any special set of skills. My university education is incomplete due to my activities outside the school. The conviction and prison time have, in effect, ended my former life.*

His thoughts came to a jarring halt, when the wagon stopped at the location just off *La Rambla de Cataluña,* where the driver would deliver his lot. Antonio thanked him and offered his apologies; he had no money for a tip. He picked up his bundle of clothes and started to walk towards the street which would lead him to his parent's house on *Passieg de Gracia,* one of the main boulevards of Barcelona.

The changes startled him. *All of this in just two years?* With every step it became clearer that the city had undergone quite an architectural renaissance. It was still the same street but totally improved, things were different. Houses had balconies with floors surrounded by huge black wrought iron banisters. Colorful edges had been added to most windows that faced the street. Entrances to these mansions were no longer traditional Catalán; they flourished with new designs and shapes he had never seen before. His mother had told him that a new extension for Barcelona had been planned, the *Eixample,* and it would eventually include the finer homes and businesses of the city.

But some things just couldn't be changed so quickly. Antonio saw a Barcelona still recovering from a rebellion that had lasted years and which had been crushed savagely by General Juan Zapatero, the chief military governor. Many of the businesses, caught in the crossfire of the insurrectionists and the military forces, were in disrepair. Pock holes, traces of bullets, and iron shrapnel remained visible. Elegantly designed windows were broken; paint had faded on the walls of many of the homes and commercial establishments. As Antonio walked to his parent's house, he saw evidence of the past strife. Years ago, he had been one of those demonstrators that had picketed the government for a reform of the labor laws and the working conditions of the factory hands. He had not been detained in the clashes between the police and the strikers, but he had been seen at these demonstrations by those unsympathetic to his politics. In a way, he was just like those buildings forever bearing the consequences of that rebellion.

When he finally arrived at the family home, Antonio contemplated Casa Roche, an imposing three story structure built in the 1840's, renovated in a new style. The house featured iron balconies on all three levels. The façade of granite and pink limestone gave the impression of being more like a castle than a family residence. Large flying buttresses near the roof gave it the appearance of being impenetrable. A heavy black iron gate adorned with black metal flowers made the portal seem more regal. Antonio shook his head at his parent's pomposity remembering where he had spent his last night in prison, on a straw mat on the floor.

He stopped in front of the entrance gate where a servant served as a gatekeeper. He rang the bell and waited. The servant approached and regarded him from head to toe, but did not recognize Antonio.

"What is your business? Please give me your name," the servant said, not looking directly at him and sounding somewhat irritated by the intrusion.

"Sebastían, how soon you have forgotten me." Antonio swallowed hard, unable to hide his disappointment at the servant's indifference. He had always been fond of old Sebastían, and now the man didn't even remember him. He tried to smile even though he knew that his smile was forced, and not reflective of any joy.

The man squinted in the noontime sun cocking his head to one side. "Perdón, who are you?"

"I am the one and only son of Agustín Roche, my dear Sebastían."

"Ohh......, Don Antonio, please forgive me, how could I? I am so stupid, please don't tell your father," he begged, barely able to maintain his composure. Sebastían's face reddened and his hands shook.

Antonio waved him off. "He won't care, do not worry. I don't blame you. All I need right now is a good shave, a bath, and a decent change of clothes. Tell my family that I'm here, por favor."

The man opened the gate to let Antonio in, then scurried off, like a scared rabbit, skipping up the steps that led to the main door. Antonio followed slowly. When he arrived at the entrance to the foyer, he looked at the pale grey marble floor and the interior of what was his former home.

Enormous changes had been made to the first floor. A new coat of paint gave it a brighter color and matching decorations were abundant. He felt, once again, a draining sensation through his body, his legs buckled and he leaned against the wall to steady himself, gripping the back of a nearby chair. He remembered that the last time he had been in the parlor, the night of his arrest.

A few minutes later his mother appeared in the hallway. It took her only seconds to realize what was going on. Bringing her hands to her face, Manuela Rivera dropped the knitting needles she was carrying, along with an unfinished red wool shawl, and ran to Antonio.

She took him in her arms and sobbed, her warmth renewing his strength. She had always doted on him, notwithstanding his father's complaints. Being in her arms again finally gave Antonio a sense of freedom he hadn't felt for what seemed like an eternity. She was his family nucleus, and that embrace was the real welcome home he would never forget.

"When did you get out of prison, *mi bebé*?"

Antonio's eyes had moistened, but he didn't want to cry. He hugged her hard and kissed both her cheeks.

"This morning, very early. A little after sunrise."

She dried her eyes and his with a small handkerchief. "Why didn't you send for someone to pick you up?"

"It happened suddenly, without much notice."

"Well now you are home for good, *Gracias a Dios*." He nodded and kept silent, unable to mention his intention of leaving the country. He would tell her when the time came.

"*Mamá*, I need something to eat, a good bath, and a bed." He put his arms around her shoulders and walked with her to the stairs. She continued to weep.

"You will have all of that and much more, my sweet son. Wait until your father comes home from work, he will be speechless."

That, Antonio realized, was true.

♦ ♦ ♦

In the evening, when Agustín Roche arrived home, he was met at the door by Sebastián, and placed his hat, gloves, and walking cane on the table near the front door. A pungent odor greeted him as he entered the hallway. A small mouse must have died, he surmised. He called out to Manuela to indicate he was home; no one replied. He followed the scent into the drawing room but found nothing. He retraced his steps, this time making a detour to the kitchen. On the floor, a pile of clothes lay and he recognized the source of the smell. *Whose clothes are those? Certainly they do not belong to one of the servants. They would know better. Look at the filth, how could anyone wear that? I must call the help.*

Before he could do anything, his wife appeared in the doorway. "Antonio is home."

Don Agustín was not surprised, word had leaked that his son would be released from prison that week. Still he felt no pleasure at the news, and now that his wife confirmed it, he simply nodded stiffly and walked to his study.

"Will Antonio be joining us for dinner?" he asked.

"I don't know. He's sleeping right now."

At dinnertime, Don Agustín was waiting, seated in his usual chair at the head of the table. Antonio sauntered in. He did not greet his father, except with a nod, nor did he shake his hand.

"Antonio, I see you are back," He had no kind words for his son, nor did he show any joy at seeing him after two years. He offered no apology for not visiting his son in prison, nor was he inclined to do so.

"Yes, father, I was released this morning."

Don Agustín signaled the servants to start serving dinner, in the formal Baroque style dining room, where at its center stood a large mahogany table edged with gold laced trim. Antonio sat at the far end of the table, opposite his father. The help just smiled and said *"Bienvenido, Señor Antonio."*

His father didn't look at him directly, but pretended to concentrate on a portion of lamb served with white fava beans and corn. Antonio had not touched the fish soup that had been served as a first course. He was not hungry and felt awkward faced with such lavish food, as compared to his recent fare. He played with a piece of bread, reenacting his prison manner of breaking it into tiny pieces to make it last longer.

"And what are your plans, now that you are out of jail?" Don Agustín tried to show interest, but conviction was lacking in his tone. Antonio had not even been asked about his health or the reasons for his release. *Plans when I've only been out of jail for 12 hours?*

"It was strongly suggested that I leave Barcelona and go to the colonies, by early next year." He did not address his father; he was looking at his mother.

"Surely you can stay here longer, no?" Manuela asked. Don Agustín didn't like the question, and looked at her quizzically.

"I don't think so, *Mamá.*" He played with the fish soup, stirring it mindlessly.

"By what date do you have to leave?" his father finally said.

"No fixed date, but sometime before the end of February, next year. It's only four more months." He kept stirring the soup hoping to change the subject.

"Well you should begin planning what you are going to do there. Exactly where would you go?" Again, Don Agustín feigned interest.

"I could sail to either Cuba or Puerto Rico. I don't know when those ships sail yet. They left that up to me. But I think I will choose Puerto Rico. *Can't he talk about anything else? I just got home and he is asking when I'm going to leave.*" As he spoke, his spirits improved visualizing the Caribbean and an adventure far away from Barcelona. The distance would be good for him, and a new environment would help erase all memories of his past troubles. It would be good to get away from his father, who had always sided against him in all arguments involving politics or the ruling class. Don Agustín had blamed him for all his troubles with the law, even for his unjust incarceration.

Doña Manuela jumped in. "Is it possible that you can take someone with you, or stay at one of our relative's houses? We have family in Puerto Rico, in Mayaguez, on the west coast."

"I suppose so," Antonio said, not specifying to what he was responding.

"Well, consider yourself lucky, the alternative of you unemployed, staying here with no visible future, would have been embarrassing to the family, much more than it has been already," Don Agustín said, as he pointed at Antonio, his left hand holding a dinner knife, a rude gesture.

"You can find yourself a good occupation there and forget all this nasty business, and given the political situation we are currently facing, it is better for the family, and even for you."

At that point Antonio couldn't hold his tongue any longer. He pushed his dinner plate away and spilled some of the fava beans on the linen tablecloth. His mother reached out and took his hand.

"That's really all you care about. Your place in society, the worthless title inherited by the family and to hell with everyone else. Forget your wife and children." He rose and threw the napkin on the untouched meal. "I did nothing wrong and someday you will cry tears of blood for how you treated me," he said, as he left the table. At the last moment he looked back and said to his father, "You have no idea what I went through those years in that rat hole you call a fort, and you didn't even bother to ask." Don Agustín looked past his son and kept silent.

Antonio realized that his outburst had been a product of his vulnerability which his father would never understand, but he didn't care. As he passed a china cabinet in the hallway, he saw a small etching of a young woman in black and white. At first he thought it was Penélope, his sister, five years his junior and a Catalonian beauty. Antonio recalled her natural gaiety and how she would kick back her head in genuine mirth, when she touched him. But the drawing, he quickly realized, wasn't of her. The etching reflected the face and figure of Paula Soler, the woman at the heart of his problems with the Soler family. He stopped, looked at the drawing closely, tempted to ask his mother why it was there. But he decided not to and went to his room.

* * *

Paula Soler's flaxen hair was unique in her family. Her peacock blue eyes made her special and she used these attributes to her advantage. Her beauty held men in a trance; she had known that since puberty. At her school, the Immaculate Conception Academy located at the end of Avenida Diagonal near the Cathedral of Santa María del Mar, she had embraced the opportunity to meet young men. Her eyes wandered even to the younger priests at the church seminary. She had been brought up in the rarified high society of Barcelona, where her parents, the Solers, held a privileged position and were esteemed by many of the entitled class. But she could care less about social niceties.

She'd met Antonio Roche during a special private function at her home. Seeing him from a distance, in a hallway filled with guests, she had headed into the crowd, made her way to him, and introduced herself. Her hair had been combed straight back in a bun. The white linen dress that she wore enhanced her appearance. As she approached, she had played with a pencil thin black satin choker around her neck.

"*Hola*, Antonio Roche, I'm Paula Soler. My parents are close friends of your parents, but we haven't met before." She noticed that Antonio seemed stunned by her. She'd liked that.

"*Cómo estás?*" Antonio had struggled to find a more suitable greeting. "We have met before. When you were little girl. You may not remember, but----."

"I wouldn't have forgotten a man like you." She had smiled at him and fingered her choker. She was a coquette, loved to be noticed and she created opportunities for it to happen.

"You were a young child." His tone was condescending.

"But I'm a child no more, as you can see." She had relished his discomfort.

"Yes, indeed, you're quite a young lady now. And *muy guapa*."

"*Gracias,* so are you. Could you get me a bit of *Jeréz*?"

"My pleasure," Antonio had said, as he led her to a serving table next to an attendant. She had stared at him while she drank the sherry, and then kept close to him as he walked towards the ballroom. Antonio had hoped to leave this precocious young woman right there. At the entrance of the ballroom he'd tried to excuse himself, however, she had stopped him and said, "Will you promise to dance with me later?" He had nodded his assent.

Something in her manner had struck Antonio. *As attractive as she is, she must be barely 17 and too aggressive for her age.* That was unusual for a young woman of her social class. To him it was tempting, but she was trouble in a dress. Enchanting, but trouble nevertheless.

As the night wore on, he had forgotten his promise to her, and couples were dancing to traditional music. There was a brass and string sextet playing at the rear of the ballroom.

Close to the beginning of the last piece to be performed, Paula had appeared, put her arm in his, and had led him to the dance floor. She had waited for the music to begin and indicated by her position that they should dance. Antonio couldn't refuse her in front of her parents, who had been standing nearby. He'd said, "I'm not familiar with this music and rarely dance at all." But she would have none of that.

As they waltzed, Paula had asked him polite questions about his family. Then she'd paused and looked him in the eyes.

"What kinds of activities fill your day?"

He had looked at her unsure of how to reply to the abrupt question.

"I love to hunt, to fish, and spend time with my friends at the *Club Cataluña*."

He had hoped that would satisfy her curiosity. It didn't.

"I meant, what gives you the most pleasure on a given day?"

The music paused momentarily, and for an encore, the sextet played at a brisker pace. It was an invitation to glide around the dance floor.

Antonio had resumed the conversation, ignoring her previous question.

"I would imagine that you have many suitors visiting you, although you are still very young."

"Not the ones that I'm interested in, and I'm not that young," she had said, fingering the pin on his velvet lapel.

Antonio had twirled her around much faster during the second dance. She'd let her head and body sway to the rhythm of the music and had followed his lead, occasionally glancing at him, but averting a stare. Her smile was fetching and sensuous; her eyes conveyed more meaning than any words could have.

"You are quite stunning," he'd said after a long silence, "But you already know that don't you?" The words had come out blunter than intended. He'd tightened his grip on her waist as he twirled her around. At first she didn't reply. After a pause she'd said, "Of course I do, but it's nice to hear it. However, you don't know anything about me, do you?"

"At your age, how much is there to know?"

"How badly do you want to find out?" She had fixed her eyes on him.

The music stopped suddenly and the question vanished as the last notes played out. She had curtsied slightly and he had returned the gesture, kissing her laced gloved hand. Paula had turned to walk away, and before he could think better of it, he'd called out to her.

"Paula, will I see you again?"

She had paused with a slight smirk on her face. "Oh, you can never tell. I may find some time between the visits of my many suitors." Laughing at her own remark, she had seemed to float to the far side of the room. Her scent had lingered in the air.

◆ ◆ ◆

Antonio noticed changes in his living quarters at home. He had occupied two rooms on the second floor of Casa Roche. The first room had three large windows which illuminated the sitting parlor, a study, and a private toilet. The second one, his bedroom, had no windows. The two walls in the small parlor were decorated with a curved silver scabbard and its sheath on one wall, and a framed painting of his favorite childhood horse, a chestnut colored stallion named *El Fiero*, on the other wall.

A large black armoire was filled with clothes that he had not used for two years. On his desk was a map of the Americas. Pins with miniature

Spanish flags represented the territories of the New Spain. He took a closer look at the sketches of the islands of Cuba and Puerto Rico. He wondered if his father had intentionally put the map on his desk.

Antonio glanced over his collection of personal belongings realizing that many of them would be discarded once he left Barcelona. The trunks that he would take with him would be filled only with his most treasured possessions; none of which were clothes. For a descendant of nobility, he had simple tastes.

Two weeks later, he dressed for dinner for the first time in years. He was prepared to announce the date of his departure from Barcelona. Antonio had secured passage on the Cisneros, a frigate that was the pre-ferred mode of transport to the Caribbean. He had chosen a triple-mast Brigantine Schooner that held 700 passengers and would take six weeks to reach Puerto Rico, after stopping to pick up additional passengers in Cádiz and a final stop in the Canary Islands. The timetable depended on the weather across the Atlantic Ocean in the winter. He arranged his departure for the first months of the New Year, a time during which most storms in the Atlantic Ocean were least likely to occur.

Antonio saw that his father was pleased that he had made a decision quickly since that evening he asked him details about his destination. He knew his father feared that if he delayed his voyage, the authorities might force his departure. That would truly be an embarrassment.

"On what resources will you rely when you arrive in Puerto Rico?" Don Agustín said. Antonio assumed that his father was trying to appear helpful

"All that I possess is in my trunks, and what I carry on my person." He glared at his father knowing that more disconcerting questions would follow.

"What I mean is, do you have money or gold coins to pay for your immediate needs? I can give you funds to book a good cabin that will en-sure your privacy for the entire voyage." The offer seemed, at first glance sincere, but Antonio wasn't convinced.

"I think I can manage with the funds mother gave me. You can save your money for something else. I don't need it, I learned frugality in prison." He forced a smile when he glanced at Penélope, sitting at his left.

"Well anyway, consider this a goodbye gift," his father said, "Spend it wisely."

His father gave a servant a large bag of coins, and pointed towards Antonio, who pushed the bag away when the servant tried to give it to him. Doña Manuela reached around the corner of the table, took the bag and put it on her lap, avoiding an argument between them.

"May I go with you?" Penélope said, startling her parents.

"Absolutely not," her mother said, before Antonio could respond.

"Of course you can. If you can't make it now, maybe in the near future. I will always have a room for my *hermanita querida*. You have a special place in my heart. I love you very much and will always protect and care for you."

He made an effort to control his emotions at this last remark. He had not expressed himself that way in a very long time. He rose, bent over and kissed his sister on the forehead.

The dinner ended quietly and Antonio excused himself from the table. Penélope followed him to his room.

"Antonio, I was serious. Please don't take what I said as humor."

"I was also serious. You can come anytime, once I 've had a chance to settle in and obtain proper living quarters and-----."

"Gracias, *mi amor.*" She kissed him on both cheeks and scampered away without letting him finish. He called her back.

"By the way," he said, "If that is a drawing of Paula Soler in the china cabinet, what is it doing in our house?"

"Doña Sinforosa, had some etchings made of her daughter, and brought us one as a gift. Mother thought it strange, but didn't want to refuse it."

♦ ♦ ♦

Paula 1869

Sinforosa Soler was a highly respected woman in Barcelona society. She had the title of Marquesa, one handed down through many generations of her own family, the Velascos, and was a noble in her own right. That distinction was worn proudly as if the tiara she frequently used were sewn permanently on her black hair. Her movements were deliberate and measured. The proper air of a noble woman was always present in her habit of keeping her distance from people she considered beneath her class. Doña Sinforosa, as she liked to be called, would cross the street if she spotted someone approaching her that she didn't particularly like. Her dresses were made of the finest linen, and many of them included lace decorations in designated areas of the arms and collar, as was the fashion. She preferred the color black, and avoided red, pink, and wine colors considering these to be vulgar; pearl white was her chosen alternate color. Sinforosa believed in the proper conduct of a woman born into society, and had attempted to instill this in Paula, who as a child, had shown a tendency to go her own way.

Paula's manner, while still refined, was earthier, which was evident in her conversations with her male friends. She loved to shock people with her expressions and often succeeded. As she grew older, this effort increased.

"Paula, I have noticed how you behave around men, and I don't like it," Sinforosa said one morning, as Paula was approaching her 17th birthday. "You provoke men as if you don't care about your reputation, and that's dangerous. I have overheard some of your conversations and I couldn't believe my ears."

Paula dreaded these tète a tétes with her mother, but this time she'd had enough.

"I am old enough to know how to act in public; I don't need your advice. You know how I feel about the pretensions of Barcelona society and of your friends. I'm not one of them and by now you should know that. I like men. I'm no longer a child. What's wrong with that? " she said defiantly.

As she spoke, the level of her irritation rose and she was on the verge of crying. She took a deep breath, dabbed her eyes with her lace handkerchief and sat down near her mother, who had approached her and put an arm around her shoulders.

"*Amor,* all I want is for you to be happy. If you get a bad reputation, you won't find a suitable husband and may wind up like your cousin, Teresa," Sinforosa hugged her gently.

"I'm not stupid, Mamá. I know exactly how to control a situation; Teresa lost her will and paid the price by getting pregnant. I'm not her." Sinforosa attempted to calm her daughter.

"I would like you to come with me tomorrow to a store that just opened up near us. It has many new fashionable imports." She massaged Paula's shoulders as she spoke.

◆　◆　◆

One person of special interest to Paula Soler was Father Juan Cervera, a newly frocked priest who had just arrived at her parish church from Andalucía. He was keenly aware that Paula was more than just a recurring penitent, since she included in her confessions details of the erotic dreams she had and then asked for forgiveness and penitence.

Father Cervera was 10 years her senior, but at age 27 his long repressed sexual desires seemed to awake from a deep sleep every time he heard Paula's confessions. He began to skip his assigned day for confessions in order to avoid her. It wasn't enough. Somehow she obtained his new church schedule and changed the day she went to see him. He was a handsome young priest with an air of manliness and a dark olive tan that Paula found attractive, no matter his vocation. His fine features didn't hurt her eyes, she mused.

"Forgive me father for I have sinned," Paula said in the confessional one afternoon. She made the sign of the cross. He had not reacted to her presence on this new day for confessions.

He held on tightly to his rosary and listened to her.

"When was your last time? Without waiting for an answer, Father Cervera continued. "Let us pray first, after that, I will listen to your confession." He clipped his words and rushed through the opening prayer.

"Speak now, my dear."

"It's one thing that I constantly dream about when I'm sleeping. Then I want to reenact the dream with a real man." She was eager to describe it and tried to discern his reaction.

"You don't have to give me details, just tell me what is bothering your soul."

He fingered his collar, it was damp.

"Father, please listen. I dream of men who want to make love to me and I don't resist. I enjoy the pleasure they create in my body, the burning sensation I feel when they kiss and touch me all over. When I awake in the middle of the night, I am wet, and not just because of the heat outside, but due to the fire inside me."

At this juncture, she watched Father Cervera carefully, trying to detect his facial expression through the screened partition, but failed to notice a change in him, except that he was perspiring heavily.

"You should banish all impure thoughts with prayer and seek God's help. Those thoughts are coming from the devil. When you wake up, immediately fall to your knees and pray to God. That will help you, I am sure. Now join me in prayer to ask forgiveness from God for your sinful thoughts." Paula was puzzled, but smiled.

"Father, I have tried to do that before and nothing happened, the dreams returned. You should know, however, that I am pure and still a virgin."

"I didn't ask you that, but it in good that you are saving yourself for marriage to the right man. Now follow me in one last prayer, you must be genuinely remorseful in order to receive absolution, you cannot pretend." She imagined that he was tempted to ask her about her dreams again, but had refrained.

"I will try," Paula promised.

"You should also recite a rosary three times a day, one just before bed. It will push any sinful thoughts out of your head." They prayed for a few minutes and Father Cervera said, "Praise the Lord, for his mercy endures forever."

"*Amén,*" they said, in unison.

These weekly confessions endured, usually held on each Saturday before Sunday Mass. When the young priest met her in church, he would cut their conversations short, citing a need to assist another parishioner, and she was aware that he was avoiding her. He told her that he had asked the Bishop to assign him other chores, and might not be her confessor anymore, however no changes were made to his confession schedule.

♦ ♦ ♦

After a few unsuccessful attempts to see Father Cervera, Paula turned her attention once again to Antonio Roche. She accompanied her mother to Casa Roche on errands or planned visits. Antonio was almost never there during the day, but her timing was successful on a few occasions. One afternoon, she stole herself away from the parlor, asking to go to the powder room as soon as she saw him walk past in the foyer.

"Antonio", she called out, reaching him just as he walked to the stable to retrieve his saddle, and then walked with him to his horse. "I see that you are an accomplished horseman. I would love to ride with you one day if you are not too busy with other matters." She swayed gently from side to side waiting for a response. She had asked him before and had not received a reply. He saddled his horse while barely looking at her.

"Of course, some other time. I have a busy agenda for today. I will first ask your parents for permission."

She realized that he was putting her off, and was surprised when he called on her a week later to set a date for an outing in the country. He had planned a Sunday ride, after church services, and informed her that he had received permission from her parents.

Chapter Two

The
Entanglement-1869

Paula Soler was waiting for Antonio to go riding with him one Sunday. While she waited, she imagined herself happily married, with children, living the good life in the high circles of Barcelona society. A wealthy land-owner or a businessman would be a good catch, one who would travel with her throughout Europe just like her parents had. They had visited most of the continent and had even sailed to Puerto Rico. If she hap-pened to marry an "*Indiano*", so much the better. She was still a virgin, as she had told Father Cervera, but that wouldn't be an obstacle for her to enjoy her youth before the inevitable arranged marriage. This was one virtue no one expected her to tarnish and thereby risk her reputation. Although she wanted to marry well, she would choose her own path to achieve that, not the one her mother had planned. Her opposing desires of hastening her sexual experiences, yet waiting for the proper match in order to marry, seemed incompatible.

She estimated that her chances of establishing a relationship with Antonio Roche were slim, however, she liked flirting with him. She put aside these thoughts temporarily as Antonio arrived. At first, they rode in silence.

"These outings are invigorating, don't you think?" Antonio said, after they had ridden for two hours throughout the surrounding countryside and had returned to the family stables.

"I enjoy the company and the fresh air, yes," she replied. She waited to see if he would help her dismount.

He dismounted, tied his horse to a nearby post, and went to assist her. As she dismounted, she almost fell to the ground, but Antonio caught her. After she was on her feet again he quickly bade her goodbye. She had expected a kiss on both cheeks, instead he chose to kiss her hand. Taken aback with his aloofness, she realized that Antonio's was keeping his distance. She found it curious that he seemed to anticipate her every move. *He is missing an opportunity for romance which could evolve into a love affair. What else can I do to break through to him? It's a challenge I can't resist. I'll have to wait.*

"Will I see you soon?" Paula inquired. It was the same question he had asked her when they first met.

"I suppose so."

"When?"

"As soon as my schedule opens up." Antonio lied, while brushing his horse's mane.

"I'm free next weekend, if you are." Paula knew that it was unfitting to insist on another rendezvous so soon, but she didn't care. She waited for an answer.

Antonio felt tempted by Paula, but he was aware of the risks he would take should he let go of his self-imposed restraint. He had observed that her flirtations with him were the same as with her other suitors. He had tried to act like an older brother, but she didn't respond in a sisterly fashion.

"I will send you a note, as soon as I can find a convenient day for both of us," he added. Antonio had no intention of doing that. He blushed at the outright falsehood, but she left him little choice. His upbringing and sense of propriety overcame any sexual attraction that he had for her. He would not take advantage of the situation. If it had it been any other woman as beautiful as Paula, things might have been different, but he would not succumb to her allure no matter the cost.

◆ ◆ ◆

Paula, notwithstanding the rebuffs of Father Cervera, continued seeing him at church, and repeatedly tried to invite him to her home to meet her parents. Cervera had not accepted any of her entreaties. He ran into her frequently at the *Boqueria* Market on Saturday afternoons, and she would approach and walk beside him telling stories of her childhood. At times he reciprocated, reciting tales of how he had found his religious calling. Father Cervera did not look directly at her manner of dressing, since many of her outfits were low cut to emphasize her figure. The resulting necklines plunged to the lowest socially acceptable level for a young woman of her position. She made sure that her bosoms were tight, well lifted, and amply visible, which made it impossible for men not to notice her.

"Señorita Paula, I see you come to the *La Boquería* almost as much as I do." It was the third Saturday in a row in which Paula and the young priest had met.

"I come here at the same hour as you do, isn't that nice?" She hid her knowledge of his weekend schedule which she'd easily guessed; he was a creature of habit.

"Yes, I suppose it is," he said. She suspected that he had doubts about the coincidences.

"Where are you going after this?" Paula asked.

Before Father Cervera could reply, she added, "I will walk with you a little longer."

She was preparing to again invite him to her home and was curious about whether he would accept.

"I'm just going to return to the Rectory to finish preparing for Mass tomorrow. It's a bit out of your way." She wasn't listening to him and was thinking about how to pick the right words so as not to sound too insistent.

"No, it's not. I'm waiting for you to accept an invitation to meet my parents and have lunch with us." She paused. "Or shall I tell them you are not interested?" *That was it, he cannot refuse. Brilliant!*

"No, please, don't say that. It's not true. I have many responsibilities in the parish and they leave me with little time for leisure. Maybe next week." That was the opening she needed and she pounced on it.

"Then I expect to see you at my parent's house next Friday afternoon, at two o'clock, and will ask my parents to prepare you a sumptuous *comida*." She shook his hand and turned to leave. He looked away, and then reluctantly said,

"*Muy bién.*"

Father Cervera walked back hurriedly to the Rectory with multiple thoughts. *If only I were not a priest. The vows I've taken can never be broken. I have just accepted an invitation that I should have refused. Paula is a temptation I've never encountered before and it's hard to resist. I must pray to the Lord for guidance and that he protect me from a moment of carnal weakness.*

◆ ◆ ◆

Paula was anticipating the luncheon that Friday. She dressed modestly to avoid suspicion. When the priest arrived at the Soler residence at the appointed hour, she escorted him to the drawing room where her parents awaited.

"We are glad to have you here," Don Teodoro said.

"I'm pleased to be invited by your family," Cervera said. They all sat.

"What province in Spain are you from, and what has brought you to our city?'

"I'm from Sevilla in Andalucía. I was offered a good position here to help my career as a priest."

"Do you find Cataluña very different from your home?'

"Yes, it's quite different, yet in many ways it's the same as the rest of Spain. I do find that Catalonians are more outwardly expressive than most Spaniards and almost fearless when they challenge authority." It was a bad choice of words. Paula saw her father stiffen at the remark, but he said nothing.

Paula knew that Don Teodoro seemed puzzled at her insistence that they have lunch with a low ranking clergyman. Her family wasn't really that active in the parish even though they kept close ties to the Bishop. The Solers gave generous grants to him whenever funds were needed for the parish, the schools, or the convent. Her father enjoyed meeting new people from various stations in life and this priest, in particular, was well groomed, educated, and from a good family. *Too bad he is a priest, she mused, he could have made a good husband. He is more handsome than most clergy.*

At the end of the meal, they gathered in the drawing room once again. Don Teodoro and Doña Sinforosa took their leave, as Paula escorted the priest to the front door. As he was about to leave she stopped him and asked when she might go to confession again.

"Didn't you confess last week?" .

"I did, but the dreams keep coming back, only now they are more vivid and last longer." She lowered voice and slowly whispered the last few words.

"I don't know what to say, perhaps the confessions aren't working for you. Maybe you should try something else to rid you of the dreams." Almost immediately, he hesitated. It was a poor choice of words, and she almost giggled.

"Please, listen to me once again, one last time and then tell me what I should do, I beg of you, Father. I can't discuss this with anyone else, not even my mother. I desperately need your help." She sounded exasperated, and the priest softened. *I may come to regret this, yet how can I refuse?*

"Come by next Saturday afternoon, one week from tomorrow, after I have done my rounds, and I will tend to you. Come to the Rectory, not the church."

As she opened the door to let him out, a fierce gust of wind hit them and the door almost knocked the priest down. She lurched forward to hold his arm and help him regain his balance. It was the first time they had ever touched. He recovered his composure but she didn't let go of him until he purposefully took her arm and removed it.

"Are you all right, Father?" He began to perspire.

"I'm fine, thanks for the dinner, now I must go."

Father Cervera suspected that her motives for seeing him again were not for the sake of confession alone. His steel gray eyes pierced her gaze, and he longed to kiss her, as dangerous as the result of that might be. Surely he would go to hell.

◆ ◆ ◆

The following Sunday, Antonio went riding again with Paula. His mother and Doña Sinforosa had suggested this particular outing, both of them thinking that Paula needed to meet more mature men, and forget the young boys with whom she was spending too much time at school. Antonio was a few years older than Paula, however that seemed to them to be enough of an age difference. The two mothers were having tea together one morning, and had come up with the idea. It was a safe arrangement, Antonio was above reproach. Doña Manuela was pleased that Doña Sinforosa trusted her son.

The couple rode for more than three hours. The path they chose took them through a meadow, passing under oak trees that towered over a field filled with golden sunflowers amid wild grass. They could hear the melodies of the different songbirds flying in sweeping circles high above them. The clouds provided a canvass for the birds and gently guided their flight. As they were contemplating the scene, Paula asked him to stop for a moment to rest. She was dismounting and suddenly cried out,

"Díos mío, me caigo." This time she managed to fall directly on Antonio, unlike the last time when she missed him.

His broad arms caught her effortlessly, and as she regained her footing, she raised her head. Her face was a few inches from his and she half expected a kiss. She prepared herself by closing her eyes and staying in his embrace, but Antonio pulled back suddenly after bending forward and almost touching her lips with his.

"Aren't you attracted to me?" Paula asked, her tone reflecting disappointment.

"No, it's not that. You're too young and our families are close friends. I don't want them to think I'm taking advantage of you. If you were older, and not a close family friend, it might be different." She stepped back.

"If you wait for me to grow older, it might be too late," Paula said, irritated and brushing down her skirt with strong strokes. "You think that I am going to wait for you or ask you to wait for me? It doesn't work that way, *querido*."

"I'm sorry, Paula. That's the way it has to be. I have nothing to gain from a passing romance with you. But you have much to lose. I have many women friends which provide me with other pleasures, but you should not try to be one of those. We can be friends, but only friends for now." He also stepped back unsure of her reaction.

"I don't see that much of an age difference between us, but if that's what you want, so be it. You may come to regret it," she said. She was failing to control her embarrassment.

Antonio was surprised at his own willpower in not taking advantage of the situation. With another woman, this wouldn't have been an issue. He was bewildered the way Paula acted. He had rejected her advances and behaved as a true gentleman, yet it had riled her.

When they returned to the Soler stables, she dismounted quickly, gave the reins of her horse to a stable hand, and left Antonio sitting on his horse without saying goodbye. . He vowed never again to see her alone; there would be no more Sunday rides.

Now he felt unsure if he would attend a birthday reception for her the following month; an invitation his family had already accepted.

♦ ♦ ♦

At her 17th birthday party, Paula met Antonio again. The Soler mansion on *Carrer d' Aragó*, a few blocks from the *Passeig de Gracia* Boulevard, was an imposing structure of stone and glass. The walls outside were blue and gray, with three floors flanked by towers which rose like spirals in the surrounding neighborhood. The house, with huge porches and bas relief figures on the outer walls, showcased the purely *modernist* Catalonian architecture that had begun to take hold.

The rooms were carved into large expanses in the house with very few places to meet privately. Even so, Paula had some private retreats where she could go when she needed to be alone. One of these was an alcove at the rear of the kitchen where the closets almost hid the entrance to a tiny room. It had a sliding partition which closed when necessary.

At the height of the party music filled the air and after a few dances with Antonio, who reluctantly agreed to dance with Paula, she asked him to accompany her to the kitchen for some warm *tapas*. She led him into the kitchen and held his hand the entire time. As she reached the open alcove, she entered.

"I think the small plates and silverware are kept here," Paula said. Inside the alcove, she pulled him in, shut the partition quickly and grabbed him by the neck.

"I need you, and tell me you don't want me." She pulled down the bodice of her dress to fully expose her breasts.

"Do you know what you are doing?" Antonio made a feeble attempt to resist, but was engulfed by her fierce passion and succumbed to her kisses. She was suffocating in a bleak landscape, without any water or shade. He was her rescue.

Paula perspired, hungry for him. She kept kissing Antonio, her tongue reaching deep into his throat, while pushing him against the wall. She ripped open his shirt and tried to unfasten his pants, but at that same moment they heard sounds very close to the alcove, and she paused. The wait staff had gathered outside the partition.

"Listen to me Paula, if they catch us, it will ruin your birthday and much more."

"No wait, they will leave any minute," she pleaded. She wouldn't let go of him.

"This is a bad idea," Antonio said, but she wouldn't listen. The fear of being detected engulfed him.

The servants lingered in the kitchen exchanging tidbits of gossip related to the festivities.

"Did you see Paula's dress?" a servant said. "This could be the night when that temptress loses her virginity." The wait staff chuckled.

She heard the remark and it managed to stop her caresses. Antonio buttoned his shirt. She was still in a state of undress, and when the wait staff left the area, she tried to kiss him again. This time he pushed her away.

"This is a mistake," he said. "If we continue, we will both regret what happens next. Don't you realize the results of what you want? I desire you too, but there could be serious consequences."

"But you like me and want me, what is the mistake? Who will ever know, except us?"

"We are not meant for each other, Paula. I don't want to play with your feelings or use you."

"Are you saying, I'm not good enough for you?" She stepped away, holding back tears.

"Listen to me. It's not that. Someday you will make any man proud to be your husband. You are beautiful. Your whole being radiates sensuality, but you want to take a very serious step in a relationship between a man and a woman, without thinking about it. I'm just saying it can't be with me. There can be nothing between us."

"Go to hell!" Paula said, in a menacing voice. "*Cobarde.*" Antonio didn't flinch, although it was the first time a woman had said those words to him.

She tried to slap him, but missed his face and hit his neck.

"What is wrong with you? I am trying to be an honest gentleman, and you insult me?"

She quickly pulled up her garments and turned in one swift motion ready to storm out. But then she faced him.

"If you mention this incident to anyone, I will accuse you of molesting me and making unwanted advances. Don't test me."

Antonio didn't doubt her words. They left him cold. This exchange would not end the matter between them, he feared. After a short time he smoothed over his shirt, walked out of the kitchen, shielded by another group of servants, and left the house through a side door. When he arrived home that evening, as he undressed, he heard the sound of objects falling to the floor from inside his shirt. One was a small pearl button that had decorated Paula's dress, the other a large ivory button from his ripped shirt. He picked them up and put them in a drawer. Souvenirs of a terrible evening.

♦ ♦ ♦

Barcelona had been immersed in strife since the mid 1800's. Laborers at the textile mills worked long days under appalling conditions, earning meager wages. They lived in crude basements with no running water, no heat, and polluted air. The outhouses were nothing more than pits sunk in the ground behind their homes, which required the last users to shovel dirt from a nearby mound and cover their bodily waste. Water was undrinkable and their food was simple, many times stale and always in short supply.

Strikes were common, and after violent clashes with the *Guardia Civil* and the military police, bodies in a decomposing state sometimes lined the streets of the city. General Zapatero, in command of the military, had launched violent reprisals against the striking workers, and barricades filled with wounded or dying men were a common sight on some of the main boulevards of the city.

During one of these strikes in the fall of 1869, Paula visited Father Cervera at the Rectory. It was mid -afternoon of the Saturday they had agreed on. As she rode in her carriage, she observed groups of men gathering stones and bricks and piling them in a heap at the entrance to the *Carrer de la Argentería* where the Rectory was located. Some of the men stopped their chores and gazed at the open carriage and its lovely young occupant. A few even tipped their caps as a courtesy. She smiled at them. They had no quarrel with a young woman of her station though, unbeknownst to them, she was the daughter of one of their hated targets, a textile mill owner.

Her carriage passed another more formidable barricade near her destination, which at first seemed to block her access to the grounds, but a small passage way had been left for pedestrians and small carriages. The barriers had been erected to make difficult a frontal assault by the mounted *Guardia Civil*, since they were reinforced by overturned disabled wagons with metal spikes in the wheels. It seemed an obstacle almost impossible to breach. Unlit torches were piled behind the wagons for easy access in the event of an evening attack. Her carriage passed through without trouble. As it entered the courtyard, she looked back at the scene through the coach's rear window.

One group manning the barricade was composed of many factory workers, all of them anarchists and anti-Catholic Church. The Rectory, however, seemed safe from attack for the moment. The rebels had their hands full with the police, but the scene made her shudder.

Once Paula had a full unobstructed view, she quickly realized that her timing was poor and that leaving the Rectory would be a far more difficult task than entering it. More strikers would assemble as the sun went down and torches would be lit, as she had observed before in other areas of the city. But she had come this far and couldn't very well retreat. She would try to make the visit a short one, even though she felt like canceling it, after all it was a contrived meeting.

"*Chofer*, will you wait for me here? I'll be back soon," she said in a worried tone.

"Of course, *Señorita*, but please don't stay too long, you can see what is going on."

She took her purse and looking back once more, walked quickly through the courtyard on a gray stone path leading to the Rectory's massive front door.

‡ ‡ ‡

33

In another part of town, Antonio was making plans for the night. He was preparing to leave Casa Roche to meet with a group of his friends at the Catalán bar, *Cuatro Vientos*. From there he would proceed to one of the barricades along the *Gran Vía de Cortes Catalanas*. It would be a day to remember, He would do something significant with his life, not just wallow in the cafes with other young faux revolutionaries. His father would disinherit him if he knew what he was up to, and would ask him to leave the family home. His father had no sympathy for the strikers and was convinced that all they wanted was revolution and disorder just for the sake of it, not for any real desire to make a change in the government.

His father stopped him at the entrance to the house.

"Where are you going tonight? It's dark now and you haven't had dinner. I hope it's not to meet those friends of yours, who are nothing but trash."

"You mean not like the boorish friends of your circle of elites? But they can afford to be indifferent to the suffering of the masses, right?"

"Antonio you are paving a path of self-destruction by opposing the Crown and associating with that rabble. It will be your downfall."

"So you would prefer that I have no ideals or convictions, and simply do nothing?" He was trying to cut the conversation short and opened the door to leave.

"I would prefer that you grow up and accept your role in this family."

Antonio's face got red and one of his hands began to tremble. His father had nothing but contempt for his ideals and his lifestyle. He was no real father to him, just a symbolic figurehead.

"I really don't care what you think; I have found a cause that makes my life meaningful." As he finished that statement, as he left he slammed the door shut with such force that two ceramic vases on the inside shelf of the foyer crashed to the floor and smashed into pieces. But a moment of doubt did enter his mind. *Has my cause blinded me to all else? Am I a rebel just to spite my father? How far can I push him? Where will this all end?*

♦ ♦ ♦

As Paula procured Father Cervera through the Bishop's personal secretary, she noticed through the window, that more strikers were arriving at the barricades, some with entire families in tow, as if it were a picnic.

She was fidgeting with her parasol and began regretting having come. Suddenly, Father Cervera appeared and gave her a winning smile and a warm welcome, which put her somewhat at ease. She followed him to his office.

"Father, I almost didn't come and just now was ready to leave. Do you wish to postpone our meeting?"

"Paula, what are you so nervous about? You are safe here, nothing will happen. If you are worried about the strikers, don't be. They have no quarrel with the church. Many of them come to Mass regularly." He spoke loudly in a sign of assurance and opened his arms. She noticed something different in his demeanor.

Paula thought he must not have read the newspapers recently or seen the manifestos that were papered on the walls of buildings and handed out on street corners. She had read the leaflets and now found herself thinking not about the purpose of her visit, but of how she was going to leave. She had lost all interest in the meeting and felt reluctant to discuss her dreams or anything else. Paula had seen dead bodies before on one of the main boulevards, but the bodies had quickly been covered over by the police as she had passed by. Blood had been spattered on a sidewalk and a wall not too far from her home, and on some nights she had heard voices shouting in the street that the *Guardia* was coming. Rifle shots had echoed in the darkness when she was lying still in her bed with the windows open, and then she'd heard the galloping of horses. Strangely enough until now, it hadn't caused her to fear for her safety.

"Father, I think we should postpone this meeting for a more suitable time, I made a mistake in coming today. Perhaps I could return in a few weeks, when the strikes end and-----."

"Nonsense, we can talk now. I have to go to Rome next month to a convocation of the clergy. All the newly ordained priests will get to meet the Pope. It is quite an honor and I cannot predict when I will return. So what do you wish to discuss? *First he had avoided her, now he was quick to agree that she should stay and meet with him. What had changed? Maybe it's his trip to Rome, or because he might not be coming back? Maybe he was attracted to her after all?.*

As he spoke, a shout was heard across the courtyard which had a ripple effect. A warning was being conveyed among the strikers. She approached the window and saw a column of mounted riders near the first barricade at the entrance of the *Plaza de Tetuán*. Shots had been fired and the smoke from rifles and pistols could be seen in the distance. Soon after, gunshots were heard near the second barricade in front of the Rectory. Fires had been lit to scare the horses of the mounted policemen. The horses galloped rapidly down the street and a few cavalry officers, with swords drawn, managed to breach the second barricade.

The battle had begun.

Paula's fears had been realized. Father Cervera and she were trapped inside the Rectory, which had closed its doors and the outside gate. There was no way to leave. She started trembling and rose from her seat to look out the window once more. By then the sun was setting. In the coming gloom, there was no sign that the battle was waning. Paula saw the mounted police and their horses regroup for a second attack.

The infantry approached, but it was repelled by the strikers. She knew they feared the *Guardia* the most. These were immensely cruel and vicious mounted soldiers with their curved front three pointed hats in black and red, bearing the symbol of the Crown. They usually attacked in pairs and were unrelenting, swinging their swords or shooting their pistols, with their horses in full stride. They were known for not giving any quarter or expecting any. She witnessed the second wave from her vantage point and kneeled beneath the window sill to avoid any ricochet gunfire.

Father Cervera rose from his chair and took Paula by the hand to lead her to safety upstairs. At the same moment, an errant musket ball broke through a window shutter, barely missed him, and pierced the wall behind his desk. They scurried up the stairs to the second floor. The sounds of battle continued, Paula cringed every time bricks and rocks were thrown against the Rectory's walls in the inner courtyard.

"Paula, you must stay the night, it's not safe for you to return home now. The doorman told me that your carriage man has left the area, perhaps frightened by the battle." He took her by both arms and looked at her to see if she understood the gravity of the situation.

"But I can't stay here all night; my parents will be worried and will want to know where I have been." Paula was on the verge of tears, she had difficulty mouthing those words as she anticipated what her father would say. There was no longer any brashness in her being.

"I will explain to them what happened, fear not."

Paula didn't know how he would explain this to her parents, and be believed. She found it difficult to swallow, her throat was dry. Trembling invaded her body and perspiration covered her entire face and neck. Once they had reached the rooms of the second floor, Cervera released her hand.

One room had a cot with a down feather filled mattress set against a wall. The other room had a very simply constructed, but more comfortable, wooden four-poster bed. He assured her that no harm would come to her. He left her alone, and closed the door.

After entering the bedroom, she removed a light linen jacket that she had worn with her dress, and loosened her bodice. She saw the room walls painted in a light cream color, with one sole window facing the inner courtyard. It was flanked with rose colored wool curtains pinned back by a bronze colored rope. There were no paintings or decorations except a simple wooden crucifix on the wall across from the bed. Several burning candlesticks shone light from a nearby table. Noticing a wash basin, soap, and a small hand towel, Paula washed and dried her face and neck, hoping to calm her nerves. But nothing could stop her jittering each time the sound of a blast came from the outside. Terrified of what might happen, she stayed away from the window. Then she undressed.

It was almost 1:00 a.m. Cervera had told Paula to try to sleep, saying that surely the next morning would be a better day. At first, she was unable to do so, but then succumbed to her exhaustion. She dozed off close to dawn.

At first morning light, Father Cervera knocked on her door, and not hearing any response opened it, after knocking once more. The candles had burned out and the room was only slightly illuminated by the sunlight. He approached Paula, who seemed sound asleep.

As he was ready to leave, she awakened, and softly called out to him. He approached; Paula rose, reached out and drew him near. He sat down on the bed.

"Father, please do not leave me alone." Her plea was genuine; she was a lost frightened soul, not a seductress.

"I wasn't trying to disturb you, I'm sorry," he said. He fidgeted.

"I was not asleep; I was resting." She looked at him longingly. He turned his face towards the door and tried to rise.

She pulled him nearer and embraced his waist from behind in a tight grip. He was wearing a yellow camisole that fit loosely and was untied at the waist. She removed her own white silk undergarment in one swift movement and sat naked before him.

"Father, please don't pull away, I don't have anyone that I can feel safe with now, except you." She was yearning for a human touch and forgot momentarily who he was.

"This is not right, Paula," he pleaded. "You cannot make me your first man." He attempted to loosen her grasp.

"I don't see you as a priest right now" She removed his frock. Cervera didn't resist.

At that moment, as the priest turned to face her, desire exploded within him and he kissed Paula first on the forehead, then on both cheeks, and finally on the mouth. He hung on to a long wet kiss prolonged by her and made more intense by her response. It held them together. It seemed that, for a moment, they had been carved in marble. He touched her breasts and her thighs and kissed her navel. She put her arms around his neck and drew him down on her. She felt his pent up desire well inside her, an irresistible force had suddenly erupted from his loins. Afterwards, the two of them lay together and drifted into a fitful sleep.

Later that morning, with the sun shining on both of them, they awoke to a new reality.

Paula could not face Cervera at first, and he did not insist, also looking away.

"Father what have we done, I'm sorry, it was me, not you," Paula said.

"I take full responsibility," he said, "I should've resisted temptation, and ------." The entire time Paula could see the look of bewilderment and confusion in his face.

"I will never speak of this, I promise," she said. She hoped he believed her.

"That won't diminish the sin I have committed against the church and against you." He put his face between his hands and cried out in desperation.

She tried to console him, but he pulled back.

"I'll get you a carriage, wait here until I call you." He said this without looking at her.

As he left, she pulled the sheets up to her chin and looked around for her clothes, realization finally dawning on her. *I just made love to a priest. I will be banished from my home, if my parents find out. They will send me away, probably to a convent or worse.*

Father Cervera went downstairs and seeing that the barricade was abandoned, and that no more fighting could be heard, asked his sexton to obtain a carriage to take Paula home.

As she departed, she said, "I'm so sorry Father, maybe someday, somehow you will forgive me."

He made no reply, helping her into the carriage. They did not swear secrecy to each other; both understood the consequences of what had transpired.

The long ride home gave her time to think about how she would face her parents, and what, if anything, she would reveal.

When she arrived home, she entered the reception area just as her mother was coming down the winding staircase still dressed in her bedclothes.

"*Hija mía,* where have you been? We thought you might have been a victim of the riots started by those *bandidos.* Thanks to *la Virgin María* you were not harmed."

"No, I'm fine. I was at the Rectory and stayed inside the entire time with other people trapped there. Once the fighting started, leaving was impossible."

"Is the Bishop safe?" Doña Sinforosa asked.

"I think so, and Father Cervera as well." Her mother had not asked about the priest. Paula realized her slip of the tongue and paused.

"Did you sleep? Have you eaten?"

"No. I would like to go to bed and not have breakfast, please excuse me." She hurried up the stairs forgetting to kiss her mother or ask about her father.

Sinforosa Soler found her daughter's remarks suspicious, especially after she mentioned the priest. She hadn't revealed everything about what had happened, that much was certain. Paula also appeared unfocused, which only meant she was upset at something, or someone, and had avoided looking at her.

She decided to let the matter rest and try to question Paula the next day, before her father arrived from Madrid.

When she finally went to Paula's bedroom the following morning to confront her, she found her daughter weeping in her bed. She approached and sat close by her. Instead of asking her questions about the day before, she remained silent until her daughter regained her composure. Without a word from Doña Sinforosa, Paula blurted her feelings.

"*Mamá*, I did something terrible yesterday. I found myself alone with Father Cervera in the Rectory, where I had to sleep because of the violence in the streets. Without thinking, I seduced him early this morning and we made love. I am ruined and may have also ruined his life. It was entirely my fault, not his."

Doña Sinforosa stunned with disbelief couldn't answer. This was totally out of character for her daughter. She refused to process what she had just heard. Paula's world had come crashing down, as had hers. *What will I do now? What will society think if they find out? Worst of all, what will my husband say? How will he react? Can I keep this matter a secret and if so, for how long? Luckily, if there are no unforeseen consequences, it could be handled.* She took a deep breath to try to compose herself. She simply would not tell her husband and make sure that Paula did the same.

Barely suppressing her rage, she shook her daughter to make sure Paula understood what had happened.

"You have sinned my child, and only God can forgive you. But most important is the fact that you must never tell anyone, not even another priest in confession. If your father ever finds out, he will disinherit you, send you to a convent or ask you to leave Barcelona. No one must ever know."

◆ ◆ ◆

The plan almost worked until Paula, four months later, started showing underneath her garments. By then, even her father, who had suspected something had gone awry, noticed. He had observed his daughter withdrawn, hardly speaking, keeping to herself and rarely leaving her room. Gone was her laughter, her sparkle, and her manner of lighting up a room with her presence. His daughter showed no interest in family affairs and found excuses to skip all social events. She had even stopped visiting her friends.

When Doña Sinforosa finally had no choice but to tell her husband what had happened, he too, was incredulous.

"How could you not say anything to me? Don't you know that she is ruined and we are too?" He was shaking and threw his walking cane half-way across the room, hitting the far wall. He sat down, then stood up and paced the foyer with a slight limp, then sat down again.

"I knew you would react this way, that is why I said nothing,"

"Father Cervera went to Rome for convocation, and was offered an administrative post at the Vatican. His belongings were forwarded to him by a fellow priest; He will not return to Barcelona. For that, we are blessed," Don Teodoro said. His face was deep red, almost purple.

"What do we do now? Dona Sinforosa asked.

"I have to think carefully about our options," he answered. "This is a scandal so huge it could forever stain our family's reputation, and Paula's, needless to say". He walked to a nearby window and stared out at the street. He paced the room nervously and returned to the window.

Can I find a last minute husband for Paula? Maybe I can buy her one. If I send her to a convent, Sinforosa will object, so will Paula, and she won't go quietly. Maybe if Paula were to leave Barcelona, it might be a solution she would agree to without a fight. What will happen to the child, will she give it up for adoption? What if Paula refuses? She is so headstrong, it's a possibility. Our family name and place in society are ruined, no doubt. All the money I possess will never restore our reputation.

♦ ♦ ♦

Without consulting his wife or daughter, he arranged a meeting with Antonio Roche to be held in his office, on the pretext of discussing a business opportunity that had become available in Puerto Rico. Antonio agreed to meet, and had come to Teodoro Soler's office on the *Via Laietana.* The office was on the third floor of an industrial warehouse and was furnished with rustic wood furniture that had seen better days.

Antonio arrived on time. He sat in a bowl shaped leather chair facing Don Teodoro.

"Antonio, I have a business proposition for you since you are the son of one of my best friends." That didn't sound sincere to Antonio, but he listened.

"I have a business partner in Puerto Rico, who along with me, is interested in buying a sugar mill in the town of Arecibo, on the north coast of the island. He needs an office manager who would be in charge of the staff, as well as the books and finances, the latter which he doesn't like doing himself. I thought you might be interested."

"I don't have any business experience. Also, would that mean living in the country, in Arecibo? Where exactly is that?"

"Experience for this job is not necessary. And I believe something could be worked out where you could manage the business from San Juan, if that were your preference. Of course, you would have to make periodic visits to the sugar mill and also hire a reliable local foreman."

Antonio didn't know what to make of this conversation.

"The roads have become better recently, thanks to us Spaniards. Travel to Arecibo can be done in one or two days, at the most. As an additional incentive, I am willing to pay your moving costs, and your passage to Puerto Rico. I can also give you an advance of six months' salary. This is not a gift. You'd earn the salary. I would also buy a home there for you. That would be a wedding gift."

"Excuse me, what did you just say?" Antonio thought he had heard the word "wedding" used.

As Teodoro Soler further explained the offer, Antonio immediately confirmed his previous doubts about the sudden surprise invitation to meet with him, and the generous unsolicited offer. He knew that there must be a condition. It had been too good to believe. Something was not right.

"You must marry my daughter, Paula, and take her with you to the Indies."

Antonio was still incredulous and suppressed his desire to storm out of the office.

"But I hardly even know her, let alone love her."

"Love will come later, I can almost guarantee it. You both like each other very much, I know that. And she's a lovely child." Antonio realized by Soler's tone that offer was sounding better and better, at least to Soler. He was rationalizing the absurdity.

"Does she want this union? Have you asked her?"

The Marqués hesitated before responding.

"She has agreed, and looks forward to being your wife. Paula has a deep affection for you."

Again not sincere, and Antonio knew by now that it was a lie.

Before Antonio could speak, Don Teodoro said, "Antonio, this is a good offer, a chance to leave for the New World and make a name for yourself, something you have failed to do so far."

After a short pause, Soler added, "Take some time and think about it, but I need answer from you before too long. I realize it's a lot to absorb. Please do not discuss this with anyone; including Paula." He looked at Antonio, who tried to mask his feelings of disgust.

'You may go now." Don Teodoro rose and extended his hand.

Antonio left the office speechless and dumbfounded, without shaking hands.

Chapter Three

The Departure

Across town, Antonio Roche was behind another barricade set up by his colleagues of the *Círculo de Anarquistas.* They had joined forces with the striking workers. He tried to sleep during the night wrapped in a coffee colored burlap sheet to protect his body against the cold, but sleep never came. That same night Paula was trapped in the Rectory with Father Cervera.

At dawn, the first mounted charge by the *Guardia Civil* began. One of the horseback riders approached at full speed and leaped over the front barricade, breaching and assaulting the ragtag forces that were defending it. The horse, a white stallion, had managed to jump over the rectangular blocks of packed dry hay placed behind an overturned wagon. The rider was shouting *"Viva la Reina Isabela,"* and had drawn his sword. The front legs of the horse cleared the haystacks, but the left rear leg of the animal got caught in the spokes of a wagon wheel, and as the horse finished his leap to the pavement, it twisted the animal's body into a disjointed shape and stopped it mid air.

The rider couldn't control the animal and the horse fell head first on the pavement with its leg broken and dangling from the wheel. The mounted policeman spun forward and hit the street with a bone crunching thud as his body crumpled at the feet of a group of rebels. The strikers, with long sickle blades and rifles, surrounded the policeman and waited for an opportunity to slay him. Antonio, seeing the developing situation, sprang to his feet, and raced to where the man lay.

"Stop, I will take care of this," he shouted. The strikers backed off.

As he approached, he drew his gun and pointed it to the ground. The men had stepped aside assuming that Antonio was going to finish off the fallen rider. Instead, he bent over and examined the man, who was no longer breathing. He touched the man's head, turned him around and noticed that he had broken his neck in the fall.

"*Está muerto*," he said as he covered the man with his burlap sheet and waved the men away.

Eugenio Ruiz, undercover spy for the Crown, made a habit of infiltrating the meetings of the anarchists and socialists, and attended rallies wearing the right clothes and carrying the red and black banner of the anarchist movement. His distinguishing feature was a scar that ran down the left side of his face, beginning just below his eye and curving outward in a half moon shape, ending just above his mouth. With the scar, his mouth bore an unnatural forced smile that was deceptive, for he was anything but kind and gentle. Once as a child, trying to show how brave he was, he had challenged a wild boar and had lost, thus the scar.

When Antonio rose up from tending to the fallen rider, he noticed Ruiz taking careful notes.   Feigning interest in the fallen guard, he addressed Antonio.

"Excuse me, my fellow comrade, how did this happen?" Corporal Ruiz asked innocently.

Antonio turned around to look directly at Ruiz. He was suspicious.

"I am not really sure; I think the horse caught his hoof on a wheel spoke. Why do you want to know, and who is asking?" Antonio was fingering his revolver tucked in the back of his pants.

"I am just a fellow compatriot sir, Armando Sotomayor. I thought the man had been shot as his horse leaped over the barrier. I report events for our cause." Ruiz smiled and Antonio detected the false note of friendliness.

"No, I don't think that was the cause. There was no shooting at that time," Antonio said.

"Of course, that must be the reason. You did not shoot him, then?"

Antonio didn't answer and watched as the man walked back to his post still scribbling in a notebook. He had seen him before but couldn't recall where. Ruiz's questions confirmed his suspicions, however, Antonio had other business at hand and ignored him.

Corporal Ruiz reported the incident to his superiors the next day and asked for more time to investigate if indeed, the *guardia* had been shot, and who might have done it. He would save the information for his own personal benefit.

◆ ◆ ◆

Antonio spent two weeks thinking about Teodoro Soler's proposition. In it, he saw advantages and disadvantages. He hoped to leave the city someday to seek a better future in another place, anywhere other than Barcelona. He had a few female friends, and assumed that he would eventually marry one of the women he was courting. That option would be lost, if he accepted Don Teodoro's offer. He wasn't privy yet to the reason why he had been offered Paula's hand in marriage, but vowed to find out. Certainly he didn't love her, and whatever she felt towards him was an infatuation, nothing more. Yes, she was beautiful, and full of life, but there must be another reason behind this sudden and unexpected development.

He had decided to reject the offer, and wanted to deliver the news to Don Teodoro in person, but only after speaking to Paula. Under no circumstances would he have accepted the offer without seeing her. He suspected that she was being offered in marriage without her knowledge or consent and wanted to know why. She was not the kind of woman who would readily agree to such an arrangement.

Antonio made an appointment to speak to Don Teodoro; this time he wanted to meet in a café on the *Nou de la Rambla*. He expected the meeting might not go well and wanted to avoid the awkwardness of speaking to Soler in his office surrounded by symbols of his authority and power.

He waited in the café. Soler arrived a short time later.

"*Buenas tardes*, I'm glad you could come, Don Teodoro, please be seated." Antonio nervously pulled out a chair for him.

The Marqués looked at the interior of the cafe to ascertain if the place was to his liking and if there was enough privacy to speak freely. He had a bad feeling about this meeting and felt uncomfortable that it was not held at a place of his own choosing.

"*Hola* Antonio. My, what an interesting choice, I've never been here, but have been told that the food is good. I didn't expect to see you so soon."

"I come here occasionally and it fits the purpose for our meeting." Antonio took his time in broaching the subject. Don Teodoro observed him to see if he could detect his mood.

"How are your parents?" Don Teodoro asked, breaking the lull in conversation.

"Fine, they are looking forward to the summer to escape to Sitges near the ocean." The small talk made Soler uneasy.

"I assume that we can now proceed to the business at hand," Don Teodoro said abruptly, rearranging the silverware on the table, as a waiter would.

"If that is your pleasure then by all means, let's talk," Antonio said. He cleared his throat.

"Have you considered my offer?" He continued to study Antonio for some sign of what was to come.

"Every day for the past two weeks."

The statement made Soler smile.

"I knew that it would interest you, since my daughter is a fine woman."

"Yes, she is. But I have not made my final decision, and there is one condition that must be met, before I do."

Soler had begun to relax and now sat up, not expecting any negotiation of terms.

"What could you possibly want in addition to all that I have offered you?"

"A chance to speak to Paula," Antonio said.

"That's impossible!" Soler moved uneasily in his chair and almost stood up.

"No, it isn't, and without speaking to Paula, the decision you are seeking from me won't come to pass."

"Then forget that I ever spoke with you. This is not a barter."

The Marqués got up to leave just as the *maître'd* arrived with the menus and a wine list. He was contemplating what to do next; he wanted to leave, yet he had to stay. He sat down and his indecision was evident, grasping the cloth napkin, folding it and then returning it to its place.

"If you don't give me the opportunity to speak to her, I can't accept a blind offer of marriage. It would make life impossible for both of us. Is that what you want, to see Paula miserable for the rest of her life?

Soler was pensive. It was a good question.

"While I can't promise you anything, if I speak to her I will consider the offer more seriously than I have so far. Again, no promises. If you don't let me see her, your offer is rejected right here." Antonio added as he started to rise slowly from the table.

Still the Marqués remained silent and did not respond. Then he said, "Let's have lunch and talk some more." He signaled a waiter.

They ordered the meal and Soler pondered his next move. *Should I tell Antonio the truth? I am so ashamed of the situation, and of Paula, that I can't. I don't trust him. I know his politics and his rebelliousness, and can't be sure that he will be able to keep a secret so delicate, regardless of whether he marries Paula or not. The truth might be better coming from Paula than from me, still it's my reputation that's at stake.*

The meal was served and after a short interlude; the café emptied. Antonio had selected the specific time intentionally. Most Catalonians didn't have lunch so early in the day.

Finally, Don Teodoro nodded.

"I will have you meet Paula at home at a convenient time later this week." He was upset that all he had planned had taken such an unusual twist, but was not altogether surprised.

"I would prefer right here, just Paula and me, no chaperones," Antonio said.

"She can't come by herself. That's all I can agree to." There was a finality to his tone.

Antonio recognized that the probability of his accepting the marriage offer was minimal, but he wanted to know the true reasons behind it, and only Paula could tell him.

Three days later, Antonio went to the Soler residence at the appointed hour and a butler escorted him to the drawing room to wait for Paula. He really hadn't prepared for this moment, and had no expectations that the conversation with her would be an easy one. He had no idea how he would ask Paula for the truth behind the marriage proposal.

After a half hour that seemed interminable, Paula appeared in the doorway and greeted Antonio in a soft voice. She seemed to be well, maybe she had added some weight, but she was still ravishing. He rose to greet her, and she put out her hand for him to kiss. They sat five feet from each other in red velvet chairs. She folded her arms on her lap and was silent, totally out of character.

The butler closed the drawing room door and an awkward silence ensued. How different from their last encounter, Antonio mused, when she had groped him in the kitchen alcove.

"I have asked to meet you for a special reason, Paula." He was struggling for the right tone and felt the goose bumps beginning.

"And what is that?" Her ignorance seemed genuine.

"I have thought long and hard about asking for your hand in marriage." He looked away at the wrong moment.

"Why would you do that?"

"I must think of marrying someone at some point in my life. But there is an added element. I plan to leave for the colonies soon after I marry." Antonio realized that he did not sound convincing and kept struggling to find the right words.

"Which one?" Paula asked, not specifying what she was referring to.

"Which woman, do you mean?" Antonio lost his edge.

"No, Antonio, which colony?"

"Oh, I have given thought to Puerto Rico. Would you like that?"

"And are you saying that you are considering me? We haven't even courted, let alone talked about an engagement. Don't you remember how our last meeting ended? Do you even like me?" Her displeasure was evident.

"You are a fine woman, and I have always had feelings for you, Paula." Another lie.

"You are hiding something, Antonio. What has my father offered you?"

A flash of heat hit Antonio with her response. He had avoided the subject of whether she would accept his offer of marriage and now she had broached it suddenly. He paused and wondered how to answer. Enough pretending. He measured his words.

"Paula, it would be wrong not to not tell you the truth. Yes, this is your father's idea, and I told him I would speak to you first, before I made a decision. I wouldn't consider it otherwise." Antonio felt better, but not relieved.

Her face became a rose colored mask. Her eyes moistened and the light in the room reflected a well of tears. He attempted to make it easier for her, using a gentler tone and pulling his chair closer.

"Listen my dear, I have no doubt you would make a good wife, even if love didn't exist at the beginning. If we work at it, time will bring love. It has happened before, look at our parents." It was a bad comparison and the words he chose were not what he meant.

"Yes, look at them. I don't want that type of marriage," Paula said.

She had lost her aggressiveness, and her vulnerability made her even more attractive to him. The tenor of the conversation aborted his previous line of thought. He had come with a mission to ask difficult questions and not to soothe her feelings. Yet he couldn't help but have empathy for her and listened as she struggled with her next words.

"You don't have to do that, Antonio, I'll survive." Gone was the coquette she delighted in playing and the sexual fantasies that she liked to act out for men. Gone was her arrogance and apparent self-confidence. He almost admired her as she held on to her self-esteem. She was crying now.

"Antonio, you are brave, willing to sacrifice yourself for a woman in my state. I must say I never imagined my father would choose you." She tried to wipe away her tears, but they kept coming. "He doesn't even like you. I appreciate that you told me the truth and the real reason why you are here." After a few minutes, she regained her composure. She got up to get a glass of water and then returned to sit closer to him.

He could not feign surprise and blurted out his question.

"What do you mean, 'in my state'?"

"I am pregnant with child from another man who won't, and cannot, marry me." It had finally been said out loud. Antonio detected a tone of liberation, not shame. It was unexpected.

"I didn't know that." He felt empty for words, and looked at the floor.

"Of course, you didn't. Father would never tell you, and if he had, you wouldn't be here." Her confidence was building, she was unafraid.

"How many months have you been with child?"

"Four." She said that proudly.

Antonio was stunned and couldn't say much more. After a few minutes, he rose and told Paula that he would contact her. He kissed her on both cheeks and quickly hugged her before leaving. Her cheeks were still wet.

On the carriage ride home, his thoughts overwhelmed him, many of which made no sense. He had expected a defiant Paula, an aggressive and demanding woman, and yet he had found a young girl floundering in a dilemma from which there was no easy exit. Her father was trying to avoid a scandal, and the only way was to engineer a marriage with him, predicated on the premise that both of them would leave Barcelona.

Antonio had imagined a different reason behind the offer, though he suspected that he was being used, whatever the motive. At first he was angry, but that feeling soon dissipated, and it led him to feel sympathy for Paula and her predicament. *Who could the father be? She didn't have one single suitor; she had many, and led a social life that included various young men who escorted her frequently to society balls and receptions. Was it one of them? How had she made such a blunder?*

♦ ♦ ♦

Paula went back to her room and sat down, thinking about what had just transpired. She remembered her first doctor's visit after she learned that she was pregnant. She didn't believe it at first, but then it had sunk in. She had left the doctor's office and crossed the street to a park nearby. The news that day had been a lead weight on her spirits.

Alone on a wooden bench, she had absentmindedly twirled her parasol letting recent events dominate her being. She had stopped her twirling and stared up at the clear sky and sparkling sun. The sunflowers nearby had bent in her direction, as if beckoning her and signaling that she would survive. She had placed her head in her hands grasping both temples with a tight grip, not wanting to let go. Paula had heard the dissonance of the songbirds in the park. They were echoes of her thoughts. *This will create a scandal for me without doubt. My life is over and I have only myself to blame. I'm a disgrace to the family, a single mother with no husband and no father for my child. I'm paying a steep price for my recklessness and I'm trapped in a deep well with no water that could, at least, end my existence. This is just a dry hole with no way out. What will I do now? Who will ever want me like this? I played with fire and got burned. Badly burned. I loved to manipulate and tease men. I thought it was all a game which I could never lose and now I have paid dearly.*

A week after their meeting, Antonio wrote Paula a letter, delivered by Sebastían, his father's servant. He had given him strict instructions to deliver it in person, and not leave the correspondence with anyone else, no matter whom it might be. If unsuccessful, Sebastían was to return the letter to him. It read:

My dearest Paula:

I hope that this note finds you well and that our meeting last week did not upset you too much. Your honesty is admirable and I respect the way you handled the subject of which we spoke. Any man who marries you will be very fortunate to have you as a wife, don't ever doubt that. You are still very young and beautiful. Motherhood will only enhance your beauty. If there was any way I could help you with your problem, other than having to enter into a prearranged marriage, I would. If we accepted your father's offer, it would only ensure that our union would fail and both of us would be very unhappy.

Puerto Rico is a lonely, primitive island where you will have no family of your own. It would make life unbearable for you and I can't be part of that. You will always be a dear friend and I care very much about you. Please know that this feeling is unconditional, regardless of the paths we each may choose. I truly hope that someday you will find happiness and real love. I'm still your friend and will never forget you.

I leave you with my kindest regards,
Antonio Roche

The day after the letter arrived, Sinforosa Soler knocked on Paula's bedroom door. There was no response. After a few moments, she entered the room calling out her name. She couldn't find her, and as she prepared to leave she noticed an open letter on a small bedside table. It was unsealed and lay open. Sinforosa sat down and read it, not caring that the letter was not addressed to her. She quickly put it down, left the room and went to seek her husband. She found him in the rear patio of the house contemplating the garden.

"Teodoro, I have some bad news."

"My Lord, what could it be now?"

"Antonio rejected your offer to marry our daughter, and apparently knows the real reason you asked."

He started fuming and it was hard for him not to curse out loud. *"Maldita sea!"*

That miserable ingrate, after the generous offer I provided him and this is how he repays me? I will see to it that he never gets a job here in Barcelona, and will do everything within my power to make his life miserable, that anarchist, self-righteous, unreliable unfeeling bastard.

The following day Don Teodoro sent a letter to his contact in Her Majesty's army and requested that Corporal Ruiz, a former employee of his, stop by his office as soon as possible. The officer who received the letter passed it on to Ruiz, who read it and went to the Soler's offices later that week.

Don Teodoro greeted him, and asked him to sit.

"My friend, I need a very special favor of you, and I'm going to go directly to the point. Do you know an Antonio Roche, son of Don Agustín Roche?

"Mi Señor Marqués, I certainly do."

"And have you seen him in any situation that would justify having him arrested? For example, have you ever seen him participating in any of the past riots or strikes?"

"I have and might be able to find something for you, *Marqués,*" Ruiz said.

"Good! What do you have in mind?"

"I'm not sure yet, sir, but it will be costly."

"I don't care how much it costs, it just better be good. I will need solid proof."

"That won't be a problem," said Ruiz. "If that is the case, I think we can make the recent death of a certain *guardia*, at which Roche was present, look like murder and make it stick. I was there, so was he, and I can act as an eyewitness and enhance my testimony, if properly compensated."

Ruiz's cooperation was all Soler needed to make a case against Antonio Roche. Relying on Ruiz' fabricated eyewitness testimony, criminal charges were brought against Antonio for manslaughter. He was arrested shortly thereafter, while protesting his innocence to no avail.

Magistrate Francisco Quijano was the sole trier of fact. Antonio produced witnesses that testified that the policeman's horse had tripped over an overturned wagon wheel and that the rider had died upon impact when he hit the pavement. Corporal Ruiz, on the other hand, testified that Antonio had intentionally shot the horse and then the rider. Ruiz had asked a group of soldiers to attend the trial in a show of support for the fallen man. He also had a fellow soldier corroborate his testimony by paying him well.

Antonio recognized his accuser from the day of the riot, but couldn't imagine who had arranged for Ruiz's testimony. There was no jury, just a prosecutor, and a magistrate who would render a verdict. He had limited access to the attorney that his father, at the insistence of his mother, had hired to represent him. Magistrate Quijano, a political appointee, after only one day of deliberations, found him guilty of manslaughter, and Antonio was sentenced to 10 years of hard labor.

He was imprisoned at Montjuic prison in 1869, and confined to a small cell that had a floor of packed hay, a narrow cot, and a bucket to serve as a toilet. While his surroundings were bleak, they were the best the prison could offer. He was the son of a wealthy businessman in Barcelona, and without his knowledge he had been given special treatment. He could exercise twice a day, and was given better meals. He didn't have to mingle with the rest of the prison population if he chose not to. Antonio spent his idle time writing in his diary, which someday would serve as a reminder of what he had suffered. That would be his guide in life, if and when he ever felt invincible or powerful. He promised himself to reread his diary frequently so that this would never happen.

♦ ♦ ♦

Months later, when faced with Paula's rebelliousness-she had fought her father's actions and threatened to go to the press and expose him with the truth about her illegitimate child- Don Teodoro relented and sent the authorities a sworn statement indicating that there had been a case of mistaken identity and calling for a retrial of Antonio Roche, who was not the person causing the death of the policeman. He had Ruiz, whom he had paid handsomely, recant his testimony as well and accept responsibility for his mistake. In return, Soler extracted a promise from Paula to leave Barcelona soon after her child was born at some secretive location. The setting aside of the verdict took two years to process before Antonio was released.

The Magistrate had prepared an Order for Antonio to be released from prison, and had offered him exile in America in lieu of any further court proceedings naming him as an accomplice. Antonio was an avowed anarchist, so there was no opposition to this new finding, nor did anyone demand a new trial.

◆ ◆ ◆

Antonio's time to leave Barcelona had arrived. It was February 1872. He packed his belongings a few days before and then bid farewell to his friends. He did not visit Paula, but suspected she had been involved in his release from prison. He spoke to Penélope a few days before he left.

"My dear sister, did Paula Soler have anything to do with my release?"

"I believe so," Penélope said. "She forced her father to have his witness recant and make sure that your conviction was reversed and that you be set free."

"How do you know this?" Antonio said, "You never told me anything before today."

"I promised her I wouldn't until it came to pass. She told me that she would insist her father do this before she ever left Barcelona, That's what her father originally wanted, for her to leave with her new born child."

"Penélope, I would very much like to have seen her one last time, but don't want to put her in a difficult situation. Please tell her I appreciate very much what she did for me and will never forget it. I'll write to her from Puerto Rico when I get the chance. Does she know I'm leaving this week?

"I'll find a way to tell her," Penélope said. He kissed his sister goodbye and hugged her for a long time. She did that very thing the next day when she met Paula at a dress shop that they frequented.

His farewell with his mother left tears streaming down their cheeks. He had hoped to avoid that, but he too succumbed to the emotion. He hugged and kissed his mother several times and promised to write and maybe visit her in a few years. The day he left, Don Agustín was nowhere to be seen. It didn't disappoint Antonio.

On that day Antonio arrived at the dock where his vessel, the *Cisneros* was anchored. He looked at the frigate and wondered how he would endure six weeks in a ship that size. Although it had to be better than the prison where he had spent two years. He would find it hard to start over in the New World, but he had to try. The cool salt scented air, mingled with the briny odor of the freshly caught fish lying on a plank at his feet, ended his daydreaming. He walked slowly to the boarding area at the dock and took one last look around to see if anyone had come to see him off. Ready to embark on a new adventure in an unknown land, he took a deep breath. He had only second hand knowledge of his destination, mostly from the stories of men who had been there and returned. He'd heard the tales of slavery in Puerto Rico, the possible abolishment of the same, and of the extreme poverty of its inhabitants. But the success stories of the "*Indianos*" gave him hope. It was an opportunity to be part of something new, something different.

As he was about to board the ship, he heard someone shout his name. He turned in the direction of the voice, and noticed that a carriage had just pulled up behind him. As he waited for the carriage door to open, he tried to guess who it might be. *Perhaps Penélope, with a last minute message?*

His eyes widened as Paula descended from the carriage. She looked more mature than the last time he saw her, so long ago, and even lovelier. She seemed more self-confident in the way she approached, than when he last saw her. She walked with her posture erect and proud, not like the woman he had left crying that day. He had often thought of her and her child during his time in prison.

"I heard that you were leaving for America," Paula said. Her eyes sparkled and she had an air of contentment. Her smile was engaging.

"Yes, I leave today." He looked at her and for the first time realized how much he really cared about her; it was much more than a passing friendship.

"I wanted to see you one more time, to tell you something you may not know."

"What is it?"

"I hope that you won't hate me for what my father put you through. I didn't know what he had done. He secured false testimony against you even though you were innocent," she said.

"I do not hate you at all, on the contrary. And what he did makes no difference now, the damage is done. I always assumed that you had helped with my release."

"I told my father that if he didn't go to the authorities and make things right, I would go to the press about my illegitimate child and later to the magistrate about the false testimony. It took him a weeks to realize that I was serious. I'm sorry it took so long to have you released."

"It doesn't matter. The important thing is that I am now free. I will never forget what you did. *Muchísimas Gracias.*"

"No, you don't have to thank me; it was my mess and my mistake. Please, can I do anything to help undo the damage?"

"You have done enough, please know that. I will start a new life and find work in San Juan. There are new industries and many companies are seeking help." He tried to disguise his uncertainty.

"And if you can't find work?"

"That won't happen, it's the only real choice I have, so I must take it. I don't expect to come back."

He didn't mean to have the last words sound so harsh.

"Will you write to me? Send your letters through your sister; we have become friends."

"Do you really want me to write?" He was surprised.

"Very much so."

Antonio was about to say goodbye, when she walked up to him, kissed him on both cheeks and embraced him. He hugged, but didn't kiss her.

"*Perdóname y buen viaje*, Antonio. God be with you."

"*Adiós*, Paula. Perhaps someday we will meet again in better circumstances. I hope your child is well"

"He is, and his name is Carlos."

Antonio turned and took one last look at the city, and at Paula. He grabbed the banister of the gangway, turned back to wave goodbye, and then boarded the ship which would take him to America.

◆ ◆ ◆

The *Cisneros* left the Barcelona port as scheduled, and headed into the Mediterranean Sea, then took a southward course bordering the East coast of the Iberian Peninsula. The first stop of the voyage to America would be Cádiz.

The first nights aboard the ship, with its constant swaying, made sleep difficult for Antonio. His surroundings did nothing to make him feel more comfortable. Despite his objections, his father had secured him a small cabin next to the Captain's quarters. The man was a distant relative of his mother. At first, Antonio had tried to change his accommodations, but was unable to do so.

Eventually, the soft rocking motion of the ship helped him sleep, notwithstanding the cacophony of unfamiliar sounds that the vessel made as it plowed through the high seas. One night, he awoke, caught in the fleeting memories of a dream.

Paula had come alive and was with him, not 1200 kilometers away. He could smell her presence, he could touch her with his eyes, she was right there. The slightly transparent white linen gown she wore swayed in unison with the ship's movements. Her naked body was visible underneath. She became a nymph in the dream and he felt a stirring in his pants. She appeared much thinner than he remembered her, her hair shorter, a lighter color, and combed differently. That was the first of a series of nighttime visions. Each night Paula came back to him, relating her own narrative as she appeared in his sleep. He often sat up with a jolt, unaware of where he was. *Where is Paula? Why is she in my dreams?*

He couldn't forget those visions for days, sometimes hoping they would continue, even though they meant little. He didn't think loved Paula, but her image, stored in the locker of his mind, did not fade with the reality of the next morning.

Perhaps it was the days on end with little to do. He had brought some books and old pamphlets, but got tired of rereading them during the long voyage. Occasionally, he shared a meal with the Captain and his crew, but usually preferred to dine alone. For now, he did not want to be noticed. At night he would write in his diary.

The *Cisneros* docked in Cádiz before commencing the remainder of the voyage, and he spent two days ashore while the ship readied itself for the transatlantic trip to America. Antonio bought more books, and ate most of his meals off the ship.

He had disembarked at the *Reina Victoria* dock and had walked thru the *Puerta del Mar*, following pedestrian traffic and hoping he would not get lost trying to retrace his steps back to the ship. He had visited the *Plaza de Abastos* in the city, where supplies such as cheeses, hams, olives, and olive oil, were stored ready to be shipped to the colonies.

Antonio traversed the *Calle Ancha* looking for a tavern with good food and entertainment. He found one named *La Tasca Marinera*.

In the bar, he met a woman who was a regular customer, and for two nights he spent the wee hours of the morning in her bed, before returning to the ship. It happened to be his first sexual encounter since before prison, but it still didn't help erase his dreams of Paula. He couldn't stop thinking of her, even though they hadn't had any lasting sexual experiences. In his mind fueled by those dreams, Paula had been his lover all along.

♦ ♦ ♦

Antonio arrived in San Juan at the beginning of April 1872, with no contacts to help him establish himself on the island. He found a small *pensión* near the Cathedral, off *Caleta de las Monjas,* as temporary lodging, and settled in for the duration. In spite of his revolutionary zeal, he found San Juan a bit primitive, and not very well maintained. He didn't mind his city surroundings or his room at the inn, but would have preferred a nicer location.

His first foray, after three days of getting used to dry land again, was to walk the city perimeter, and see if he could find a job. At first he found nothing, but two weeks later he saw a sign in a window of a restaurant, *La Taberna Española,* which was seeking waiters. He looked in the entrance and it seemed to be a fine dining establishment; the waiters all wore dinner jackets with black bowties and the tables were covered with white linen tablecloths. Antonio didn't have the spare money to buy the outfit required for a waiter, so he didn't interview for that job, but accepted a position in the kitchen as a busboy and dishwasher.

He lasted only three months in the restaurant and left after a heated argument with the chef. He had no love for the task of washing dishes, and collecting and disposing trash. Antonio had earned enough money, however, to buy a tropical cotton suit that he could use later in another occupation.

As luck would have it, he found another restaurant, *La Cueva de Andalucía*, which was seeking a wine steward. Antonio knew something about wines, especially Spanish wines, and thought the position might be a good fit. He had no training in the art of fine wines, but knew enough to get past the interview and be hired. He was required to use a business suit for work. While he thought that his position would be a temporary one, he wanted to get as much experience as necessary in the restaurant business in case he was unable to find other employment better suited to him

One year later he finally met the owner's oldest daughter, Rita Toledo. He'd seen her come and go at the restaurant. She was a tiny thin boned woman with long dark brown hair that clung to her face and neck. She wore some makeup, perfectly applied, but didn't need much of it. A fetching manner and a delicate tone in her voice made her uniquely feminine and attractive. Rita didn't flirt, and spoke to Antonio only when necessary. Usually it occurred when she helped her father in chores related to his restaurant business, since all the wine purchases had to be approved by Antonio. He liked her demeanor and looked forward to her visits. Her interactions with him were a plus to his daily duties and he wanted to get to know her. Antonio hadn't felt an attraction to a woman, as strong as this, since his days in Barcelona. He welcomed the feeling.

Antonio stopped Rita one afternoon as she was about to leave the eatery, and asked if he might speak to her in private.

"Rita, I would like to know if you might be interested in going out with me someday, not to a restaurant, but to the beach on the coast near *Loíza,* which is one of the most beautiful on the island." He was absorbed by her dark brown eyes.

"I didn't think you would be interested in going out with me. I might like that, but would have to ask my father. Remember you are his employee, which might be a problem."

"I will ask him first, don't worry. If he objects, then no harm done." She smiled at his last remark and then left the restaurant. Antonio kept his promise and asked Don Alberto Toledo for permission to see his daughter. To his surprise, the man consented to the outing, as long as a chaperone was present.

The first date with her went well, and that led to a second and third date before Rita and Antonio became serious. There was talk of an engagement in the not too distant future, and just about that same time Antonio found work more to his liking, office work. He had helped his father, as a teenager, working at Don Agustín's offices and the chores were more familiar to him

He had been in San Juan for three years before he had the courage to apply for a position in an office that managed a sugar mill in Arecibo. The opening was for a clerk, with a promise of advancement. The sugar mill was up for sale and the incoming partners wanted new management and staff, so Antonio's timing was good. The new company would be named Aboy and Hnos. He didn't know who the new partners were, and didn't really care. The decision to hire him took two months, but he waited patiently, and it happened.

On the day he was advised to report to work, on the spur of the moment, Antonio proposed to Rita. He later took her to dinner at the same Spanish dining establishment, where he had washed dishes in his first job. Her mother and father joined them for the celebration. The wait staff looked bewildered to see Antonio so elegantly dressed, but received them graciously and gave him a bottle of fine wine as a courtesy. Antonio was wearing his new suit to symbolize a change to his lackluster beginning on the island. They were married three months later in a simple ceremony and honeymooned in the mountains near Luquillo, the rain forest of *El Yunque*.

◆ ◆ ◆

A cholera epidemic struck the island in the winter of 1876, and despite precautions taken by the residents of San Juan, the epidemic contaminated certain water sources in the old city, one of which belonged to Rita's friends who she often visited. During her last visit to that family, she drank the contaminated water and became gravely sick two days later. Antonio rushed her to the local hospital, but despite the brave efforts of the physicians, she succumbed to the illness at the age of 21.

Antonio spoke to the only good friend he had in the city, Roberto Morales, a worker he met at his first job. A week had passed since the funeral. He was beside himself and could hardly concentrate on anything besides Rita. They had been happy together and had even planned to have children given the chance. There were never serious arguments between them, and they both loved to go on trips to the interior of the island. Gaiety had returned to his life.

"I came to the island to seek a new life and to find a good job. I finally found one and then married my dear Rita. After getting some order and peace, I lose her. What have I done wrong to deserve this? It never stops." His hands covered his face and he sobbed.

"Nothing Antonio, you could have not prevented her death, don't be so hard on yourself. You spent two happy years with her. Treasure those memories, they are all you have left," Roberto said, as he put his arm around Antonio.

The next day Antonio asked for a leave of absence from his job, and even though he had been working there less than a year, it was approved and he booked passage to Spain, hoping that returning home would restore his spirits.

◆ ◆ ◆

While the trip back to Spain was less demanding on Antonio than his departure, it had been five years since he left Barcelona and he had no expectations that it would be a trouble- free visit. The ship taking him back, the *Alfonso XXII* was faster than the *Cisneros,* and the accommodations were an improvement, but it still was a long ocean voyage and by no means was bad weather avoidable. He arrived home planning to stay two months at most, but was prepared for a shorter stay depending on his family's situation.

"Antonio *querido,* it's so nice to have you back," his mother said, surprised and elated when she first greeted him. "How long will you stay?"

"I planned this visit for one month, mother, maybe more." He hesitated to mention the real length of his stay.

"Penélope will faint when sees you. Do you know she's engaged to be married, ------- finally?"

The last word produced a quizzical look in Antonio. *Finally? That doesn't sound good.*

"I did not, the last time she wrote to me she didn't mention it."

"Well it's true, and we are all so happy. He's from a good family." *Of course he is,* mused Antonio.

"Where is she? And where is father?"

If we had known, you gave no notice; we all would have been here. Penélope is touring Europe with her fiancée's family, and your father is away on business. He may return before you leave."

Antonio sat with his mother and explained the reason for his visit and the loss of Rita. He noticed that she was upset that he had never informed her of his marriage. He asked her to forgive him.

"In a certain way, I'm glad I'm here alone with you, it will make my stay less difficult."

"Don't say that, my son. In any event, you can do as you please. You have to grieve and only you will know when it's time to move on. I forgive you for not telling me about Rita"

"*Gracias, mama.*"

Antonio spent exactly 45 days in Barcelona, and never saw his father. He managed to share his entire stay with his mother, and the last week with his sister, sometimes talking to Penélope into the wee hours of the morning.

He had asked Penélope about Paula but did not try to meet with her. His sister told him that Paula now had a little boy named Carlos. Before he left, Antonio sent Paula a note with his deepest regards to her and her son.

He set sail for San Juan, again with no regrets about leaving Spain.

Chapter Four

The Indianos

The village of Tossa del Mar was lined with small shops and houses whose red tile terracotta roofs and stark white walls were similar to those found in the Andalucian province. The town, 52 miles north of Barcelona on the Costa Brava, was a sleepy town with a sweeping beach front that hugged the peacock blue waters of the coastline. It was marked on its far shore by of a former Roman villa, the *Vila Vella*. The medieval steps from the old upper part of town descended to the *Plaza del Pintor Villalonga*, an area where artisans sold their wares. The Plaza also served as a social gathering spot for the townsfolk.

On a bench in the plaza sat Félix Prats contemplating the future. Young, ambitious, and restless, he was a distant relative of Juan Prim Prats, a famous businessman who had served as a Spanish soldier in Puerto Rico in the 1850's. Félix had never met Prats, but his mother, who had, told him stories about the man. Those stories were laced with Prat's commercial successes after he had left military service and returned from the colonies a wealthy man.

"Félix, look at your relative, he became rich in America," his mother would say. "You should think about going there and not wasting your youth here."

He usually waved her off. "Mamá, I don't know anyone there. It's too far from all that is familiar to me to give it serious thought." But he had. The more he thought, the more he was convinced that he had no future in Tossa del Mar.

Many friends of his, former soldiers who had returned from the military, all came with similar fascinating tales. They had been in Puerto Rico and Cuba, and Félix wanted to follow in their footsteps. Still in his mid-twenties, he had a part time job selling dry goods in a local merchant's store in Tossa del Mar, but the job wasn't satisfying in the least.

Félix had been born out of wedlock to Ramona Prats, and she had put her maiden name on his birth certificate, not the one of his natural father. This didn't bother Félix, he felt no loyalty to him and planned to change his surname anyway, to something that reflected much more distinction than a father with which he had no ties. Being a sales clerk was beneath him, and due to the accident of birth, society would never welcome him without some recognition, like a title of nobility. He planned to acquire one by any means necessary, and even if the title was of a lesser rank, it should be enough to give him respect. He would make this change when he left Spain to begin a new life.

Félix was very light skinned with prematurely gray hair. His nose was the only discomforting feature, large, red and bulbous. But people liked him as soon as they met him, and this helped with his assigned chores at his work.

"I think you are right about me leaving Spain," he said a few days later to his mother, with whom he shared a cottage. "My only regret would be leaving you alone here. I could send for you once I have established myself, so you need not worry."

"How do you expect me to survive a long ocean voyage with my arthritic knees and back? It's hard for me to move around the house, let alone spend many weeks at sea," his mother said.

"It won't be a problem, Mamá; they are trying to make voyages to the Caribbean more comfortable and faster." He exaggerated the point to ease her worries. The more he gave his plans thought, the closer he was to taking the leap. He counted his savings and asked the owner of the dry goods store for a leave of absence. He didn't specify how long he would be gone. He planned to leave Tossa, via Barcelona, on a ship that was set to sail in one month.

Félix booked passage on the *Regina*, in September 1877, a new two mast ocean vessel that was making the journey to Puerto Rico. It carried fewer passengers than other ships, thus it was a faster voyage, reducing the travel time to the Caribbean by two days. On the passenger list, he registered his name as Félix Raphael Hidalgo. It was an aristocratic sounding last name that let him pretend he had a noble bloodline. If asked, he would say that the title was inherited from his ancestors, but did not come with a fortune.

At the last minute, Félix had a local artisan create a fake heraldic coat of arms with an obscure pattern on a skin colored parchment, which he framed along with an imitation certificate of authenticity. It had been an expensive purchase, but it looked genuine. Félix bought the artisan's silence by paying him an additional fee. The funds to purchase this title had come from a purse accidentally left behind by a customer in the dry goods store. Félix had taken the purse with him on his last day of work, not fearing any consequences since he was leaving Spain. It was his first theft.

Félix had a good friend in Tossa that had once worked in the same dry goods store. Vicente Ferrer had met Félix when they were both 14 years old. Vicente came from a poor family that could not afford to let him study beyond age 16, so his parents dismissed his tutor, a *preceptor*, and made him find work. He found a job where Félix was employed, but did not remain there for long. He had cultivated a distaste at having to be polite to strangers just because they were customers. He also had an uncontrollable temper at times, once cursing at a woman who had changed her mind six times about the right cloth to buy for a new dress. He had thrown a bundle of cloth at her and as a result had been terminated.

After that incident, Vicente found work as an apprentice mailman for the village. He was good with numbers and remembered building locations in an uncanny manner. He habitually saved a few *pesetas* to meet with Félix. They would go to the village fairs held during the year where the main topic of their discussions was their future. Vicente loved the

outdoors, the farms where he had grown up, and he thrived when la-
boring in the fields close to nature. Traveling to another country, a more
primitive country, was his dream. He wanted to start his own farm and
be his own boss. Like Félix, he longed to change his life, even if it meant
leaving behind all that he cherished. At one of these meetings weeks later,
he encountered Félix and was surprised at his friend's news.

"I have come to the conclusion that I should leave Tossa and go to
America," Félix said. "I hope to become rich. But if I don't, what do I have
to lose? Are you interested in joining me on the voyage to start a new future?" The question caught Vicente off guard.

"I haven't given it much thought lately, but I'm open to the idea."

"I have already booked passage, so make your decision soon."

In this manner and by discussing his plans in detail, Félix convinced
him that they both should leave Spain. Vicente booked passage on the
same ship, departing the same day for the Indies. He made arrangements
to share a berth with Félix in second class accommodations, rather than
traveling in steerage and sleeping in the hull with the other passengers.
The only fare cheaper than steerage was sleeping on deck where they
would have to brave the elements. The day before they left, they bid farewell to their families, not knowing if they would ever see them again. The
crossing of the Atlantic was expected to be uneventful, but it was that time
of the year when a hurricane could ruin their voyage, so they were alert to
any stories from other experienced passengers about storm crossings.

Once on board, they spoke to each other in *Catalán,* not wanting
strangers to understand their conversations. Most of the passengers
were Spaniards from other provinces, some were Portuguese, so they
did not understand the friends' language of choice.

As the ship crossed the tempestuous Atlantic, the waves became rougher. During their passage several gales hit the ship with all their fury. Other
than seasickness, no lamentable injuries were sustained by either one.
By most standards, the crossing was not too difficult. The food on the
ship, however, was inedible. Many other passengers had brought some

of their own foodstuffs, but not nearly enough supplies to last the entire voyage without spoiling. Thus for many, the only choice was the food on the vessel.

Vicente had a good rapport with Félix, even though they did not share the same perspectives on life. He was content with his childhood and upbringing, while Félix harbored resentments toward people he didn't even know, especially the wealthy. Notwithstanding this, Vicente heard Félix say that he wanted to be part of that same despised class; the rich had it all, plus the freedom to do whatever they desired. That was the power that money provided. Vicente listened to him silently, he didn't care much about money.

Even in their physiques they were different. Vicente was tall, with strawberry blond hair and hazel eyes that made him look like an Irishman. Félix was rather short, with his face dominating his body disproportionately. People quickly noticed his nose.

One evening, Vicente and Félix, were alone on the deck.

"Félix, what do you suppose we will find over there?" He didn't expect a quick answer, since the question was rhetorical, but Félix gave him one.

"It is quite primitive, they had their own Indians once, the *Taínos*, but they are long gone. I think they may still have slaves, I'm not sure. I suppose we will see a town, unlike Tossa, but which will grow into a large city someday. We can be part of that future if we work hard, and not succumb to the challenges and difficulties we will face. It certainly isn't *España*, and in many ways I'm glad."

"I hope it's as different as any place can be from Spain. I've heard that it's largely unspoiled and thinly populated." Vicente spoke of his dreams of farming land far from the bustle of any city.

"You know Vicente, our paths may take different directions, but I hope we will always be friends. I trust you; that is the reason why I wanted you to come with me. Keep your wits and whatever happens, you will be fine." Vicente turned away from the banister and looked at Félix. He put his hand on his shoulder. "I trust you as well, and know that we will always be the best of friends."

At that same moment, a young woman approached the deck near them and started heaving violently, with so much force that she could hardly remain on her feet. Félix and Vicente looked at her, and when it seemed that she was about to fall on the deck, Félix rushed over to steady her. He held her up against the railing and then walked her slowly to a bench, where she sat down. Her dress was covered with vomit, and she was embarrassed, but thanked him for assisting her.

"*Gracias, señor.* You didn't have to do that."

"My name is Natalia Díaz from San Juan. I'm *Puertorriqueña*, born there of Spanish parents. I'm returning home after visiting relatives in Valencia."

"And I'm Félix Raphael Hidalgo, of Tossa del Mar, on the Costa Brava. I go by my first name, Félix."

" Hidalgo eh? Are you of noble birth?"

"I suppose so," he answered, and made a feigned attempt to kiss her hand, but upon smelling the vomit on her dress, backed away. He tried to hide his disgust.

She laughed. "Don't worry; I know I look awful and smell even worse."

The way in which she said it, in a self-deprecating manner, made her more charming to Félix, even in her distress.

During the remaining weeks of the voyage, Félix started looking for Natalia as part of his daily routine. He enjoyed their conversations and even though she spoke with a lisp, he didn't mind. Her long brown tresses, creamy skin, and hazel eyes suggested a descendant from a good family, which made her even more interesting.

Natalia was shy and delicate, but possessed the air of a self-confident woman, one who might someday effectively manage a family and raise disciplined children. He didn't know her status, but it seemed strange to him that a woman of her age would be traveling alone. She wasn't. Her aunt, Minerva Díaz, was returning to the island with her.

"What do you plan to do when you arrive in Puerto Rico, *Señor* Hidalgo?" Natalia inquired.

"I hope to find work in any food export and import business that there might be, especially between Spain and Puerto Rico."

"Where on the island will you look?"

"In San Juan, at first. Later, I may start my own business and expand to the island's interior if all goes well. Do you have an occupation?"

"I'm a seamstress for part of the week, but do have plans to become a teacher, if the right opportunity presents itself. I have been studying with a tutor." He wondered how she could teach with her noticeable lisp.

"Are you spoken for?" Félix was smitten, now that he realized she was not beyond reach, thus he sought an answer. It was a rude question.

"*Sí y no.*" The answer was intentionally ambiguous.

"What does that mean?"

"I have a gentleman that calls on me from time to time, but he has not asked for my hand in marriage yet. Why do you ask?"

"Do you plan to marry him?" Félix ignored her, and had asked another impertinent question. He paced the deck as he waited for her to respond.

"It depends on many things," she replied. She stood up, waved good-bye and walked away.

"I hope to see you soon, please get well," he said in a loud voice so she could hear him. He was disappointed that his questions had startled her, but planned on getting to know her better. *Maybe she was an impossible catch, on the verge of getting married.*

Vicente and Félix made few friends on the passage to San Juan, but were amiable whenever the occasion called for it. Félix had made a wise choice in booking better sleeping quarters. "Quarters" was perhaps too fancy a word for where they slept, he thought, since there were no doors or portholes to view the ocean. The berth was a series of canvas partitions and a narrow sleeping hammock for each of them. Located in the second level below deck, where the movements of the Brigantine were less severe than in the hold of the ship. The sleeping berths came with a rudimentary wash bowl for passengers to wash their hands and faces, but no toilet. For their other necessities they had ugly brown wooden buckets with metal handles. The stench they generated was intolerable. When Vicente got sick, he would go above deck rather than use the buckets. Those contraptions only made him feel worse. Félix himself fell sick on many days of the voyage, but fortunately good weather occasionally provided a respite from the choppy seas, once the ocean storms had passed.

Most of the passengers kept to themselves, but in the evenings- below deck -men drank fortified wine and played games of chance to pass the time. Women didn't participate in these games, so Félix and Vicente went to the main deck to breathe fresh air and spend as much time as they could in female company. Félix sought to be alone with Natalia, as often as he could. He was then able to discuss subjects that might prove awkward in mixed company.

"*Señor* Hidalgo, do you have someone waiting for you once you arrive in San Juan?" Natalia asked. It was her turn to be inquisitive.

"Please address me as Félix. No, I'm single, and plan to stay single for now. As for my other plans I will tell you, but only if you describe what the island life is like, where you live, and your impressions of San Juan. I hope to set up a business that will benefit everyone, not just me or the upper classes like in Spain. In the New World, everyone is equal, no?"

"Not everyone, my friend. There are many poor people barely getting by and then there are the former slaves. Slavery was recently abolished on the island, but they are still the poorest of all. My life is simple, as is life on the island. I do not go out much, like most folks who are not rich. The poor are just like the poor in Spain. San Juan shows promise, but needs to develop more." She expressed genuine concern for the welfare of the needy. Félix found it refreshing for a woman of her background.

"Equality will take time to implement my dear, if I know my countrymen well. As long as there are no rebellions or riots by the former slaves, I personally don't care if they are free or not. Riots could bring other consequences." No one would ever suspect his humble origins hearing him say this.

"Spoken like a true aristocrat, if I may say so. But it sounds cruel."

"No, I hold no prejudices, as long as my position and status are not affected." Félix liked his well-spoken bluff.

"The rich will always be rich, *Señor* Hidalgo."

Félix remained silent, and nodded his head.

His conversations with Natalia were not conducive to impressing her, he thought, but they helped to get to know her better. She might be interested in him as long as the boring sea voyage lasted, but he was unsure if their budding friendship would continue once they arrived in Puerto Rico. She had a life there, and the young man she had mentioned would most likely be waiting for her at the Port of San Juan.

"All I have are my belongings, my savings, and the desire to succeed at any cost. Nothing and no one can stop me from succeeding. I fear nothing." Félix emphasized his bravado to impress her.

"You will face many challenges as an immigrant and new arrival," she said.

"I'm well aware of that, but I have the willpower to overcome any obstacle," he said with even more conviction.

"I think you will be just fine." In her tone he noticed that this was not feigned praise, and that she believed him.

The weeks passed, and both Félix and Vicente were growing impatient with the slow movement of their ship towards the Caribbean. They had encountered one big storm, a *ciclón*, during the crossing and it had made the passengers miserable for the two days that it lasted. The body fluids, on and below deck, added to the foul air and caused more seasickness. On more than one occasion, Félix, despite his eagerness to leave Spain, regretted making the trip. Had he known that a storm on the open seas would be so violent, he might not have booked passage.

Vicente did not mind the storms; it interrupted the boredom, and provided fodder for conversation with the other passengers. When Vicente could, he assisted others. Some passengers, even in their miserable state, declined his help to avoid appearing weak. These were mostly men. Félix was not one of them.

A few days later, the Captain indicated that the port of call, San Juan Bautista, was only seven or eight days away and the rest of the journey should be subject to better weather. Many passengers didn't believe him, but Vicente trusted his experience. He was on deck with Félix, looking at the open seas, which now were calm.

"Vicente, I never have been so sick in my life, I wish someone had told me about the storms."

"Do you think that the company that owns these ships is going to tell you the truth? Only the sailors with experience will, and I believe what they say. We will be there in a matter of days, Félix, so don't lose your faith."

"I haven't been able to see Natalia or help her, you know how sick she gets."

"My friend, I think it is you who needs help. Do you want me to go find her? And by the way, when was the last time you had some food?" Félix almost retched when he heard that word.

"You would do that for me? Please don't say anything to her if you see her by chance, then just walk towards me and we'll see what happens. *Gracias.*"

"Stay where you are, don't move. Here is some water." He left Félix alone on deck. When he returned with Natalia, he left her with Félix and moved to another part of the ship.

◆ ◆ ◆

Both men didn't know that by 1872, Puerto Rico had already experienced its first rebellion against Spanish rule. The colonists, *criollos*, had first written petitions to the Military Governor asking for self- rule and tax reform. The petitions were sent to the Spanish Courts and were then forwarded to the Crown. Most of these pleas fell on deaf ears, with the Spanish government acknowledging, at best, that some form of autonomy would be granted to the island in the near future. Sadly, nothing happened. This narrative was repeated by many of the passengers returning to the island. Félix first heard it from Natalia, who claimed she was not into politics.

Félix was unaware that the expensive title he had bought with his savings would soon lose all its value and prestige.

Vicente could adjust to any political situation, since his main desire was to become a farmer, and not get involved in politics. If he had to move to the interior of the island, so be it. He learned from other passengers about the tranquility of the central mountain range, the *cordillera*, and of the beauty of the Caribbean Sea bordering the south coast. His was not a struggle with political aims or to gain a place in society; his was a struggle to build a better life than the one he had in Tossa del Mar. In contrast, he observed that Félix's only worry was whether any insurrection by rebels or slaves would destroy his plans to become wealthy. It became a factor to think about as the ship approached their destination.

They arrived in Puerto Rico, just as the sailors had predicted, a week later. That morning as the sun arose a passenger on the bow of the ship started shouting. He had seen from a distance, the mountain peak on the east end of the island of the mountainous *Sierra de Luquillo,* also known as *El Yunque.*

The news spread amongst the passengers and a few ran below deck to alert those who were still sleeping. Soon a crowd of people appeared on the bow of the *Regina* and took in the majesty of the verdant mountain range, with its forest of emerald green topped by light grey clouds at the crest.

Most of them stared in silence, while a few emitted sighs of relief and amazement that their journey was almost over. They would land in San Juan harbor within hours, after many difficult weeks at sea. A few of the passengers refused to go below deck again, so not to miss the glorious views. They feared the vision they saw might disappear if they looked away, even for a moment.

Vicente, who had been absorbing the scene ran below deck with shouts that woke Félix and everyone else.

"Félix, we have arrived in Puerto Rico, you can see the island from the tip of the bow, if you hurry. *Corre amigo, para que veas lo bello que es tu nueva isla.* It's beautiful."

"Vicente *calma*, we are still not there and it's not my island yet. Maybe it will be."

He followed Vicente to the front and joined the rest of the people there who would not step aside to let them approach the railing. The scenery left him speechless. Not ever having seen a tropical island, he imagined he had died and gone to heaven. It was Paradise.

Félix managed a wide grin when he looked at Vicente.

There was still more than 60 nautical miles to sail before reaching port, but it felt like a pleasure trip from there on. A cherished dream would soon become a reality for many of the immigrants.

The palm trees and the sugar- colored sand were visible as they approached the island. The palms beckoned the passengers by dancing in unison and swaying in the wind, as if mimicking the sirens in ancient Greek mythology. The surf lapped softly on the beach. They could not yet hear the waves, but those sounds would soon be part of a symphony announcing their arrival in the Caribbean. The day was clear with a sky that was swathed in light blue and dotted with white specks of clouds. The only suggestion of rain was the dark grey clouds at the peak of *El Yunque*.

Vicente approached Félix, hugged him and kissed his cheek, a gesture that was unfamiliar to Félix and caught him by surprise. Once he spotted Natalia among the crowd, Félix walked over to her and kissed her hand as if saying that the trip was a success and also indicating, with that kiss, a special type of fondness for his newfound friend. Awkwardly, he tried to embrace her, but at the last minute desisted. She laughed and thanked him, but offered no reciprocal gesture. She looked at him steadily, longer than usual. Félix felt that the look reflected a certain fondness for him, but he had no way of confirming it.

At dusk, as they reached the harbor in San Juan; the twinkle of candles and street lamps in the old city could be seen. The stars in the night rose just above them, like a canopy. The ship anchored outside the harbor waiting for the signal from the Captain of the Port that the *Regina* could approach and occupy the berth assigned.

Félix said to Vicente, *"Esta es nuestra casa ahora, amigo mío."*

Chapter Five

Borinquén

The local newspapers of Barcelona had varying descriptions of San Juan, the capital of Puerto Rico, a Spanish colony since the times of Ponce de León. Félix and Vicente had bought all the newspapers and articles that they could find before boarding the *Regina.* Their fellow passengers had lent them journals which had colorful descriptions of life on the island. Félix had read that the capital had become a center for trade with Spain. A well planned city, it had built its first Catholic Church in 1524, named *San Jose*, on a promontory near *El Morro* castle. The street leading up the hill to the church, *Calle del Cristo*, had been paved with blue gray cobblestones made from a ballast foundation, the same ballast used to provide dead weight to the Spanish ships, to avoid floundering in the storms of the Atlantic Ocean. Reports stated that San Juan's streets were lined with two story buildings, built in a colonial style painted in floral colors, with wrought iron balconies on their second floors. The ground floors on the main streets, such as *Calle Fortaleza* and *Calle San Francisco*, were mostly for commercial establishments.

The port of San Juan was a busy commercial center between Spain, Cuba, and the other islands of the Antilles. The Spanish government exploited the natural resources of this island. Among those was agriculture, specifically sugar, coffee, and tobacco which were the main exports to Spain. Some locals, known as *Peninsulares*, had returned to Spain once they had accumulated their wealth. Others had stayed as long as they prospered, and the remainder had made the island their permanent home.

Once the *Regina* anchored at the port of San Juan, it disembarked its passengers in order of class of fare, the highest fares were first. Many travelers leaving the ship were not prepared for the stifling heat and humidity of the tropics. Most of the men were dressed in black, the color of the times. After only an hour or so in the boiling hot sun, they started removing items of their clothing. The young women arriving were dressed with high neck collars and long sleeves. These were the most affected by the heat. Broad hats for women and wide brim hats for men helped ward off the sun, but not everyone wore them. By the time the ship docked, Félix and Vicente had stripped down to their shirts and were perspiring profusely.

The two friends were among the last to leave the ship, they wanted to absorb the change of scenery and view the crowds that had come to greet the passengers. Félix, for one, wanted to see if a young man had come to welcome Natalia Díaz. He missed the chance when he lost track of her among the passengers that had already left. Finally, he disembarked the ship.

Both of them walked to an office at the port where they signed a log of incoming passengers. The log had a space to indicate the name, age, gender, home address, and destination of each immigrant. Félix and Vicente just jotted down the words *"pensión"* for an address where they would be residing. They entered the date, July 24, 1877. Spanish customs officers checked their entries and place of birth, glanced at them briefly, and waved them on.

"We are in Borinquén after all," Félix said, using the native name for the island, and his mind filled with thoughts of Natalia. He regretted not having asked her for an address.

"Yes, and so far it is beautiful, except for the streets around the port. Did you see how ugly they get after the rains and mud?" Vicente said.

"Yes," Félix nodded dismissively, still lost in thought. "I lost track of Natalia when we disembarked. I should have followed her."

"Be patient, you will see her again. Right now we have many chores ahead of us to get settled." Félix looked at Vicente, but was staring right past him, wishing he'd had one more chance to speak to her.

"I guess you are right, that chance meeting on the ship was probably just that."

The old colonial city, with its flower vases on porches and brightly colored homes, was quite a sight to behold. The rotten garbage left out in front of the houses, as well as the putrid odors of animal waste, however, soon burnished the image. Vicente hoped that the entire city would not be in this state of neglect. Conditions in the streets improved slightly as they walked to the center of town, towards the *Plaza de Armas,* where the Spanish government had its administrative buildings.

As they walked, Vicente spoke to Félix about his plans.

"Félix, I have set my goals. I want to secure an apprentice job in a business here in San Juan, and later move on to the island's interior with some money and become a farmer. I want to get back to the soil, the earth that I love so much." As he said this, it became Vicente's turn to daydream. Félix turned to him and took his arm.

"You hadn't mentioned anything aboard the ship, when did you make that decision?"

"Before I left Tossa del Mar, but I preferred not say anything until we arrived, given the distance involved, the journey, and not knowing what to expect. What if we hadn't arrived safely?" Vicente's pent up anxiety surfaced. He took a deep breath and stopped to take in his surroundings and the unfamiliar sounds and sights of a colonial town.

"My friend you are far ahead of me in knowing what you want. I admire you. That's how it's done."

Félix hugged Vicente for the first time and told him that he would look for work in those companies specializing in imports from the mother country.

San Juan had little attraction for Vicente; it was already crowded with immigrants from Spain and other countries living side by side with limited space inside a walled city. While recognizing the beauty of the city's colonial architecture, he was not overly impressed by it. The population density was not to his liking, and he vowed to stay only the time necessary to put his plans into action. He would seek his future in the interior mountain region of the island.

They walked up the hill to the *Pensión Buena Esperanza* located on *Calle San Francisco.* Once they arrived at the *pensíon,* they paid for a shared room, giving the innkeeper an advance on the rent. The inn had a small courtyard outside the main entrance. Inside there were 12 rooms, six on each of two floors with the innkeeper and his wife occupying rooms on the first floor. It was clean, affordable, and while it provided no food service other than a morning coffee and bread, it seemed satisfactory to both of them.

The first task was to seek employment. Félix needed to work in a dry goods store, to add to his experience. Vicente told him that he would work anywhere; it was only a temporary arrangement.

On their fifth night in San Juan, after seeking jobs all day, they decided to have a meal at a better establishment, recommended by the innkeeper. They went to *La Palma de Mallorca*, a restaurant they normally could not afford. It was a place favored by the elite *San Juaneros*, but it also had an inexpensive tavern in the rear. As they entered the establishment, both of them glanced at the long bar adjacent to the formal dining room. Huge 20 foot tall rectangular mirrors hung on three walls reflecting their images. Just off the dining room was a garden with a small sculptured fountain, several wrought iron chairs, and a dark mahogany bench. The restaurant sought to replicate, in every detail, the finest eating establishments in Madrid. In the back, past the bar through a dimly lit corridor, the entrance to the tavern was visible.

Félix and Vicente sat down and contemplated their surroundings. Even the tavern had a touch of elegance to it, dark wooden tables and chairs, topped by wine colored cloths. The room generated a feeling of comfort that gave them satisfaction.

"Only now, do I get a real sense that we did the right thing in coming to *Borinquén,*" Félix said.

"I know, I feel the same way, too. If I had stayed in Tossa, I would have been a messenger for the rest of my life. Here there seem to be less obstacles to earning good money through hard work, At least, I hope so."

"I only regret not insisting that Natalia give me her address," Félix was still thinking about the lost opportunity with her.

"As I said before, you will see her again. This is a small city, you may still find her. Did she have an occupation?" Vicente put his arm on Félix's shoulder and patted him as a gesture of reassurance.

"Yes, she's a seamstress, but wants to become a schoolteacher. I think she is engaged, but I'm not sure-----" Félix's voice trailed off.

"You have really been stricken; you spend too much time thinking about her. Trust me, next time you see Natalia, she won't have a boyfriend. All you have to do is keep your eyes open and ask about her from time to time. Eventually, you will meet someone who will know her. Stop dreaming, we have work to do." He asked the waiter to bring the menus.

Félix found little consolation in his words.

"If she remembers me. You are the one who is dreaming, my dear Vicente, but it helps. Now let's enjoy our first *cena* in Puerto Rico and toast the future with *vino*."

"To us, and to our success in this beautiful land," Vicente raised his wine goblet.

"*Salud, amor, y pesetas.*"

◆ ◆ ◆

Vicente was the first to find a job, when he applied for work in the main offices of Aboy and Hnos, the company that managed, *Central Cambalache*, a sugar plantation in Arecibo. He entered the front door and addressed a man sitting at a desk.

"*Buenos Dias*, my name is Vicente Ferrer, from Tossa, in Cataluña, I saw your sign outside."

The desk supervisor asked him to sit down.

"We are in need of a courier to deliver documents and packages to different parts of the island, mostly to Cambalache, Arecibo, our main business. The voyage to that town is long and arduous. It's not easy."

"I don't mind." He recounted his experiences delivering mail in his hometown.

"Do you have references I can contact?"

"Not in Puerto Rico, I just arrived."

"Finally, do you have any criminal record from Tossa or any other province of Spain?"

"No."

"The pay for a messenger is not much, but if you are thrifty, you can live on the salary. Is that acceptable?" He told Vicente what the salary would be.

Vicente thought about the offer and realized that it was the type of job that would help him get to the interior of the island on a regular basis. Whether he traveled on horseback, or in a carriage, was unimportant to him. It was a chance to gain a foothold in his new home and begin working towards achieving his dream.

"It's acceptable, I can manage, and I have some savings."

"If Don Antonio Roche, our manager approves, could you start next week?"

"*Claro que si.*"

Vicente smiled and clapped his hands. A job so soon after arriving! He couldn't wait to tell Félix.

◆ ◆ ◆

Félix had more difficulty in finding work. He tried his hand as a watchman at the San Juan Pier, and for a short time as a garbage man, and later a street cleaner. *Anything to earn income, so I won't get into serious debt.* His pride was an obstacle that forced him to quit each of these endeavors before too long, so his search for a suitable job became a continuous one.

He'd heard from the innkeeper that there was a large dry goods store in front of the *Plaza de Armas* which sold mostly imported cloths and fabrics. The location was on *Calle Crúz*, a street perpendicular to *Calle San Francisco*, three blocks from *La Fortaleza,* the governor's mansion. The business, *Importaciones Mundillo*, was adjacent to the building that housed the Spanish government's municipal offices, and was easily identified by its huge red and yellow sign, the colors of the Spanish flag.

Félix walked slowly past the store various times before he could muster the courage to enter and ask for the owner. One morning he finally went in and inquired if the owner was present. A clerk told him to wait near the front door.

Angel Márquez was short and overweight, with most of his bulk around his waist. His girth was made evident by the long black jacket, two sizes too small, that he insisted on using, which made him appear even more obese. He set his eyeglasses on his nose at all times. On this particular day, he appeared to Félix to be in a good mood, and he interviewed him on the spot.

"What line of work did you do in Spain?" Márquez said.

"Dry goods, *Señor.*"

"Specifically, did you perform any administrative or clerical work?"

"At times, when the owner was away on travel. I was mostly responsible for the warehouse, but also tended to the customers."

"How long did you have that job, and why did you leave?"

Félix could see that Márquez was studying him carefully.

"I worked there for five years, never missed a day of work. I was not let go. I left Tossa del Mar on my own to find a better life and try to be part of something new."

"Life here is different from Tossa, I hope you realize that."

"That's why I came. I'm not afraid of hard work." Félix was not bothered or put off by Márquez's questions, or by his gruff exterior.

He hoped his candor and his apparent experience would sway the proprietor. He tried his best to be likeable and to seem eager to learn the business.

"Young man, I will think about it for a few days and will send you a message if I decide to hire you. If you haven't heard from me in two weeks, that means I found someone else. Leave me your name and address."

No working arrangement was discussed other than the fact that Félix would be paid in Puerto Rican *pesos,* not Spanish *pesetas.* Félix didn't care. He hadn't thought much about what his *pesetas* were worth on the island, but would soon find out.

◆ ◆ ◆

Vicente started traveling to Arecibo the day after he began his duties. He reported to Antonio Roche, who had emigrated from Cataluña years earlier, much like him. He liked the man, even with his aristocratic air, typical of Spaniards of high birth. While he dressed elegantly but casually, Roche was not above working at the same tasks as his employees. Vicente listened as Roche explained many of the operational details of the sugar mill in Arecibo. The employees were treated with respect he stated, and most of them seemed to enjoy working there though the wages paid by the company were barely enough to make a living.

Vicente frequently traveled to the interior with him in the company wagon, and occasionally had the chance to talk to him on what had led Roche to leave Spain.

"Don Antonio, do you miss Barcelona?

"I miss my mother, my sister, and my friends. Also, I miss some of the entertainment that exists there. I don't miss the politics or the government, or the high society that is entrenched in everyday life."

Vicente thought it best not to press the issue.

"How long have you been here?"

"I arrived in April 1872, and have been here since. I settled down and went back to Barcelona only once. It took me time to find an occupation that suited me, since my schooling in Spain had been incomplete. But at the same time, I was in no hurry to work at just any job. Then I began to run out of money. Finally, after one bad and one good job, I applied to work for Aboy and began as a clerk."

"Do you still have family there? Vicente asked, ignoring the last part of the conversation.

"Only my mother and sister," Antonio replied, not mentioning his father.

◆ ◆ ◆

One afternoon on Vicente's third trip to Cambalache, while he waited for his boss to finish his business, he met a young woman that worked as a maid at the residences, and served as a part time cook. Belén Aponte was well formed, with shoulder length dark brown hair that she wore in a neatly woven braid while she labored at the Central. Her skin was a light caramel color and her deep brown eyes reflected a gentle soul. The bangs from her hair fell on her forehead and added to her childlike appearance. She spoke with barely a whisper, and it seemed to Vicente that if he ever touched her, she would break. He took off his hat when he addressed her, even though it was not customary.

"Where are you from *Señorita* Belén?" he asked, on a day he finally found the courage to speak to her. Before that he usually greeted her with a *"Buenos Días Señorita"* and moved on.

"I'm from Sábana Grande, a town in the foothills of the mountains in the southwest. I live on a coffee farm."

"Yet you work as a cook here?"

"Yes, and I also clean the foreman's residence as well."

"A coffee farm, what is that like?"

She explained that the mountain towns were famous for their coffee farms. They had been established by small property owners who could not compete with the sugar or the tobacco industries. Sugar was the main crop, now called *"Rey Azúcar"* and tobacco was the runner up, a prince of crops. Coffee was a distant third, one of the most difficult to cultivate successfully and sell for a good price in the markets.

"I didn't know that there were so many coffee farms in the mountain region," Vicente said.

"It's a good living and my family has survived thanks to the coffee bean. I have to go now, Don Vicente." He remained standing there and watched her walk away as long as he could.

Belén wore simple white cotton dresses, with a red bandana wrapped around her neck and shoulders to add color to her garments. With her natural beauty, she was a unique find in an isolated sugar plantation.

After a few trips to Arecibo with short but frequent conversations, Vicente developed a strong attraction for her, even though the time they spent together could be measured in minutes, not hours. He would stop her and exchange pleasantries and talk mostly about topics relating to cultivating coffee. He looked forward to those exchanges and it gave him needed information for his main interest, determining if owning a coffee farm was even possible for a man of limited means.

"Belén, are you promised to anyone?" he asked her one afternoon just before he left the sugar mill.

"Why do you ask?"

"It's none of my business, but I'm curious."

"You're right; it's none of your business. And the answer is no."

She then looked at the ground and walked away without further conversation.

The following week, he was able to speak to her again on her lunch hour. He approached her slowly and apologized for his rude questions earlier. She waved him off.

"Tell me more about your home town, how far is it from here, and what's it like?"

"It's a long day's ride by wagon or on horseback. I don't think you would enjoy the town very much; there is almost no life after dark, especially if you don't live near the plaza. It is very small and provincial. All the social activity revolves around the church." She was trying to be realistic but that didn't dissuade Vicente.

"What does your father do?" he asked.

"My father works for a *criollo* landowner; and is the foreman of the coffee farm."

"And how big is your family?

"We are nine brothers and sisters. I'm the youngest. Don't ask me how old I am," she said, forestalling the next question.

"A gentleman never would. Is it possible that I might visit your home? With the permission of your father, of course."

"I will ask *Papá.* It would have to be on a Sunday, and he will want to know the purpose of your visit." She looked at him to detect fear; he wasn't scared.

"Tell him that I plan to become a farmer, and that I would appreciate his advice."

Belén looked at him, and this time she smiled.

After that, every chance he had he would visit the family farm and spend the day, so that they would get to know him. This was only possible when he was at the sugar mill for a more than a week.

After two years of traveling from San Juan to Arecibo, Vicente was transferred permanently to Cambalache. It proved to be more efficient and economical for the company, and it was better for him.

He began a real relationship with Belén, and made plans to ask for her hand in marriage, once he could afford to have his own home. He was living in the employee quarters of the Central, but they were not fit for a married couple. Belén kept her usual job and slept in one of the dormitories which were divided by gender.

She told him that her parents did not like the idea of her sleeping away from home, especially on the same plantation as her suitor, but they had little choice. Frequent travel to and from Sábana Grande, through barely passable country roads was too difficult.

Vicente bided his time. Once they were married, he would leave Arecibo and move to Sábana Grande, a plan he hoped would find favor with her family.

♦ ♦ ♦

Félix was working on his bookkeeping chores in the *Mundillo* store one Monday morning when the chimes of the front door suddenly rang. The store was nearly empty, since it had just opened for business. He looked up to notice a young woman in a floor-length lavender dress with a broad matching hat. He glanced at her and continued his work assuming that she would be attended to by another store clerk. Most women who came to the store favored female attendants, who knew more about clothes, designs, and fashion, than the men who worked there.

Moments later the woman was standing before him.

"*Pero, Señor Hidalgo*, don't you recognize me?"

Félix looked up startled, and there she was: Natalia Díaz, the woman from the ship. It had been a long time since he'd arrived and she had almost faded from his memory. But now standing before him, she looked as lovely as he remembered her, if not more. He composed himself, rose and straightened his jacket. Then he took her hand and kissed it gently.

"I have never forgotten you; I just assumed that by now you were married to that young man you mentioned once. I thought that you had moved away from San Juan."

"I understand perfectly, and I remember you. My father is a very good friend of *Señor* Márquez, the owner of this store, who mentioned you by name not too long ago. Every time I tell the story of my last voyage to the island, I also talk about the man, Félix, who came to my rescue when I was sick. You see that I didn't forget your name, either. Do you remember mine?"

"Of course, I do, Natalia. How have you been? Where do you live now?"

"I live here in San Juan with my family, in an area known as *Puerta de Tierra*. I am not married, which was going to be your next question. My suitor returned to Spain. Both his parents died suddenly and he had to assume control over the family business in Madrid. He never proposed and we parted as friends." Félix noticed her smile as she said the last words.

Her answer made Félix glow inside. He admired her boldness and thought about his next question before asking it, not wanting to be too inquisitive.

"Do you still sew or are you now a teacher?"

"I do both, as time permits. I also love playing music, something I had not done for a long time."

"I didn't know that. What instrument do you play?"

"The harp." She looked around her as if searching for something.

"I'm sorry; I forgot that you may not be here for a social visit. Can I help you with anything?"

Márquez had been looking at them and Félix didn't want to waste company time.

"I'm looking for several cloths to fashion a dress for my niece on her birthday, and I have the time to sew it myself."

Félix took her by the arm and led her to a stack of imported cloths from Spain and pulled out several rolls for her to examine. All the while he studied her, the delicate way in which she touched the cloths, and her reactions to the different colors and textures she examined. He stood back while she finished.

"Do you need some time to make a decision?" he asked, after she had chosen two samples.

"No, I think I found what I came for." He took that to mean the cloths, not him, but he was pleased to hear her say those words.

"Can I have someone deliver these to your home so you won't have to carry them yourself?"

"That's very kind of you; I have other errands to run. Here is my address."

"How did you know I would still be here?"

"I made some inquiries." She gave no details.

"Will I ever see you again?" He couldn't anticipate how she would respond. Until that moment she had been overly polite, maintaining her distance, as did he.

"If you personally bring the cloths to my house, you will."

"That, I can do." She bade him goodbye, and with a nod of her head, departed. Félix was elated; Vicente's prediction had come true.

◆ ◆ ◆

By 1879, Antonio Roche had been residing in Puerto Rico for seven years. Now in his early thirties, he looked back on his first years on the island. The idea of becoming an *Indiano*, and returning to Barcelona a rich man, faded as he grew accustomed to life in the Spanish colony and the rewards it offered anyone willing to take risks. He relished the relaxed style of the local culture and the inherent happiness that the islanders seemed to possess, even those who lived in squalor. The islanders had a saying *"A mal tiempo, buena cara."* The spirit of living life to the fullest was contagious, and he had adjusted easily to that.

One morning the resident partner, Jacinto Aboy, who also happened to be from Barcelona, and was good friend of Don Teodoro Soler asked Antonio whether he happened to know the Marqués. Antonio said he did. He swallowed hard after that and tried to change the subject. He had never realized that those two men were close friends.

"If you know my partner, then you must know his family including Paula Soler, his beautiful daughter," Aboy said.

"I do, I met her many years ago, when she was very young. I didn't know that Teodoro Soler was a partner here"

"He acquired an interest in the sugar mill years ago. Paula is now a widow and a mother. Sadly, her husband died in Cuba while serving in the Spanish Army." Antonio had to mask his surprise at Aboy's words. He shifted uneasily trying to focus. "She has expressed an interest in visiting Puerto Rico in the near future."

"Does Don Teodoro know that I work here? "Antonio ignored the man's last remarks.

"He does, he knows the name of all of our employees."

If he hasn't gotten rid of me, is this Soler's way of seeking forgiveness and atoning for framing me? Or am I being set up for another fall? Did Paula intervene on my behalf when she found out I wanted to work here? She must have. That must be it; she still feels in debted to me.

♦ ♦ ♦

Puerto Rico, as a Spanish colony, had suffered from oppressive rule, and the Spanish Crown had continually turned deaf ears to the clamor for reform by resident islanders. They were developing a love for their new land and, as colonists, could not understand why the island was not treated like other provinces in Spain, especially in view of the riches it provided to the mother country. Tariffs on products that originated in Puerto Rico were excessive, and unfair to the local businesses and the industries. Much of the profits derived from local labor left the island to fill the coffers of the Crown and the native *criollos* were left with the crumbs. These complaints circulated in the circles that Antonio frequented and the arguments sounded familiar as he recalled his days as a rebel. But this time he would stay on the sidelines. He had no intention of reliving his days in Barcelona.

Insurrection had been considered by the locals and a few years before Antonio Roche arrived, in 1868, an aborted attempt to overthrow the Spanish government had taken place in the town of *Lares*. The rebellion had been poorly planned and executed, and the expected uprising by the *campesinos* had fizzled. Antonio had learned of these events by a series of articles in the local newspaper, *Gazeta de Puerto Rico,* and from the many discussions among his business acquaintances.

Many of those rebels in the *Lares* incident had been summarily executed by the Spanish soldiers once the uprising was crushed. Others had died in jail awaiting trial. As he read about these events he knew that his days of anarchy and rebellion were behind him. He still identified himself with the lower classes, notwithstanding his background, but tried to banish all thoughts of helping any efforts at rebellion, although he sympathized with the ideal of self-government for the island. Antonio wanted to stay away from politics and hoped that any upheavals would leave him untouched.

◆ ◆ ◆

At the Aboy offices, no further word about Paula had been mentioned until one afternoon several months later, Antonio overheard Mr. Aboy speaking to a clerk about her.

"Pedro, did you know that Paula Soler and her son are on their way to the island?"

"No, I didn't."

"She is scheduled to arrive in two weeks. Please have the offices and the storage room prepared in case she asks for a tour of the facilities. After all, she is my partner's daughter and future heir."

"Certainly, *Señor* Aboy."

Antonio was stunned by the news. He had struggled to forget Paula, though he had written to her a few, mostly formal letters. She belonged to the memories of his past life in Barcelona, and he refused to dwell on them, yet he often continued to dream of her even after Rita's death. It was an inconsistency of his nature.

Now that he knew that Paula was coming, he wasn't sure what to think. She hadn't married, according to his mother, and he was a widower. Although he had never felt anything more than a passing attraction for her, he still couldn't explain his dreams. It had been many years since their last meeting and he wondered if she had changed. *Is she still as beautiful as the day I bade her goodbye in Barcelona?*

He wrote to his mother to find out more about Paula, but assumed that she would arrive well before he received a reply. Correspondence took more than five weeks to arrive from Spain and then another week to reach the intended recipient.

As he prepared for the eventual encounter, he anticipated that a visit by Paula to her father's investments was inevitable. *What will I say to her?*

Will she act kindly towards me, as she did in our last meeting or will she act as though she hardly cares? I wonder what the child is like. Does he look like Paula, or his father?

When he returned from a trip to Cambalache one Friday evening, a letter was waiting for him at his apartment on *Calle Norzagaray*, a street that bordered the north end of the city, where he had moved after his wife's death. It had been posted seven weeks earlier and was covered with stamps depicting the image of the Spanish Queen Isabela II. He took a small sword shaped letter opener, inserted it, and read the contents.

> *My esteemed Antonio:*
>
> *You will probably receive this letter shortly before I arrive in Puerto Rico. It has been a long time since we last communicated, but I know of your business endeavors from both my father and Penélope.*
>
> *I have decided to relocate to the island and start a new life, something I have wanted to do since the birth of my son. He is eleven years old now, and I want to make sure that he grows up in a place where the circumstances of his birth do not place any obstacles in his path. You should see him; he is a handsome young boy, with fine features and a keen mind. I have a feeling that he will become a lawyer, or a doctor, or maybe a successful businessman. But none of that would happen here. As much as I love my Cataluña, I see no future in Spain for Carlitos or myself. As you can see, I made my father wait a long time for me to leave Barcelona.*
>
> *I have always held you in high esteem, even though you may not think so. Whatever happened between us in the past should stay there. You should know that I still appreciate your friendship and my hope is that we may renew the same when I see you.*

I will not stay in the capital very long, since I plan to go to Ponce and live with relatives for the time being. Maybe that is where I will eventually settle. I will visit San Juan for a few days to rest from the ocean voyage, and I trust we can meet and discuss the island, its people, and your experiences. I have many questions to ask of you and hope you can answer them.

The ship that I'm arriving on is named for our country, Cataluña. You will see the anticipated arrival date in the shipping lines schedule. It will be sometime in early March. I look forward to seeing you once again.

Cariñosmente,
Paula Soler

Antonio finished the letter and placed it in his vest pocket. At least he knew that a rendezvous with Paula would not be unpleasant. What he couldn't anticipate was his reaction upon seeing her again.

◆ ◆ ◆

Paula arrived in San Juan the first week of March 1884; twelve years had passed since she last saw Antonio. She had secured temporary quarters with the help of Jacinto Aboy and had obtained suitable lodgings for her and Carlitos. Two days after arriving, she sent a message to the Aboy offices, announcing that she would be calling on Antonio the following day. All she requested was to be given an hour when it would be convenient for him, and to send a reply message.

The messenger returned later that afternoon and brought a note from Antonio that he preferred to call on her the next day at the inn, after business hours, if it was acceptable. He also mentioned that he wanted to meet her son.

The following evening. Antonio walked to the inn and knocked on the main door. The inn was located on *Calle Sol*, built in typical Spanish colonial style with its own inner courtyard and a marble water fountain in the center. He looked at the façade. The rooms had twin balconies on the second floor. The exterior walls of the building were painted in rose, which contrasted nicely with those of nearby houses, painted in dark blue-gray colors. Antonio surveyed his surroundings and compared the inn to the mansion in which Paula had been raised in Barcelona. *She must have changed, now that she is a mother. That can bring a bevy of unexpected new experiences.*

He was lost in his thoughts when the innkeeper, an older woman dressed in a plain pink frock, asked if he was there to see anyone. He mentioned Paula's name and said he would wait in the courtyard. A few moments later he heard steps behind him. He turned and there she was. He hesitated before he spoke. She was still captivating.

"Paula, you look lovely and haven't changed a bit," he said finally.

"Nonsense, I am older and look the part."

Her hair was longer and her face was one of a fully mature woman, not the young girl he once knew. He did not detect any wrinkles. She had blushed when he called her by name, and he approached her warily not knowing if a handshake would be too cold a gesture, or if a kiss was too familiar after such a long separation.

"Come here, and give me a proper embrace." Paula said.

She was even more beautiful than he remembered, and when he hesitated in kissing her, she closed the distance between them, hugging and kissing him on both cheeks.

"Antonio, I can't believe it's you. You look well, but I see that your hair is thinning. Oh my! What a terrible thing to say after so much time." She blushed and giggled, and Antonio couldn't help but chuckle himself.

"It's the truth, so don't worry, I've seen it coming for years now." He passed his hand over his head.

"How is life treating you? How do you like Puerto Rico, as compared to Barcelona?

He paused before answering, to make sure he didn't say anything negative.

"It has its advantages and disadvantages like any other place."

"I never imagined you would stay so long, many of the *Indianos* make their fortunes in a few years and then return to Spain. I was expecting you would too." He knew that the question was an innocent one, not one meant to measure his progress or lack of success.

"I know, but I'm not like them. This is my country for as long as it will have me. It's my home now. I don't miss Barcelona that much, and have only returned there once for a brief visit with my family. Sorry that I never looked you up, I sent you a note since I didn't want to intrude." He felt guilty after saying this, but she did not react.

"I received it. Also, I heard from Penélope that you had married and lost your wife to an illness, I'm sorry."

"It was difficult at first; we were married for only a short time. She was the victim of cholera." After a pause he asked, "Do you see my sister often?" The mention of Penélope had made him smile.

"Yes. We became good friends after you left. In fact, I'm surprised that she didn't follow you to the island."

"I invited her many times, but she never acted on her desires to leave Barcelona, I think she fell in love with a compatriot. But I'm still hoping that she will come visit me someday. May I meet your son?" He really didn't know what he would say to Carlitos.

"Why didn't you remarry?" As an unexpected question, it caught him off balance.

"I never found the right person after Rita. I have had women acquaintances, but nothing serious. My work consumes me at the present, however, I don't plan to become a priest either. She giggled.

"How come you never married?" He instantly regretted the remark, but Paula didn't seem bothered. "How are your parents?" he added quickly.

"No, I never had the incentive to marry. I became a *jamona!*" She laughed at the phrase. "Mother is well, but Father has been ill lately and has begun to take a passive role in his businesses. He spends his time reading and socializing with his group of friends. I'm not sure that he is content with that. The doctors have recommended that he retire completely. He may even have to sell his interests in his overseas investments."

Antonio was surprised by her remarks, but tried not to show it.

"Enough about the past, what do you plan to do now that you have moved to *Borinquén*?"

"Not sure. I will spend some time with my relatives in Ponce, and then decide, once I have obtained proper schooling for my son. I know that Ponce is not Barcelona, but I don't care. I needed a change. Now come with me, I will introduce you to Carlitos."

Antonio followed Paula into the inn and waited in the drawing room that also served as a reception area. He sat down while Paula went to fetch her son. A few minutes later, she appeared with the child. He leaned on her and hesitated in stepping forward to shake Antonio's hand. His skin had a light olive color much like the inhabitants of southern Spain, and his pear shaped face was framed by his bowl type haircut with short bangs. Carlitos looked at Antonio with his large dark brown eyes then averted his glance by looking out at the courtyard.

"*Hola*, Carlitos. *Gusto en conocerte.*"

"*Hola, Señor* Roche."

"Welcome to Puerto Rico, where there is never a winter to worry about," Antonio said.

"*Que bueno!*" Carlitos replied.

"Tell *Señor* Roche what you want to be when you grow up," Paula said. She nudged her son.

"A *conquistador* or a general in the *caballería*."

"That means you love horses, right?" Antonio asked.

The boy nodded.

"We shall see," Paula said.

As their encounter drew to a close, Antonio asked Paula if both of them could dine with him before they left San Juan. She agreed. He bent down and shook the boy's hand, mussed his hair a bit, and with much more self-confidence kissed Paula goodbye.

As he walked home, Antonio was pleased that the meeting had gone so well, and that there was no mention of their past in Barcelona. *Perhaps we can be friends after all. Yet I'm uncertain on how that friendship will develop or where it might lead.* As he pondered whether he would visit her in Ponce, he thought about the long journey from San Juan, through the mountains of Cayey towards Salinas, and then westward on the southern coast. It was not a trip that he could make often.

Part Two

Chapter Six

Slavery and servitude

Rosalina Pabón was born to slave parents in the town of Vega Baja. A scrawny little child when she first viewed the world, she grew up quickly into a comely young woman. At age 15, she started working in the main residence of a sugar plantation as a servant helping her mother, Lucinda, in the kitchen. She had fine features, her nose and lips were thin and her hair was silky jet black, always worn in braids. Due to her mixed racial features, people incorrectly assumed that she had been the offspring of a Spaniard and a slave woman. At an early age and with a full figure, she had begun catching the glances of men who worked at the sugar mill, but they kept their distance since her father was well known and had a special status among the slaves.

Rosalina's parents shared with her the daily grind at the *Central San Jacinto* owned by the Marqués of Vega Baja, Miguel Riberas Pabón. They awoke before dawn, in the palm fronded shack that was their home, and with a meager breakfast started the day. The plantation foreman expected them to report to work by six in the morning, Monday through Saturday

After the main meals at the master's house had been served, Rosalina helped with the chores of cleaning their humble abode, and later prepared the ingredients for a simple meal of rice, chicken, and yucca, for her mother to cook when she returned at dusk. The family was not treated badly, except for some isolated instances, but the living conditions at the Central were far from pleasant.

In 1873, when Rosalina was 13 years old, the Spanish government in Madrid abolished slavery. It took months for the news to reach Puerto Rico, and the local Spanish authorities decided to implement the decree in stages. They wanted sufficient time to free the slaves in an orderly manner and to gradually indemnify the owners for the loss of their laborers. They would be hard to replace since most *criollo* workers shied away from the work assigned to slaves.

For some, mostly the landowners, the delayed implementation in freeing the slaves was welcome news. They knew it was inevitable and would have preferred otherwise, but it enabled them to adjust to the economic impact of losing slave labor. Also, it assured them compensation from the government for the liberated field hands. Although the law now required the landowners to pay former slaves with wages for their labor, in reality nothing changed. Many of those liberated continued to work where they lived. Their wages were minimal, and the landowners no longer had to provide them free shelter and food, meaning that their salaries would be spent as soon as they got paid. Slavery had become indentured servitude; the debts that freed slaves owed for room and board exceeded their compensation. The initial wages were paid in Puerto Rican *pesos* not Spanish *pesetas,* which represented a decrease in value of the coin. In addition, the owners implemented a journal diary system that recorded the wages paid to each worker. The freed slaves were required to keep one to be employed in any capacity, and thus they became known as *jornaleros.*

Rosalina was too young to understand this change in her status even though her parents explained it to her as best they could. *What does it mean being free? Can I go anywhere I please? Do I now have to work for pay, as well as help my family with chores?*

"Rosalina, it is a new day, we are free," Lucinda said.

"Yes, but free to do what?"

"We can do as we please, my lovely child."

"We own nothing, have no money, and still depend on the *blancos*," Rosalina said. She sounded harsh, but that was how she felt.

"*Niña,* you have no idea what it was like coming over on the ship, kept in chains like animals, sleeping in our filth, with no food, no clean water!" Her mother's voice cracked.

"But that was before I was born, so I don't know." She grew impatient with her mother, but lowered her voice.

"Many of the slaves on the ship died and the others like me were violated both in body and spirit."

Rosalina remained silent. Her mother had rarely discussed those events, and she wasn't going to ask for details.

"We were fortunate enough to be bought by Don Miguel, compared to the fate suffered by other slaves." She saw her mother close to tears. Rosalina went to her mother and put her arm around her shoulders and hugged her

"That I do know *Mamá,*" she said.

All the while, Bernardo Pabón, her father, who had taken the family surname of the plantation owner, observed the scene in silence. With no schooling and illiterate, he could only explain to Rosalina, in simple phrases, what he thought it all meant. He was a grizzled figure, with lines carved into his face, like chiseled marble. His full head of hair was prematurely white, and thus his nickname, *copo de nieve.*

"*Hija,* it means that we no longer have to do what the *blancos* ask us to do. We will actually receive *pesos* for our labor."

"Will we move away?"

"Not for now, there is nowhere to go. I will look for work in San Juan, where I have heard many former slaves are going to, or maybe in Arecibo, where I know someone. I need to find a job. It will take time and then will we can go."

"What will we do in San Juan or even in Arecibo, *Papá?*"

"*No sé,* Rosalina, but I will tell you once I find out." Rosalina knew that Bernardo was facing uncertainty for the first time in their family life. He would have to make difficult decisions and chart their future.

"How soon will you know?" Rosalina insisted.

"Enough questions. As I said, I will tell you."

To Rosalina, this change in status meant her dreary life might be over, if her father managed to find work in another place. Apparently, from his words he believed that there might be a good opportunity in the sugar central in Arecibo, on the north coast, ten miles away. She was not so sure that it would be a better alternative than San Juan, but her father said he knew people at *Central Cambalache.*

♦ ♦ ♦

The time came for the Pabóns to leave San Jacinto after the last harvest, *la zafra,* was completed. Bernardo was aware that the owner, Don Miguel, would not need his services for the remainder of the season. Fortunately, at the same time, the official notice of the end of slavery arrived from the capital with a timetable for freeing the slaves at *San Jacinto*, along with the estimated amount of owner's compensation for each slave liberated.

Bernardo's foreman at *San Jacinto* was traveling to visit other properties, and he took the opportunity to speak to Don Miguel and announce his departure.

"Buenos Días, *patrón*," Bernardo said.

"*Hola*, Bernardo, what can I do for you?"

"I have come to let you know that my family and I are moving to Arecibo."

"After all these years with me you want to leave?" Don Miguel was genuinely surprised.

"You have treated us well, but now I'm a free man, and must find other work and start a new life." Bernardo had never said these words before and it felt strange, but good.

"I can give you a raise, if it's money that you want."

"*Gracias*, but no, I want more than money. I want to be owner of the last years of my life for whatever God has planned for me."

"I see. You should know that as a 'free' man nothing will really change. You will still be poor with no guarantee of wages."

"That may be true, but I have to try." Bernardo's voice was hardening and his throat tightened.

Don Miguel had plenty of other workers and could manage without the Pabón family. He shrugged and signaled to Bernardo that he could go. For the old former slave, it was his first decision as a free man. If he stayed in Vega Baja, he would always be considered a slave and continue to be treated as one. The *patrón* would never recognize his new status. In a new environment he could bargain for his wages, act freely, and attempt to find a new beginning.

The wagon ride to Arecibo was long, but doable in one afternoon. Unbeknownst to his family, Bernardo had taken a prior trip to Cambalache and spoken to the foreman, who indicated that there was a job for him based on his experience. When informed, Lucinda approved of the decision, but Rosalina stated that it would be just another small country town, no different from Vega Baja, and with no friends. Slaves like her didn't have much of a social life. Nothing would really change, she told them. Her parents didn't respond.

◆ ◆ ◆

At the beginning of 1886, almost two years after Paula had arrived in Ponce, news came from Barcelona that Don Teodoro Soler had died. By the time she received notice, the funeral had already taken place. In a letter from her mother, she was instructed to consult an attorney in San Juan for all matters pertaining to her father's estate. Sinforosa Soler had not included in her letter many details, or much information regarding her own future plans. More documents, the letter said, would be sent to Paula regarding her father's business and property interests on the island. Under Spanish inheritance law, Paula, and her two brothers, Pablo and Lorenzo, would inherit all of her father's assets. The new counsel to be hired would explain the precise distribution of the Soler estate.

Paula immediately made plans to travel to San Juan and obtain preliminary advice from the company attorney of Aboy and Hnos. Carlitos would accompany her.

Upon arrival she stayed at the same inn she had previously used. Although she had written to Antonio occasionally and had received a few letters from him, their communication was infrequent. She had seen him only occasionally in the past years. Nevertheless, she called on him before she met with company counsel.

As she entered the Aboy offices, she observed Antonio bent over his desk studying some documents. He didn't see her approach.

"*Hola,* Antonio, I thought I would come by and say hello."

Antonio looked up at her and seemed taken aback at first. He regained his composure, put his pen down, stood up and greeted Paula with a kiss.

"It's been a long time." He began to sweat for no apparent reason and his pulse quickened.

"I know, but that's your fault, you promised to come to Ponce and visit me and never did, plus your letters were scarce."

"I've been very busy, and company travel to the island takes a toll on me. I have thought of you often, but never seemed to get a chance to visit Ponce for more than a day."

"So it was a weekend or nothing?" Her sarcasm was evident, but she continued smiling.

Antonio winced. "I didn't say that." He continued to perspire though the office wasn't very warm.

Paula was as lovely as ever. She was wearing dark blue from neck to toe, which Antonio found odd given that the summer heat was in full swing. He looked at her; she caught him staring.

"Do I look that bad?" she said playfully.

"Oh no, not at all, on the contrary, you are always beautiful, that has never changed. What brings you to San Juan?"

"Have you not heard that my father died?"

"No, I knew that he was ill, but did not know he had passed." His tone was low and deliberate, the news didn't produce any effect in him, but he saw that Paula was sad.

"I have come to San Juan to meet with the company attorney and find out what's in my father's estate. I know he was partial owner of this business, and he owned land in both Arecibo and Salinas, but to what extent, I'm not sure."

"Your father bought out his partner two years ago. He owned the entire sugar mill of *Central Cambalache*, and the acres of land where the sugarcane is planted. The same applies to the land in Salinas, in the Southeast."

"I didn't realize that," she said.

"Yes, Paula, you and your brothers have a small fortune at your disposal, along with the huge responsibilities that come with it."

"I don't know how much interest they have in Puerto Rico, or whether they will come help me manage the sugar business."

"They will come, rest assured, especially if it means money going into their pockets." As soon as he spoke the words, he regretted it. She was flustered by the comment but remained silent. Paula shifted her stance and looked away.

"*Lo siento*, I didn't mean for those words to come out that way. I meant no disrespect."

"I accept your apology," she said coldly.

"Can we meet at some point during your stay?"

"Maybe, Antonio, I'll let you know. It was nice seeing you again."

"How is your son? Did he come with you?"

"Yes, he did. He has grown fast."

She turned on her heels and left. Antonio could kick himself for ruining the moment with such an insensitive comment, but it was done and he would have to make amends. Paula was the new owner of the business and it would now define their relationship. If he'd ever had any designs on her, it was too late. He'd had the chance earlier in his life to marry her, had turned it down, and had let the past two years slip by. It may have been a mistake, not that he would have wanted a relationship based solely on the Soler fortune, but he had no regrets with his original decision not to marry Paula.

A few days later, Paula came back to the Aboy offices to meet with the company attorney. On her way out, she told Antonio that she needed to talk to him, preferably outside the offices. They agreed to meet for dinner at *La Compostelana*, a newly popular restaurant in the old city.

That evening she arrived by carriage, stepped out to the curb and looked at the entrance of the dining establishment. Not the type of place she would have frequented in Barcelona, but those days were gone. It appeared that this town was her future. She straightened her dress and entered.

Antonio was waiting for her at the end of a mahogany bar where local intellectuals held discussions on literature, art, and politics. Tonight the dining room was quiet and Antonio found a table near the rear of the salon where he could speak to Paula undisturbed. She smiled, took her time sitting down, taking off her gloves, and storing her handbag. She wore her hat at all times. Paula looked at him, not averting her stare, knowing full well that present circumstances resulted in him seeing her in a different light. .

"How are you dealing with the new events, Paula?"

"As well as can be expected, I suppose."

She knew he was concerned, not for her, but for himself. So be it.

"Did you get good advice from the attorney?"

"Yes, it so happens that I have a lot of decisions to make and some of them can't wait until my two brothers decide to come, if they come."

She could tell that he looked uneasy and fidgeted with his empty wine glass.

"Like what?" Antonio asked the question bluntly.

"One decision is whether I will stay here as owner, or sell my stake to my brothers, or someone else. Another factor to consider is that my brothers may not want to be involved in the business of sugarcane and move here, so I may have to buy them out, then maybe sell."

"If you decide to stay, would that mean that you would be moving to Arecibo or to San Juan?"

"I have already visited Arecibo, and I wouldn't live there, it's too primitive and isolated. If I stay in Puerto Rico, it will be here in the capital."

"If I can help with your decision let me know." The remark sounded insincere, even to himself.

"What I wanted to speak to you about Antonio, was whether you would be able to work for me if I stay as the new owner, or if our past relationship would present problems?" She poised herself for his response.

"That's a question I have to think about, Paula, I can't give you an answer right now. I really enjoy what I do, and the responsibilities that the position carries, but I have been my own man here, with no one telling me how to do my job, or second guessing me. Your father and the other gentleman were passive owners, and let me run the business, without much supervision. I made good money for them, and earned their trust. The Central has always posted profits, except for one year when a hurricane destroyed almost all of our crop."

"I realize that this is a big change for you, as it is for me, but I am hoping that we can both adjust to the new reality." She looked down at the menu, not having an appetite. He ordered a bottle of *Rioja* wine, while she was lost in thought.

"First, please answer one question. Did you play any part in Aboy hiring me when I first applied for work?" Antonio asked.

After a few minutes of silence she said, "I did, but it was only out of the desire to help you after what had happened in Barcelona. You were qualified anyway, it wasn't really a favor. I hope you will not hold that against me and consider staying. I really mean that, Antonio."

He looked down at the table, removed the napkin from his plate, and mulled over what she had just said. He didn't look at her until he answered. "I will certainly give the matter the thought it deserves."

She reached over the table and in an unexpected move took his hand. He looked at her for a moment. She could tell that he found her alluring and attractive, it was in his eyes. He smiled and she then released his hand to reach for her wine glass.

◆ ◆ ◆

Bernardo Pabón arrived at the *Central Cambalache* with his family in tow. They had made the trip with all of their belongings stuffed in three cloth bags. After hitching a ride on a farm wagon headed to Arecibo, they were left three miles from their destination. They walked the rest of the way with their bags on their backs wearing leather sandals that made the walk less difficult. The dirt road was surrounded by sugarcane fields with the stalks over seven feet high and with no visible inhabitants. The late after-noon sun was a fiery orange ball that drenched them in perspiration, as if they had just taken a bath. A light wind provided some relief.

At Cambalache, they reported to Vicente Ferrer, the foreman, an ami-able Spaniard, something the family had not encountered before. Usually, foremen were former slaves or *criollo* workers from the lowest rung of society. Vicente was altogether different; he had good manners and treat-ed his underlings well, something other sugar plantation owners did not encourage. He had taken the job at the urging of Antonio Roche, who recognized that Vicente was smart and was being underutilized as a mes-senger. Although he was earning a better salary, along with the pay came longer hours and less time off. With the title of *capataz,* he reported di-rectly to Antonio, which meant he had a lot of discretion in supervising the workers. He greeted the Pabóns warmly and showed them the Central and their living quarters.

Rosalina found Vicente quite handsome. When he first saw her, she had just turned 17 and he was amazed at her refined features and shapely legs. She wore her garments tighter than most women, with her full fig-ure and derriere protruding sensually, hinting at the body underneath. Her breasts were full for her age, but she covered them carefully with a shawl. It was hard for Vicente to not notice her, and he diverted his eyes frequently to avoid awkward situations. She was an African princess with pea green eyes.

The Pabóns were each given duties similar to those they had at their former plantation. Rosalina was assigned to the cleaning of the dormitories, and her mother was the new cook in the main house of the Central, replacing Belén Aponte who had taken on other duties.

Vicente had his own lodgings and no longer lived in the servant quarters. Running the mill and supervising the field hands was time consuming. He made sure they earned their pay and ran a strict schedule. Former slaves and *criollo* field hands were treated equally, making no distinction as to their heritage. Vicente knew this made some *criollo* workers feel resentful, but he made it clear that all workers were equal at Cambalache.

Cambalache was similar to most sugar mills, but much more grandiose in its spread and in its construction. A tall dark brown brick smokestack dominated all the buildings. Next to it were the sheds where sugarcane was cut and processed for preparation to recover the sugar, with the machinery necessary to extract the cane juice. Behind the sheds were the warehouses for storage of the product. The mill also had spacious living quarters for the field hands, much better than most mills, as well as a central office to conduct its business.

The sugar mill was twice the size of Bernardo's former place of work. He liked his new boss and sensed that he was a good man who treated everyone fairly. He never used the whip or any type of physical punishment with his laborers. When field hands disobeyed an order or behaved impudently, or when they were caught stealing, Vicente simply fired them. At the same time, Bernardo did not notice the growing attraction between his boss and his daughter.

Late one morning, Vicente stumbled into Rosalina in his living quarters.

"Rosalina, what brings you here at this time of day?"

"Nothing, *Señor* Ferrer, I just wanted to help your maid, who is not feeling well today. She asked me to cover."

"What is wrong with Amalia? She didn't mention anything to me."

He couldn't help but stare at her breasts. He caught himself, but too late to stop her from seeing where his eyes were fixed. She smiled and seemed pleased.

"I think she's in the family way, *Señor,* I may be wrong. She doesn't show yet, but she has all the symptoms." He felt the desire to linger with her, but his better judgment kept him at bay. *What is wrong with me, she just got here?*

"*Bueno*, if she doesn't feel better by tomorrow you may substitute for her until she can come back to work. Please tell her to get well."

"*Vale.*"

"You are using a typical Spanish word, I like it."

"So do I." She looked at him fetchingly. As she left, she brushed past him slightly touching his pants.

"*Excúseme* por favor, *Señor* Ferrer."

"Please call me Don Vicente, which is fine." He smiled at her and let her pass.

She gazed into his eyes directly, and didn't bow her head as she had been taught. Her hair was parted over her forehead and brushed back showing the roots in the middle of her scalp, giving her a broad forehead that shone in the sunlight. Vicente looked at her, and felt a tingle in his groin. He placed his belongings on the bed. He hadn't felt that sensation since he first kissed Belén, his fiancé, thinking at the time that there would be no other woman for him, and that he could never be unfaithful.

A week later, he invited Rosalina to meet late at night in a spare room behind the offices of the sugar mill that had a small bed and sink. She accepted.

◆　◆　◆

Félix Hidalgo's responsibilities at the *Mundillo* store had increased now that he had worked there for more than a year- a sort of probationary pe-riod- and they included basic bookkeeping.

The more he became involved in the store, the more he realized what a good business it was, something he wanted for himself one day. He accepted cash, *pesetas or pesos*, from customers and kept a book on accounts payable and receivables, a duty that Márquez had entrusted to him. On many occasions, large amounts of cash were received when the owner was out of the store on other business. Félix was tempted to pocket some of the cash, and not credit customers' accounts, especially when they didn't ask for a receipt. At first, he resisted the temptation, but with the owner's frequent absences, along with his deteriorating memory and absentmindedness, Félix became emboldened and pocketed some monies to see if the owner would notice. Insignificant amounts from the customer payments morphed into larger amounts from the direct sales of merchandise. He also learned how to forge the inventory lists.

Félix began to accumulate the embezzled funds in a box located in a floor compartment underneath Márquez's desk. He had planned to store them there, easy to recover if the owner noticed any funds missing. The next step was to *"borrow"* money from his stash to buy gifts for Natalia, whom he now visited regularly.

"Natalia, I have a small gift for you," he would say.

"*Mijo*, what did you buy this time? We are just friends, and I don't need jewelry," she said, as she failed to hide her delight.

As a teacher of a Catholic elementary grade school, she earned a paltry salary, not enough to buy any luxuries. She began to look forward to his frequent visits.

"Shouldn't you be saving money to start your own business?" She said this with concern in her tone, not as a polite remark.

"I am saving, but this is part of a bonus I received this week for my hard work. I get them often."

If she knew the source of the money, Félix realized, she would be shocked and it could prove fatal to their relationship.

"I am grateful, and happy that your plans are succeeding, but I think you have given me enough for now. Please stop."

The gifts grew more expensive, and after a year of courting Natalia, he bought her a silver colored gold ring with a large diamond. It was half a carat, with a distinctive cut, one of the most expensive rings sold in San Juan. When he presented her with the ring and asked for her hand in marriage, she accepted.

Soon after their engagement, two men walked into the *Mundillo* store on a Monday morning, and asked the clerk for a *Señor* Hidalgo. The clerk called Félix, who went to the front of the store and introduced himself.

"*Buenos Dias*, I'm the acting manager of the store, Félix Hidalgo. What can I do for you?" He could tell that this wasn't a routine visit.

"I'm *Licenciado* Lorenzo Cátala, and this is my brother, Eugenio. I am *Señor* Márquez' legal counsel and Eugenio is his auditor. We are here to examine the accounts of *Mundillo* and make a complete audit. Márquez is thinking of selling the business, due to his poor health."

Félix froze at those words. He hadn't been informed of an audit; it had been years since any had been performed for *Mundillo* Imports. He looked at both men dressed in dull grey suits with matching vests and bone white straw hats. Their manner was brusque and no one smiled during the introductions.

"I knew about the owner's poor health, but I didn't expect your visit. When was this planned?"

"*Señor* Márquez had requested an audit some time ago, but recently asked us to move it up and-----. Did he not mention this to you?"

"No, not at all. If he had, I would have had all the books prepared for your review. Now it will take a couple of days before I can organize them." Félix was beginning to feel hot flashes. The visitors noticed his discomfort.

"No need. We will start today. You don't have to prepare or organize anything. Just give us a place where we can work in private. The owner's office will be just fine."

Félix's scalp was dripping wet. He wiped it with his handkerchief and mumbled something about the intense heat. He led them to the owner's office, offered them coffee which they declined, and then asked the clerk to bring all the ledgers of the store and place them on the large wooden desk. After they had been seated, Félix took the liberty of sending the store messenger to Márquez, to verify if these men were indeed his advisors.

The messenger returned an hour later and confirmed who the men were, and he told Félix that the owner asked him to take a vacation for two weeks, and name an assistant as acting store manager. The message made Félix dread the revelations that were about to be unleashed. He anticipated that his deeds would be uncovered and would probably lead to his being charged with embezzlement and his eventual disgrace. That same night he tried to access the office and retrieve the remaining stolen funds from their hiding place, but the area was blocked. The desk had been moved by the auditors and covered his secret access to the stash. Three nights later he returned to the store. He tried to enter, but found that the locks on both the front and back doors had been changed.

His chest tightened, and he had difficulty breathing. His pulse pounded in his ears, a prelude to his frequent and severe headaches. Visiting Natalia was out of the question, He feared that his countenance would betray his anxiety. Revealing what had happened was impossible, the disgrace was sure to cause a rupture with her. *Should I confess, be honest and pay the price? Or should I avoid detection and prolong the lies, hoping for a chance to replace the missing funds without being caught? Must I choose between losing Natalia and going to jail or should I just disappear?*

He went to her house and informed her that his work would keep him occupied for some time, due to an audit and an inventory at the store. He said he might not see her for a few weeks. She was amenable.

Two weeks later he was summoned to the home of *Señor* Márquez, and was expecting to be fired. The look on the owners face didn't reveal any emotion; he just stared at Félix while the latter sat uncomfortably in a chair waiting for the owner to speak first.

"I know what you did, my esteemed *Señor* Hidalgo," Márquez said. (He had never referred to Félix that way.) "My lawyer recommends that I report you to the authorities and have you prosecuted for theft. They say I should let you rot in jail. You have violated my trust and worst of all, you have abused my generosity and friendship. What do you have to say?" Márquez's face was so red that it looked ready to burst.

Félix looked at him and struggled to gather his thoughts before answering. He had difficulty clearing his throat. Once again, he felt lightheaded.

"I have nothing to say, except I'm truly sorry, and somehow, someday, I will pay you back. All I ask you is that you show mercy and forgiveness, and that you not send me to jail."

"Why did you do it? And what did you do with the monies you stole from me, which amount to hundreds of *pesos?* Why didn't you just ask me for a loan, if you had money problems?"

"I spent some of it, and hid the rest in your store, in a place that I will show you, if you let me. The reason why does not justify what I did."

"And what will you do if I don't have you arrested?"

"I will find another place to work and will pay you back, every single *peso.* You have my word." Félix was grasping the seat of the chair and began to tremble.

"I have your word? What word? You are a thief, how can I believe you? Who will employ you without a reference? This is a small town and all the merchants know each other. One word from me and you will be out on the streets begging for food."

"I know that," Félix said. Now he could barely keep from fainting. Márquez brought him a glass of water.

After a few minutes of silence, Márquez changed his tone and calmed down. His next words were tempered and deliberate.

"You were a good worker, Félix, and for a long time you ran my business well. I have no one right now who can replace you. So here is what you are going to do, if you want to avoid prison. You will work under my supervision until I sell the store, and your wages will be used to repay your debt, along with returning the unused stolen funds to me. You will get a receipt of what you earn for each month, and receive no money until your debt is paid, except for a small allowance for food and shelter. If you should violate any of these conditions, you will certainly end up before a magistrate. Your work hours will be from sunrise to sunset, with only Sundays off. For all intents, you will be my personal servant in the store, with no titles or position. You will help in whatever duties I assign to you including, sweeping the floors, cleaning the shelves, the windows, the toilets, and collecting the garbage. Your place of work will be the stockroom, not in the store. I do not want my customers to see you. These terms are not negotiable. Do you accept them?"

"I do," Félix said quickly. There was no difference between the conditions imposed and involuntary servitude. He had no choice, but perhaps he eventually might make good on his marriage promise to Natalia. It was a slim hope, but a chance nonetheless.

The arrangement with the owner did not last. A few weeks later a fellow worker, in anger, called Félix a thief. He was unaware that the stock boy had heard about the embezzlement, but if that man knew about it, so did the others. Félix couldn't bear the shame, and he struck the man in the face. When the man fell backwards, he knocked over a ceiling-high rack of crystal goblets and wine decanters placed in storage. The accident caused damage to other goods, including the fine china that was also stored on an adjoining rack. Félix, in desperation, ran out of the store and headed straight to Natalia's house. *Surely I will be fired, and the police will come after me.* Before he disappeared, he wanted a chance to explain to Natalia what had happened and would not lie anymore, not to her.

He found her on the balcony of her home in *Puerta de Tierra*. She had been sewing some garments that needed repair and she smiled at him as he approached the front gate, but detected that something was off. She stood up, left the garments on the chair, and walked towards him. As soon as she reached him, he fell into her arms and started sobbing.

"What is it, my dear? What has happened to you? She was unprepared at this display of emotion and her eyes moistened.

"Natalia, I love you and you should always remember that. No matter what people say about me, that's how I feel. I will love you until the day I die."

"Don't be foolish, why are you saying that? What's wrong?"

She listened to him as he began to explain how the day's events had unfolded. As he spoke, she looked down on her engagement ring and fingered the gold chain around her neck stroking the fruits of his criminal acts. Once Félix had finished, she backed away from him followed by a long interlude in which no one spoke. She then turned to go back to the house, but he held her by the arm.

"Please try to understand, I did it for you, my love," he said.

"You did what? For me, are you crazy? It's not like I needed all this fancy jewelry. I didn't care about that, I cared about you, and thought you were different from other men. You have now dishonored yourself and your noble title, assuming that's a real title. I doubt it. You led me to believe that you had savings and that the gifts were bought with your own money." Tears were flowing down her face.

"I promised *Señor* Márquez that I would pay him back. He even let me stay working for him until the debt was repaid. After today, I don't think he will want me to return. I struck a man who insulted me and when he fell it resulted in heavy damage to many fragile goods-------." She had stopped listening.

"Please leave, Félix, before I lose my temper. I don't want to see you anymore and here is the ring, and the necklace you gave me. The other items I will send to your home by messenger."

"I won't be there; I am leaving San Juan tonight."

"Where will you go? How are you going to hide from the authorities?" She began to fear for his safety, at odds with her anger.

"If I knew, and I don't, I wouldn't tell you for your own good."

She was struck by the fact that she might never see him again. It added to her despair. She wiped away her tears and stopped crying. She struggled with her next words.

"Goodbye Félix. I hope that someday you will seek your future in an honest way and find some redemption. You are not a bad person, but you have made a huge mistake and will have to pay for it, one way or another. The mistake will only get worse if you flee. As for me, I don't know if I can ever forgive you."

With that declaration, Natalia pulled herself away from his grasp, went inside her house, and closed the front door without looking back.

Félix fell to his knees sobbing and saying "No, no, no." He struggled to stand, then slowly turned around.

He was at a loss on what to do. The only alternative that came to mind was Arecibo. He would talk to Vicente, to see if he could provide him temporary refuge. No other choice seemed to make sense. He couldn't go back to Spain, booking a passage on a ship would take time, and immigration officials would have been alerted to his physical description. The police would be watching the port of San Juan, since they were ever vigilant for any criminals who tried to leave the island.

He left for Arecibo that same night without notifying anyone. As for Natalia, he realized he had lost her by his deception and lies. The gifts to her meant nothing. Before leaving her house he had tossed the ring and the gold chain on her porch after placing them in a small velvet bag he always carried. His life and his dreams had come crashing down. There was no one to blame but himself.

Chapter Seven

Encounter

Paula Soler had become an important person in the San Juan community. In less than five years after she became the sole owner of Aboy and Hnos, now renamed Soler S.A., she had moved into a large house in a neighborhood just beyond Puerta de Tierra, across from a lagoon, where the elite classes of San Juan had homes.

While Paula had no prior experience in managing an enterprise such as a sugar plantation, she'd had plenty of teachers. She had undergone a sharp learning curve on her way to master the intricacies of the sugar cane business and relished the work. The day to day management of the Central was left to Antonio who in working alongside Paula had witnessed another side of her. They often traded glances as the work day progressed, and sometimes the looks were not those of business partners. She was a mature businesswoman, no longer the girl who was trying to attract suitable male companions. On the contrary, she had found one. Her pulse quickened at the sight of Antonio, and she caught herself straightening her hair and looking in mirrors whenever she was about to meet him for a social occasion.

They were having frequent dinners and she often asked for his advice on matters that did not directly concern him, such as the education of her son. The relationship between the two men in her life was a close one, and the fact didn't escape her. Sometimes she wondered if her feelings for Antonio were much more than simple affection, especially on those occasions when he kissed her goodbye upon taking his leave. She understood those were not kisses of a romantic nature, but she enjoyed them.

Antonio visited her usually on Sunday afternoons, right after Mass. They talked about the island's society, politics, and business. Occasionally, Carlitos went with them on visits to other towns. The three of them went to different Patron Saint's Day festivals not too far from the capital. One day upon their return from an outing, Paula asked Antonio to stay for dinner.

"Antonio, I am so glad that you decided to stay with the company. I have come to depend on you so much."

"I'm happy. You've let me run the sugar mill like I used to before you took over. More than that, on a personal level, I have grown very fond of Carlitos."

He said nothing about their relationship, and she hesitated before continuing.

"Don't think I haven't noticed how well both of you get along. Yes, the best thing that I did was to stay in San Juan."

"Carlitos is a fine boy, I think he's being raised properly. Any advice that I can give to help prepare him for adulthood, I will gladly do so. I wish I could be more of a father to him, but that's not the case."

"I think he already sees you as a father figure."

"I'm glad. If he were ever to join the business, I know for sure that he would quickly learn the ropes. He's quite intelligent," Antonio added.

Carlitos was just shy of 16, and showed the first signs of becoming an adult and having his own opinions. He wasn't too preoccupied with the Old World, which seem to fascinate his mother, since she made a conscientious effort to teach him the history of Cataluña, and their family legacy. She had enrolled him in a Catholic school run by Franciscan priests, the Saint Francis of Assisi School on *Calle San Francisco* in San Juan. Studying there in a strict repressive environment, only fortified his resistance to the Spanish way of life. He resented the harsh discipline that was imposed on the students by both priests and nuns. School felt like prison and he frequently said that to Antonio. The youth's expressions of frustration and anger at the school's faculty and their inflexible attitudes reminded Antonio of his youth and he would tell stories to Carlitos about his own experiences in the Catholic schools of Barcelona.

Antonio, while not yet sure of the magnitude of his feelings for Paula, felt a deep emotional attachment to her and Carlitos, one that he did not fully comprehend.

Carlitos and he were sitting quietly on a bench outside the family house, when suddenly the boy spoke.

"I think that I might like to go into politics someday, Don Antonio," Carlos said.

"You don't have to call me *Don*, Antonio is alright."

"*Mamá* would not allow me." He grinned.

"Well then only when we are alone, it will be our secret. If you study hard,and get a good education, nothing is beyond your reach, son. But there are other professions like medicine, and the law, which you might consider."

"I want to be like you, my own man. I have heard that you were a rebel, and actually participated in strikes and protests in Barcelona."

"I used to be, not so much anymore." Antonio didn't expect this comment and looked away.

"I love stories of conflicts. Maybe I'll try to be a journalist."

Antonio then asked him if he would like to go to the Old Spanish Fort of San Cristóbal for a visit.

"Yes, and lets invite *Mamá*."

Antonio tried to avoid discussing politics with Carlitos, but it was a failed effort. The boy's growing interest in the autonomist movement was evident even at his early age. When he learned in school that slaves had gained their freedom by a Spanish government decree in 1873, he commemorated the anniversaries of that day in this own particular way, by shaking the hands of all the black people that he encountered on the streets of Old San Juan. He embraced little black children walking with their parents, actions that left those parents and onlookers in a state of disbelief.

A few weeks later, on a Friday afternoon, Carlitos was wandering the halls of his school, when he noticed a priest dressed in a Franciscan frock, staring at him. He was an unfamiliar and older priest, with a stooped back and unkempt gray hair that covered his entire head and reached his shoulders. He kept his eyes fixed on Carlitos and made a weak attempt to wave at him. Carlos waved back, hesitating. When he returned home that day he told his mother about the stranger and his odd appearance. Paula was stunned. She had received letters from her mother that sometimes contained hints of the whereabouts of Father Cervera, even though she never directly asked about him. Her mother's last letter had mentioned that Cervera might be going to the America. *It couldn't be.*

"What did he look like?" Paula asked her son.

Carlitos described the man.

She had heard among her friends which had children at that school, that a Spanish envoy, a priest from the Vatican, would be visiting the Catholic schools in the city. He was there to determine if the catechism and curricula taught in the parochial schools was current by Vatican standards, and then he would evaluate each school accordingly. *It's impossible. Mother had told me that he traveled frequently outside the Vatican, to several Spanish colonies. No, it couldn't be him; the coincidence would be too great. The description doesn't match.*

◆ ◆ ◆

Father Cervera had served the Vatican loyally for the more than a decade, but aspired to have his own church and rise in the ranks of the priesthood. In Rome, he had been assigned to routine administrative tasks which he soon grew tired of. Often praised for his attention to detail, he felt that he deserved his own parish, preferably in Spain. He was told to be patient. One Cardinal had suggested that he volunteer for trips to America, or Africa, to add field experience to his credentials. An assignment like that would help him advance in the church hierarchy, he was advised. After one such trip to Africa which lasted three months, he returned to Rome feeling ill. He had coughed up blood one night, and later asked to see a physician. The diagnosis was bad. He had contracted tuberculosis, and it was beginning to spread in his lungs.

When the opportunity arose to go to Puerto Rico in 1887, for the evaluation of the Catholic schools, he volunteered. Perhaps the warm weather would help him battle the disease. His doctor advised against the trip, but he decided to go anyway. To go to the island was against his better nature and his instinct. A fellow priest, who had worked in Barcelona, had brought him news of his former parish. Cervera had asked him if he knew the Soler family, since its patriarch was a huge contributor to the church. The priest told Cervera that he did in fact know them. Cervera's curiosity about Paula trumped his caution and he had asked about her. She had moved to Puerto Rico, was the last thing the priest had heard.

After his arrival on the island, Father Cervera was given lodgings at the Cathedral Annex in San Juan, on *Calle San José*. He later met with fellow priests and school administrators assigned to the Diocese. One day during Mass at the Cathedral, while sitting near the priest celebrating the liturgy, he spotted someone who resembled Paula. At first he wasn't sure, the woman was older and a bit heavier, but he imagined it might be her. She was sitting at a sharp angle from him in the third row behind a wide pillar. She could not see him. He observed her for the better part of an hour. He remembered the striking woman with whom he'd had sexual relations that night long ago.

Sitting next to Paula was a young boy, an adolescent, who had olive colored skin just like his fellow Andalucíans. He was intrigued by the boy's features. To meet her accidentally was his fanciful wish, but he didn't want to open a door to memories of that fateful incident, a door that had been closed for so many years. Plus, he feared that the outcome of such an encounter would be unpredictable and painful.

◆　◆　◆

After Paula heard about the priest's arrival, she was curious about his identity, but refused to believe it might be Father Cervera. Yet she couldn't put it out of her mind. After she spoke to Carlitos, she made plans to visit the school using as an excuse that she was seeking opportunities to volunteer for charity work.

On the day of her visit, as Paula entered the school grounds, she looked quickly around her and caught a glimpse of a man who could be the priest Carlitos had described. He was sitting on a bench in the small patio just beyond the school entrance. She entered the lobby, as if seeking information were her only motive, and approached a nun at the reception desk.

"*Hola*, My name is Paula Soler and I understand that you may need volunteers." The nun looked up at her.

"That is true, are you here to become a volunteer?" the nun asked.

"Yes, I am. What exactly is the nature of the work?"

"It is helping feed and clothe the children who are poor and abandoned, and taking care of the *ancianos* in the asylum."

Tending to old, infirm people did not appeal to her, but she said "That is exactly what I would like."

After a few moments, as the nun wrote her name down, she said nonchalantly,   "Who is that priest outside? I've never seen him before."

The nun rose from her stool, peered around the corner of the wall, and sat down again.

"That is Father Juan Cervera from Rome, a Jesuit priest, and an emissary from the Vatican to the Bishop of San Juan."

The nun's declaration stunned Paula; she felt dizzy and had to lean on a chair to regain her composure. The sister asked her if she was ill. Paula responded that she was fine, left her personal card with the nun, and slowly left the reception area, headed toward the garden. She steadied herself and studied his figure for a few moments. Once she overcame her anxiety, she took a deep breath and approached him, carefully observing his silhouette. *It is him, there is no doubt.*

"Father Cervera?" Paula asked, from a short distance away.

The man turned around slowly, looked at her, but did not respond. He seemed unnerved by her voice.

"I'm sorry, do I know you?" He finally said, with an audible tremor. He faked lack of recognition, but it didn't fool Paula. She could tell that he had actually recognized her.

"Do you remember a young woman by the name of Paula Soler from Barcelona? She was a member of your congregation at the Immaculate Conception church in 1869, where you were a young clergyman.

He was at least 50 years old, Paula surmised, but looked much older.

Paula took off her scarf and hat and defiantly said, "I am her."

Father Cervera reacted slowly; she could tell that he had been jolted by the exchange. His initial reaction confirmed it. He rose from the bench and took a few steps toward her.

"Yes, I remember." His left arm started to shake; he touched his throat, as if he needed air.

"Father Cervera, as a result of our night together, you have a son. A son who does not know you are his father, I'm growing weary hiding the truth. His name is Carlos and his last name is Soler, my maiden name."

Father Cervera, still in shock, didn't reply. The trembling of his hand, and now his arm, increased. He folded his arm on his chest and sat down in a wrought iron chair a few feet away from her.

Paula saw him wince as if in severe pain and approached him sitting down nearby. "Father, are you not well?"

"No, it's just I didn't know. What can I say? Are you here because you want to accuse me of something or to have me recognize him as my son?" He looked at the ground fully absorbing the content of what he had said and awaiting her response. After several minutes of silence Cervera looked at her.

"I would like to meet him."

Paula blanched. Moments later, she was in tears.

She hated herself; the unwanted pregnancy had been her fault, not Father Cervera's.

"No, I don't want him to know who you are. He would never understand and there is nothing you can say that would change that. I just wanted you to know that you have a son."

With those last words Paula got up, took a last look at Cervera and walked away quickly. Father Cervera, with desperation in his voice, called after her.

"Señorita Paula, please listen to me, don't go."

She was weak and confused with her mind numbed by a multitude of thoughts from the encounter. She had lost self-control, something she had promised herself not to do. His plea made her turn to face him. She could by his ashen face that he found it impossible to believe the news after all this time.

"I am dying, *Señorita* Paula. I'm suffering from consumption and have very little time left on this earth. I want to see him one time; just one time. I will never reveal who I truly am. Please concede this last wish for me. If I am truly his father, I have that right. Whatever I did wrong, I will atone for that and will face my Savior when the time comes."

Paula didn't answer; she walked back to the company offices knowing that she had not given much thought to the effects of a confrontation with Father Cervera. She struggled to find the keys to her office, still in tears. She entered quietly through a back door and closed it gently.

♦ ♦ ♦

Father Cervera sat down again in the courtyard and gathered his thoughts. All of this seemed like a nightmare to him. Yes, he had seen the young man at the Sunday Mass. His only thought at the time was that he looked Andalucían, and was sitting next to Paula. *How could that have happened in only one night with her? Why did I even come to the island, when I already suspected that Paula might be living here? I deserve to be ashamed and humiliated.* He could not come to grips with the fact that he had a son. He walked silently back to the Cathedral to pray for guidance.

He would request an early transfer back to Rome, saying that his work in San Juan was done.

Cervera received a message from Paula a week later, asking for a time and day for a meeting with her and Carlitos. It was unexpected. His pulse raced as he read the note realizing that what he refused to believe was true.

Carlitos and his mother arrived at the Rectory of the San Jose church which Cervera had chosen for the meeting. The boy did not fully understand the purpose of the visit.

"*Mamá,* why are we meeting with this strange priest? I have no classes with him."

"He wants to meet with a few students on a more personal level, before he makes his final evaluation of the school system here, and you were one of those chosen."

"Is he going to ask me questions about my catechism lessons? That's my least favorite subject. I hate it."

"No, I think he just wants to know more about how it feels to grow up in the colonies, and what you really think about the school," Paula said.

"I don't like this. If I tell him how I truly feel, I'll be expelled."

"Nonsense"

When they arrived at the Rectory they were led into a visitors' parlor. Father Cervera came in shortly after that and introduced himself, but did not shake hands with either of them. He attempted to keep his composure. He simply smiled and extended his arms motioning to them to sit down.

"I'm glad I was able to meet with both of you," he said, as he greeted them. "Can I offer you coffee or something else?"

Carlitos looked at the man and closely examined his features.

The coloring of his skin and his accent made it obvious that the priest was from southern Spain, much like his father, so he had been told. The man appeared sick and coughed frequently into a handkerchief. *Why am I even here? Why is he interested in me?*

"I wanted to meet a few of the students," Father Cervera began, guessing at the question evident on the boy's face. "What is your name? And how do you like our school young man?"

"Carlos Soler. The school serves its purpose," he said dryly. The priest was surprised at the answer, given the boy's age.

"What he means is, that he is content with the classes and instructors," Paula chimed in, trying to ease the obvious tension.

"That is fine," Cervera said. "Carlos, what plans do you have when you grow up?"

"That's a long way off, but I like politics and journalism."

"Have you considered the clergy?"

"Never in my life. Sorry, I mean no."

At that remark the priest forced a smile.

"And in your free time, what do you do?"

"I often accompany Don Antonio Roche, a family friend, to parks, festivals, and art galleries. He's almost like a father to me, since I never met my real father, who is dead." Father Cervera almost cringed at the last words.

"If you could change one thing in your classroom learning, what would that be?

"Less religion and catechism, more current world events."

At that moment, Paula rose to signal that the meeting was over, and Father Cervera nodded. He leaned over to touch the boy's hair and then shook his hand. Paula watched carefully and saw Carlos eyeing the priest steadily. They bid their farewells and Paula felt relieved that the encounter had not gone badly.

Carlitos wasn't convinced by the reason given for the reunion with Father Cervera. The priest's eyes, nose and mouth were similar to his own, only with wrinkles. *I haven't been told the truth about this priest. Someday I will figure it out. This meeting was not by chance.*

Neither Carlos, nor Paula went to Mass for more than a month, after that. They never saw the priest again.

◆ ◆ ◆

Oelvera put in his papers requesting a transfer back to Spain, but weeks passed without his receiving word from Rome. His health continued to deteriorate, and the Bishop insisted that he be hospitalized at a sponsored hospital in Santurce.

Three months after he had met Carlitos, a news item appeared in the San Juan *Gazeta,* which read:

> **Father Juan Cervera, age 57, a Spanish priest from Andalucía, and Vatican envoy assigned to the San Juan Diocese, died last Friday. The cause of death was tuberculosis. He died at the Hospital Auxilio Cristiano and left no known relatives. A Mass in his remembrance will be held this coming Sunday at the Cathedral in San Juan at 10:00 a.m. Donations in his memory are welcomed.**

Paula read the obituary and reflected on the unfortunate events that tied her to the priest she had known, the father of her child. She made plans to attend the Mass and asked Carlos to go with her. She had resolved to face the past, without shame, after that last encounter with the priest.

The Mass included choral music and was attended by many parishioners, since the Cathedral was the most important church on the island. The worshippers listened to the homily, took Communion, and sang in unison the hymns selected for the memorial. They prayed for Father Cervera's soul.

Paula broke down at the mention of his name by the Bishop, and cried at different intervals during the service. This was the end of a sad chapter in her life, yet she felt no ill will towards Cervera, who had become a victim of her own recklessness. At the end of the Mass, she passed by his casket, touched it gently and laid a yellow rose on the white satin cover.

Carlitos held on tight to his mother's hand. Paula knew it was hard for him to believe that this was the same priest who had met with them only a few months before. His tears welled up at the same moment as his mother's. Some day she would tell him the truth.

◆ ◆ ◆

A month after the funeral, Antonio invited Paula to dinner one evening in late October, when the high humidity and heat of the tropics had subsided somewhat, and when walking the streets of the capital was not so oppressive. He had suggested a new establishment that had just opened on *Calle San Justo*. She told Antonio that instead she would prefer to have him come to her home. The following evening Carlitos would be visiting relatives in Ponce, where he was going to spend the weekend, and they would have more time to talk privately.

The sun was setting as he arrived at her waterfront home. The sky was a mosaic of bright orange, violet, and pink just before the sun dipped below the horizon. The lagoon, just outside the former San Juan walls, sparkled with the fading reflection of the light. It had become a luminescent mirror.

Paula met Antonio at the door. She was dressed in a summer white cotton frock with three quarter length sleeves. Her freshly washed hair, still moist, fell beneath her shoulders and created a frame around her face accentuating her fine lines. She pecked him on the cheek as she greeted him and asked him in. They proceeded to the patio in full view of the lagoon and silently watched the sun depart.

"You look splendid tonight, Paula."

"No, I don't. You're just being polite. My hair is a mess."

"That is something I would not say, if I didn't feel it."

"*Gracias*," she said as she poured him a glass of *Jeréz*. "So do you."

"This is nice, that we can meet here in the evening away from the office."

"I feel the same way."

As dusk finally stole the light, oil torch lamps lit the patio. Antonio wondered why he had taken so long to appreciate Paula's refinement and class. She was just 30, and with her figure, no one would guess she was a single mother.

Antonio couldn't take his eyes off her, and tried to avert his gaze when she turned her head, but she caught him staring once again. Nothing was said. All the time wasted, all the years, the empty ones that had passed between them, and yet here they were alone in a new country far from where they had first met. They had a good life, with many friends in Puerto Rico. Friends had become family as they remade their lives away from their native land, yet there was something missing. It could be a somewhat desolate existence, but at least now they had each other.

"Would you open this bottle of *Rioja* wine for me, so I don't have to call the help?" Paula asked suddenly.

Antonio responded, opened the bottle and they toasted the past year, the good and plentiful sugarcane harvest, and the prosperity they had achieved through their own efforts. They were beholden to no one.

They drank more wine, and a servant appeared to ask if they were ready to be served dinner. Paula waved the servant away. *"Más tarde."*

"Finally," she said, "We can enjoy each other's company without being limited by people, time, or other things."

"Vale. Paula, do you remember our last meeting at the port, in Barcelona, the day I left Spain?"

"Of course I do, how could I forget? I felt so terrible for you and blamed myself for your forced exile. It was a sad goodbye."

"It wasn't your fault. I could have given you a kinder farewell and mentioned that I accepted your apology and that I was leaving Barcelona with few regrets. Good fortune made that goodbye a temporary one. I dreamt about you many times on the transatlantic journey to the island."

"I also thought of you Antonio, while I was in Cataluña, especially after I gave birth to Carlitos. I had my regrets, but was not ashamed of my situation, even if my parents were. I never cared about anyone else's opinion of me, except maybe yours."

She paused.

"Antonio, I have something to say. The man, who is Carlitos' father, was in San Juan recently."

"What?"

"Yes, I recognized him, once I saw him up close at Carlitos' school. He was visiting from the Vatican conducting a study of Catholic schools here."

"Are you saying that he's a priest?"

"Yes. He was. I am sorry that it took me so long to tell you."

"That explains many things about how you handled this matter. Did you ever inform your parents who he was?"

"Yes, but they made me promise not to say a word, or they would disown me. They threatened to banish me to a convent and put my son up for adoption."

"I'm so sorry. Do you plan to do anything about the priest now?" He didn't ask his name.

"I spoke to him at the Rectory months ago, and took Carlitos with me for one meeting with him. I have not told my son who he really was. Then the priest died of consumption last month here in San Juan." As she said this, she bowed her head and began weeping softly.

Antonio rose from his chair and walked over to the wooden bench where she sat. He took a seat beside her and instinctively put his arm around her. She looked up at him. He wiped away her tears with his handkerchief.

"My dearest Paula, life hasn't treated you any more kindly than me." Without thinking, he pulled her to him and kissed her. He remembered their last kiss so many years ago in Barcelona. This one was very different. She was willing and as he pulled away, she pulled him close again and kissed him with so much fervor that it surprised him. They embraced. For that one moment in time, he was her anchor and she hung on trying not to be swept away by the waves of her emotions. Their life experiences had separated and transformed them, but they now had finally found each other.

They parted for an instant; she stood up and took him by the hand and led him to her bedroom chamber. They made love during the night. A special magic that had been denied them drove their urgency. Paula appeared even more sensuous to Antonio when she had totally disrobed, and he was amazed that her lily white satin skin had no blemishes or wrinkles. Her maturity was apparent from her breasts. She had gained very little weight notwithstanding childbirth and was glowing with a look that only a woman in her prime can possess.

They did not have dinner that night and slept until late morning with no one disturbing them. As she woke and contemplated Antonio, she was overcome with her feelings for him and her eyes moistened.

"Antonio, *querido*, are you awake?" He didn't answer, but cuddled up to her body. As she caressed his hair she realized, at that precise moment, that she had fallen in love with him from the very first day they met. It had always been that way, even though she had tried to block those feelings for so long. She got up, dressed, and remained looking at him as he slept. She then bent down and kissed his forehead before she left the room.

After he woke, Antonio joined her for breakfast on the patio where they sat the previous night. She blocked the noon glare with her fan, as she looked at him while he ate, not knowing what to say. She half expected him to finish eating, stand up, and say goodbye. Instead, he rose from the table, came and knelt down beside her and kissed her.

"I think that last night made us realize that we cannot continue to live as we have. Living apart, looking and desiring each other from a distance, is not the answer. Those days are over. I want to marry you," Antonio said.

"Do you know what you are saying?"

"I think I do. This isn't the first time it has crossed my mind."

"But do you even love me?"

"I believe so. What I feel now is what matters. Do you have any feelings for me?"

"I do, and I've had them for a very long time, but managed to hide that for many years, before I came here and even afterwards."

"Could you see yourself as my wife?"

"I could, even though I may not be able to bear you any children. I may be too old."

"Nonsense, and that is not the reason I want to marry you."

He bent down and kissed her once again as the bright noon sun announced a new day. He then recalled an entry in the journal he had made while in prison. The book was dusty and the pages filled with green mold but he had kept it at the bottom of a large trunk that he brought from Barcelona. The entry read, *Will I ever find my one true love after this ordeal? Is it Paula? How can I ever be happy and live the life that I so desperately want?*

◆ ◆ ◆

Félix had been living at Central Cambalache after he fled San Juan, and had remained there for three years. The authorities had not pursued him to Arecibo, even though he expected them to do so, and he had changed his surname back to Prats, and used his middle name Raphael, hoping to go undetected. His relationship with Vicente was good; since he had told him the true reason for his leaving San Juan abruptly. His friend had provided him shelter in the servant quarters and had assigned Félix some duties at the sugar mill. When asked, Félix would simply state that he was in exile and that he had a claim to a noble title in Spain, which had produced conflict with the government, and it had forced him to leave. No one had asked for details.

He had recently noticed that Vicente had become distracted from his work and he knew why. Vicente was engaged to marry Belén Aponte, the young *criolla* from Sábana Grande, but was more focused on Rosalina, the former slave girl, than on his fiancée. He was not being attentive to the many business details that should normally occupy his day.

Vicente kept postponing the date of wedding to Belén, and Félix could tell that she was getting anxious, not suspecting the real reason for the multiple delays. She threatened to break off the engagoment if Vicente postponed the wedding one more time, so he agreed to set a firm date for the nuptials.

Félix sought to counsel his friend, as he was deeply indebted to him, but Vicente brushed away any discussions of Rosalina.

"Vicente, you are not concentrating on your chores. The workers notice and they are following your example. They are naturally lazy, you know."

"What are you saying? How could you know that, you don't even work with them?"

"But I hear things," Félix said.

"What do you hear?"

"You are not hiding your interest in Rosalina, and the workers have seen you kissing her behind the warehouse, and sneaking into the store room behind the building late at night."

"That's not true," Vicente said unconvincingly. "Whatever I do in my time off is nobody's business." He began shuffling papers nervously.

"Not even Belén's?"

"I'm not paying you to act as my confessor, leave me alone." He walked away.

Félix feared that Vicente's lapses on the job would imperil his tenure as foreman at Cambalache. Labor troubles were brewing on the horizon, and even though union activities were forbidden under Spanish rule, the circulation of various publications featured articles on workers' rights. Many of the laborers at the mill were illiterate and not able to read these manifestos, but they were read out aloud to them by others. Publications such as the *Proletarian Voice* and *The International Worker's Weekly* were filled with socialist and anti-government propaganda. While those ideas were not fully understood by the labor force, the slogans used resonated with many of them. Félix worried that the workers might cause disruptions at the Central.

Vicente had charged Félix with running errands for him and paying the Cambalache workers their monthly wages. He carried with him the coin of the realm, the Puerto Rican *peso*, a hybrid currency used in the Spanish colonies. Félix felt uneasy carrying out this task, given his natural tendencies, but he had to help his friend.

Vicente, on the other hand, continued delegating tasks and trusted him, notwithstanding the embezzlement Félix had committed in San Juan. He knew better than to try to steal from his benefactor. Vicente had told him that sometimes people do stupid things, but that everyone deserved a second chance.

As the wedding day approached, Vicente struggled with his feelings for both Belén and Rosalina, and this tortured him. He loved Belén as his future wife and mother of his children. Yet he loved Rosalina for the passion that she stirred within him when they lay together. She was sensuality incarnate and beguiling. It hadn't been hard to seduce her, she had nothing, and Vicente provided her with special privileges. With Belén it was different; she was destined to become the head of his family and he would entrust her with all his earthly possessions to administer for their future children, his only heirs.

Vicente was aware that Belén would never accept Rosalina as the "other woman" as many other spouses did. She had told him that her friends had suggested that she accept the inevitable; that Spanish men had to have their mistresses *"on the side"*. She had replied each time that if that was the way they wanted to live, that was their choice. She would never accept such a fate. Belén had repeated this often to Vicente; it wasn't a bluff. He knew her to be stubborn and proud.

As time passed, Vicente continued wrestling with his conscience, not breaking off his relationship with Rosalina. In an attempt to buy Belén a wedding gift like no other, he sent Félix incognito to San Juan. Félix at first resisted the idea, even though he had grown a long beard and a large handlebar mustache that made his appearance dramatically different. But Vicente insisted and he had to agree. His friend assured him that no one would recognize him during one brief trip, and recommended that he return that same night to Arecibo, and not linger in the capital.

Félix's travel plans went well except that on his return trip he stopped on the road outside the town of Bayamón to water his horse and adjust a wheel of his carriage. In the moonlit night, two unknown assailants approached him.

"My friend what have you there, do you need help?" One of the strangers said.

"No, I think I am all right, *Gracias.*"

"No *compadre,* we insist on helping you," the second man said.

As he stood up to face the men, one of them came from behind and kicked him to the ground. Félix attempted to fend him off.

"I'm the Marqués of Arecibo, I am royalty, and if you harm me, the police will hunt you down." They ignored him, quickly overcame and pinned him to the ground.

"Marqués *de mierda.* Who cares?" One of them said, mocking him.

"Please don't do this, Félix pleaded, "I can pay you well, if you let me go."

The first assailant said, "Why should we accept a simple payment when we can have it all?"

At that point, the second man, who was sitting on Félix, pulled out a long steel dagger and plunged it into his chest. Félix lost consciousness with the jolt and pain of the knife wound.

The robbers fled, after taking Belén's wedding gift of porcelain dishes, and dinnerware imported from Spain. They also grabbed his shoulder purse with its stash of *pesos* and gold coins, including that week's payroll for the Cambalache workers. Félix's carriage was left by the side of the road. The last thing he would see, as he tried to get up after recovering his senses, was his horse being led away by the thieves.

Luckily for Félix, the dagger did not penetrate his chest completely; it was partially absorbed by a small medallion that Félix carried on a chain underneath his shirt, so the dagger did not hit his heart, or an artery, but broke several of his ribs. He was severely wounded and the warm blood oozed inside his shirt. As he lay on the ground bleeding, some townsfolk rushed over after hearing the commotion. One shopkeeper took Félix and lifted him with the help of two other men. They carried him to his shed and laid him on a straw mat. Félix, who was awake but could barely speak, mouthed the words *"Ayúdame por favor."* He lost consciousness once more and a deep sleep enveloped him.

The shopkeeper's wife tended to his injuries and stopped the flow of blood, by plugging the hole the dagger had created. She looked at the medallion now covered in blood and broken flesh. As she removed the chain on his neck and put it aside, she saw a royal shield carved in its center. The fake medallion had saved his life. She put it next to his body and went in search of a physician.

Vicente, having not heard from him, imagined that Félix had fled with his money. At first, he refused to believe that Félix had stolen from him; but later he attributed his conduct to a return to criminal behavior. He finally asked the authorities if they had seen him or heard of an accident that may have claimed Félix, but no one could say.

He continued with his plans to wed Belén, postponing the wedding one last time, using as an excuse, that he had lost his entire wedding funds to his best friend, who had betrayed him.

Chapter Eight

The American
Colony - 1898

During the middle of May 1898, under a splendid deep blue sky that only can be seen in the Atlantic Ocean, north of where it meets the Caribbean Sea, the bombardment of San Juan began. Antonio, who was now living in the capital for most of the week, could hear the sounds of bursting shells. They originated from 11 ships anchored off Fort *El Morro*. The attack was led by the American naval forces fighting the Spanish American War. According to news accounts he had read, the Americans had invaded Cuba, the Philippines, and finally had their sights on Puerto Rico. The principal invasion force had been reserved for the southwest coast, a strategy adopted by the American military. The local media did not hide this fact. Once the invasion started, reports started coming in by messengers that Guánica, the least defended part of the island, had succumbed, showing little resistance to the U.S. Army.

As these events unfolded in the island newspapers, Antonio kept abreast of the nascent conflict. He prepared for the imminent change of sovereign governments and predicted that it was just a matter of time before the island fell to the American forces.

In San Juan, as the bombardment continued, the skies were red and orange with the incendiary glow from the fires that the bombs created. The vibrations from the shells striking their targets were felt for miles.

Antonio ran outside the home he shared with Paula and their two children, María Penélope and Rubén. Carlos was away in Arecibo.

Antonio returned to the house and informed Paula of the situation.

"This is the moment of truth, Paula, the invasion that we expected has begun and the *Americanos* are just offshore near the port."

"My Lord, what will become of us?" Paula said.

"We will be fine, if we accept the inevitable and adjust to the change. We owe nothing to the Spaniards. They exploited this island for 400 years."

"Aren't we just changing masters? The flags will be replaced, but what else?"

"I, for one, welcome any change for the better. We shall have to wait and see." Antonio yearned for a truly free Puerto Rico, achieved without violence, but suspected that would not come easily.

"I fear for the children, and for our home," she said. "You know how conquering armies treat the population of defeated countries. Look at our Spanish history."

"Don't be foolish, Paula, it's not like that. The *Americanos* don't slaughter people when they win a war. They won't hurt us, believe me."

Paula wanted to rely on his assurances but she wrapped her arms around both her children and hugged them as if it were the last time. Her fear was palpable.

The entire campaign to seize Puerto Rico lasted only 19 days, with a low number of casualties on each side of the conflict. The newspapers related the details of the final battle to seize the island and how easy it had been for the Americans to seize Borinquén from the Spaniards.

♦ ♦ ♦

Carlitos Soler Roche had left for Spain when he was 18 to study abroad. Puerto Rico had not yet established a university of its own, and he felt that pursuing his studies in Spain would broaden his horizons. He had joined his family's business at Cambalache after finishing his university studies. Still single, he had dived into the sugarcane business, making journalism his only other outside interest. He was in his late twenties and not too concerned with the current conflict. When he heard that the Americans had successfully invaded the island, his belief that the Spaniards would someday be forced to leave the island was validated. Other than by force, they would leave only after stripping it bare of its natural resources and taxing the population into poverty. He felt no sympathy for the crumbling regime and received the news of the fall of San Juan, with great expectations that it would be good for Puerto Rico, his home.

His main concern at Cambalache was the fledging rum production which the Central had belatedly turned its attention to, given the fluctuating demands on the world market for sugar and the heavy tariffs imposed by the Spanish regime. The product had a limitless future since the markets were embracing the refined rum business more than ever. The invasion by the Americans would bring economic benefits to the sugarcane industry, or so he hoped. He wanted to become a leader in this effort, a sort of pioneer.

Even though traveling soon after the hostilities had ceased was perilous, he made the journey to San Juan and was guided by his instinct on which roads to travel to avoid military operations. As he arrived at his parents' home, he spotted Antonio on the front porch. His adoptive father waved.

"My son what are you doing here? How were you able to make it to San Juan?"

"*Papá*, I came with almost no bags or extra clothes and stopped only briefly to give the horses some rest. A new day is coming and I wouldn't miss it for anything."

"You made that trip in record time, my son. Come inside to have something to eat and I will bring you up to date on recent events."

"Do you think that our Central business will survive the change of governments? Can it prosper?"

"We are a resilient people, my son, we can survive anything. I fear not, for the Americans have a different, if not a caustic way of governing. They are known for promoting democracy."

"I can see no downside to their takeover. Maybe it will bring a change in our fortunes, even though it's probably won't bring the island's autonomy we had hoped for," Carlitos said.

"Time will tell." Antonio put his arm around his son and led him inside.

◆ ◆ ◆

Vicente Ferrer was present that 25th day of July 1898, when the U.S. troops came ashore in Guánica. He was among the members of the welcoming committee that had been organized by the townsfolk which included residents from nearby Sábana Grande. He had always considered himself a true Catalonian, not a Spaniard, and now he was a *criollo*. He resented the entire Spanish Government, Royalist or Republican. Surely this invasion would provide relief to the small landowners and farmers who were paying exorbitant taxes to the Spanish Crown. They had quietly accepted the dictates from Madrid, without violence, even when their legitimate protests were ignored. He shared the belief that U.S. markets would be open to Puerto Rican agricultural products such as coffee.

At the Gúanica port, he shook the hand of the first officer he met from the U.S. Army, Major John Albert, originally from Boston, Massachusetts. Vicente knew some English, but not enough to sustain a long conversation with the officer.

"Welcome to Borinquén, *Señor Mayor*. We are happy that you have come to liberate the island. We love the word *Libertad*." Vicente exclaimed.

The Major smiled and responded with a handshake. He said, "We hope to help your people recover from the abuses of the Spaniards."

"*Así sera.*" Please let me escort you to the *Alcaldía* where the Spanish mayor had his office."

Major Albert followed Vicente to the center of Guánica and some of the troops settled down inside the town hall. Another contingent of troops followed the fleeing Spanish garrison. A third platoon of infantry dressed in both khaki shirts and pants marched eastwards on the south coast to Ponce. A few of the soldiers wore navy blue wool top coats, in the style of previous U.S. military uniforms dating as far back as the American Civil War.

Vicente lingered for a short while, bid his farewell to the Major and returned by wagon to Sábana Grande, traveling through the unpaved mountain roads. On the way, he spotted flags of the United States, flying from some *bohíos* along the way to his farm. On occasion, a tricolored flag was flown next to the Stars and Stripes. The flag of Puerto Rico had been proscribed by the Spanish; it represented the national colors and its movement for independence. Designed in the exact same pattern as the Cuban flag, but with the colors reversed, it bore wide red and white stripes and a huge blue triangle on its left side featuring a prominent white star. Vicente had read in the newspapers that the flag was designed in New York, but he had never seen it displayed openly.

As he traveled back to his home, his thoughts focused on what the future held for his family and for his farm, as well as the future of Cambalache, the sugarcane plantation in Arecibo where he had worked for so many years. He had moved to Sábana Grande after marrying Belén Aponte and had hired Rosalina, as his domestic servant, to help with the chores in his new home.

As his mistress, she had already borne him a son, who Belén thought had been fathered by another man. Vicente let her believe this, though his affair with Rosalina was not a well-kept secret. The reality of his marriage, after seven years, had changed. Belén had gravitated toward living a separate life from him after they began a family and after the initial attraction between them had vanished. She had given birth to his three children and had taken on the role of family matriarch, with little time left for Vicente's complaints, advice, or for any intimacy. She had told him earlier in their marriage, that she would never accept the existence of a mistress, however, the affair with Rosalina continued, and she turned a blind eye.

The raising of the American flag and the lowering of the Spanish banner at San Juan City Hall on October 17, 1898, after the War ended and the Treaty of Paris was signed, was attended by a large portion of the city's residents. It included both incoming and outgoing military and political appointees. Antonio was accompanied by Paula, and Carlos at the *Plaza de Armas*. He stood next to Vicente, who had traveled to the capital at Antonio's invitation, to be present on the occasion. There were two platoons of American soldiers, and three platoons of Spanish soldiers on the opposite side, facing the center of the plaza.

The Americans wore their distinguishable khakis, while the Spanish troops had on tricolor uniforms worn only on special occasions. Flags ruffled, banners were displayed and people lined the surrounding streets and balconies to witness the symbolic transfer of power. The sun was bright, there was a slight breeze, and the only other feature was the scent of gunpowder that came from the discharge of several rifles in a mock salute to the Americans.

No one applauded when they lowered the Spanish colors, after their band played its familiar dirge. The Spanish garrison then withdrew. A few moments later, the U.S. banner was raised on the roof of the *Alcaldia,* and was accompanied by the rendition of the Star Spangled Banner, played by the U. S. Army band assembled for the ceremony. After the anthem ended, massive applause broke out from the crowd. Antonio looked at Vicente and shared a glum smile with him, more reflective of the unknown future than of any real joy.

◆ ◆ ◆

While important changes were taking place in the political future of the island, nature had charted its own course for the inhabitants by creating a hurricane that struck the island only one year after the American invasion.

Vicente was the first one in his household to hear the howling winds which started at 3 in the morning on an overcast day in August 1899. The day before, flocks of birds of different species were seen flying in a northwest direction from the southeast, in a massive V shape formation. They were screeching incessantly like ravens

He woke up his entire family to seek appropriate shelter from the storm, but there was no better place to ride it out than his own home. And by then it was too late.

Winds increased in their intensity. There were no warnings, no evidence that a major catastrophic hurricane was about to hit the island. The rustling of the palms, swaying to a degree where the fronds almost kissed the ground and the flying debris of *bohío* roofs were the only signs.

Hurricane *San Ciriaco,* the name given to the storm, hit the island in a devastating manner. It's furor destroyed most of the coffee crop grown on Vicente's farm and adjoining ones on the surrounding mountains. It ravaged vast acres of sugarcane that were waiting for the harvest of that year. When the storm had passed, all Vicente could see for miles was total destruction.

Carlos had remained at Cambalache when *San Ciriaco* hit Arecibo. It had entered through Humacao with a swath that covered the entire island with powerful wind gusts, so strong that it demolished a multitude of residential and commercial structures. The storm inundated low lying areas of Arecibo with incessant solid sheets of rain, making all roads impassable. Even if Carlos had wanted to leave the Central, he couldn't have. The damages to the sugar mill were so crippling that Antonio Roche instructed Carlos to close down operations at the sugar mill for the rest of the year. They would try to save the remainder of the crop in order to process it at another sugar mill or perhaps sell it to a third party. Carlos realized that the losses to the Central were staggering. Cambalache had no back up crop as a substitute and rum production had barely started. There was no income to be derived to sustain the plantation, except from the outstanding accounts receivables that were owed to the Soler family entity, renamed Soler-Roche and Sons, after the wedding of Paula and Antonio. He realized that in order to continue its operations, the mill desperately needed an investor who might provide financial help.

Antonio met with Carlos in San Juan, a week after the storm hit to assess the damage. Paula sat with them in silence.

"It wasn't enough that the *gringos* came and grabbed the island, now we have to rebuild and start over thanks to *San Ciriaco*, as if we had never been in business," Carlos said. His initial enthusiasm for the American takeover had cooled.

"One bureaucracy has been substituted for another."

"This too, will pass," Antonio said, "We cannot give up, too much is at stake. It's not just money, it's our family name. We have enough to survive for a while, and maybe enough to replant the fields, but we have to find funds to pay our workers."

"I think we can rehire some laid off workers when the planting season comes next spring. We will see what happens; it all depends on harvesting an abundant crop. The only fortunate thing about the American invasion is that we now have the United States as a market for our sugar. It's a huge market, and that may help us," Carlos said.

"Both of you are right," said Paula, breaking her pensive mood. She was worried about her family's future given all the challenges that they now faced.

"We have to look for new investors, friends and business associates, who might be willing to take risks, but who will be amply rewarded when the Central recovers. We will explain what we will do under the American administration, and exactly how we will rebuild Cambalache with the help of their investments. I know for certain that there will be interest among our friends at the *Club Español*. I can think of two families right now that I have no qualms about asking for capital to help rebuild our business."

"You mean the Ollers, and the Rodríguez family?" Antonio asked.

"Well, they are two of our very best friends, right?" she replied. "It's worth asking. We know there are five big families that control the sugarcane industry on the island, and those two in particular are probably the most likely ones who can help. That would give those two families a large stake in our business."

Antonio paced around the living room. "These are hard times, Paula. Yes, they're our friends, but everyone has to fend for themselves right now. What makes you think they would be willing to invest?"

Paula stood up trying to put on a confident face for Carlos's sake. Their son was becoming a businessman; she knew he paid close attention to these discussions. His desire to learn had never ceased, and right now it was her duty to reassure him that all was not lost.

"For one, they have similar backgrounds to us, even though the Rodríguez family is not Catalonian," she said gesturing with her hands. "Both families have seen hard times and have come from humble beginnings to become wealthy. Secondly, we can suggest selling them a portion of our land, or borrowing their capital with the land as collateral. Another alternative could be that we sell them some company shares and they become shareholders along with us."

Antonio and Carlos both stared at her for a moment and she had to hide her incredulity. *When will they learn that I'm as smart as them? These men hadn't built their investments by themselves. She had proven herself a businesswoman long ago.*

"When and how should we approach them? Carlos asked.

"Let me think about that. I want a discreet, yet persuasive approach, for the best effect," Paula said.

"We could organize a social event here in San Juan, and have people come as overnight guests, since one of the families is from Ponce, and the other is from Salinas," Carlos suggested.

"Only after they have agreed to consider investing. I don't want to appear that we are desperate or begging for help. We are too proud to do that and there is nothing worse than going to a *fiesta* and being solicited right then and there. I know the feeling, believe me," Antonio said. "I don't want to waste our time, or theirs."

"Carlos, I agree with your father, and I will give you an important role in the planning. I want young people to come too, not just the parents. It's important to include the next generation. They are potential successors and rightful heirs."

"I like the thought," Carlos replied.

◆ ◆ ◆

New political forces had been unleashed with the American invasion, and some of the political parties under Spanish rule were seeking a role in the colonial administration. Leaders of these entities were preparing to participate in island politics, although the field was muddied and some parties had changed their political platforms to conform to the new reality. Others, like the Liberal Party, had quietly morphed and modified their platform since their whole purpose under Spanish rule was to have a voice and vote in the Spanish courts. The Liberals had done what they could to represent the island, hoping that Puerto Rico would be named an official province of Spain with a large degree of local autonomy. Those efforts had failed.

Now the United States was in charge, and the Americans quickly named the political leaders of the colony, all appointed by the President of the United States or by the Governor of Puerto Rico, himself a political appointee. The Treaty of Paris included in its provisions that Spain would cede possession of Puerto Rico to the United States. No clauses were included in the treaty insuring a transition to self-government like those pertaining to the Philippines and Cuba. This had sealed the island's destiny. It became an American possession, a non- incorporated territory, with no provisions for the island's transition to either statehood or independence. Antonio and Carlos had read the details in the local press and were disappointed by the terms of the treaty.

The first Puerto Rican colonial government was modeled on the American system, but modified to adjust to the former Spanish colony.

As the members of the Soler -Roche family were facing a new future, with a possible resurgence of their sugar plantation, other members of the social and political establishment were unsure on how to proceed.

Antonio Roche had joined the Autonomist Party earlier and contributed some money to replenish its coffers. He was no longer the revolutionary anarchist of his youth, but was far from being a conservative. The party asked him to occupy a leadership position, but he declined at first, fearing that his past murder conviction would come back to haunt him.

He had not yet received word from his parents that his name had been cleared, a goal his mother had stated she would pursue.

Carlos, on the other hand, was an independence sympathizer and had been one all of his youth, but refrained from arguing politics at the dinner table. He had no reservations, however, in discussing the subject with his friends and associates and was considered a militant because of his views. His political group, the Union Party, soon abandoned the statehood ideal, which suited Carlos just fine. He had joined a party that was considered moderate, not radical. Although his private political beliefs were more leftist, he was careful not to disseminate them widely. He was aware that his political beliefs could affect his business interests under colonial rule.

"*Papá*, do you have plans to seek an appointment to any of the government positions?" Carlos asked. "Could you serve the new master?"

"It's too early to say, son. It will depend on how the government is organized, the measure of authority it will have under American rule, and what position I am offered, if any. I would never compromise my principles." He didn't mention his criminal record in Barcelona.

"I'm glad to hear that, I feel the same. But what if nothing changes?"

"I doubt that. The Americans have a different mentality than the Spaniards, and they will try to help the island, at least at first. But how those intentions will translate into action, is anyone's guess."

"There are two different schools of thought on what should happen to the island, if it's not to remain a colony," Carlos said. He was trying to be candid with his father with his own perspective. "One is for statehood; the other is for outright independence."

"I'm well aware of that, and I don't have an answer on what I would do, if those were the only choices we had."

"Neither do I." Carlos passed his hand over his head as if trying to banish unpleasant thoughts not yet fully formed. There was no need to worry Antonio any further with his own misgivings.

◆ ◆ ◆

After the old walls of San Juan were demolished in 1897, to further the expansion of the city, much of the population moved to the southeast, to an area that led to a lagoon separating the island city of San Juan from the main island. Antonio and Paula selected the area named *Puerta de Tierra,* a gate to land, to build a new home. It was not far from their present home. The shoreline near the lagoon was bordered by the sea, which was both emerald green and navy blue. The surrounding land was nearly flat reached by the lapping ocean waves. It contained a marshland on the opposite shore with dark murky sands that needed landfill and development, but the area held the possibility of an expansion that would spur the growth of the capital. It was here at the edge of that lagoon that the Solers began construction of their new house in 1900.

Once the home was completed, they moved into the two story white stucco mansion that had a red Andalucian style roof. This new dwelling was the estate that Paula had envisioned all of her life. Not a home in the modernist style of Barcelona, but one inspired by those on the surrounding hills of Sevilla and Granada. Each window of the new mansion had its own private balcony with tile bordered archways that led to a view of the private gardens facing the lagoon. She could now have a real social life and entertain as she once did in Barcelona. This would be her domain. As she reminisced about the days of her past, she realized how much her life had changed and how dramatically it had been altered by her first pregnancy. She couldn't imagine life now without her children.

♦ ♦ ♦

Vicente Ferrer had joined the Liberal Party offshoot in Sábana Grande founded by a well-known autonomist and abolitionist, Rafael Labra. He had met Mr. Labra at a gathering convened before the actual invasion of the island by the United States. He listened with enthusiasm to the reformer, as he spoke of his dreams for a truly autonomous, and perhaps someday, independent Puerto Rico. Labra had been at the forefront of the fight to liberate the island slaves, and now led a movement to establish a true democracy on the island.

Vicente, mesmerized by his pronouncements and eager to be involved in the island's struggle to seek its identity, became a follower. At one of these meetings a bearded, white haired man, with a pronounced stoop in his back and a slow gait, approached Vicente and greeted him. The man was dressed in an old wine colored shawl and leaned on a maple colored cane.

"*Hola,* Don Vicente, I was hoping to see you again in better circumstances than the last time I saw you."

"And who may I ask, are you?"

"You do not remember me?" Vicente stared at the man and managed a slight glimpse of recognition, but couldn't place him.

"Félix, Félix Prats Hidalgo, I came over with you on the ship *Regina* from Barcelona. We used to be good friends." The man started to weep as he mouthed the words. Vicente touched him on the shoulder.

"Félix?" I thought you were dead. How long has it been? Ten years, maybe more?"

"Yes, it has been a very long time, and part of the reason I never came back to Cambalache after leaving, was due to the fact that I lost your monies, the payroll, and wedding gift to *Señorita* Belén. I thought you were never going to believe what happened to me. I was robbed at knifepoint and seriously wounded by bandits on the road back to Arecibo. I remained unconscious for a very long time, but was brought back to life by some *campesinos* in Bayamón. They nursed me back to health, and I am forever in their debt. I had no choice but to stay with them. I paid them back for their generosity by working on their farm during the hard times that followed."

"I don't know whether to believe you or not. You could have sent for me; I might have been able to help. But after so many years you just show up? Why was there no word from you?" Vicente's tone was sharp and his face was turning red.

"I was ashamed to return to Arecibo, thinking you might not believe me, because of what I did at the *Mundillo* store in San Juan." Félix was shaking and began sobbing.

Vicente softened.

"You're probably right. I might have not understood, but with some proof how could I not have forgiven you? The assault was not your fault, if that's what really happened. And you didn't lose the payroll; it was in another leather bag that you left at the door of my house. If you had another bag with you that night, it had no money."

Some of Vicente's incredulity remained. He took out a handkerchief from his vest and handed it to Félix. *This poor wretch, could any part of what he is saying be true?*

"Thank God for that. My hope is that you will forgive me now. Here is a purse containing the exact amount of *pesos* that were stolen from me that day, it's at least the value of the wedding gifts that I bought for you. I know that it cannot really repay you after all these years. I don't have the payroll money, so I'm relieved."

Félix coughed violently, and covered his mouth, his entire body shaking as he held out a purse. He could not continue speaking. Vicente was unnerved by the whole incident and delayed his response.

"I really don't need this money anymore, you can keep it; you may have to use it someday."

"Please, Don Vicente, I can't accept that. The money is not mine, and I don't want to go to my grave owing you, and being branded a thief. Please give me a chance to atone for my past behavior. *Por favor se lo pido.*"

The anguish in his voice was hard to ignore. Vicente accepted the money, thinking he might later give it to Rosalina. He then spoke without anger, and he was truly moved by Félix.

"What will you do now?" Vicente asked.

"I will go back to Bayamón, and wait for my time to come."

Vicente struggled with his next words, and the pity he felt as he remembered his days with Félix on the ship. They had been so happy and excited in their adventure to a new land.

His thoughts dwelled on the night, during their first days, when they ate at the nice restaurant in San Juan, full of hope.

"Please come visit me at the farm, if only for a few days, and meet my family. I have three children now, and own a coffee farm on the mountain road to Maricao. It might be good for your health. Here, I will write down address for you."

He handed Félix a piece of paper with his address and directions.

"I will try, my friend." Félix shook hands with Vicente and parted after clasping his right arm. Vicente looked at him, stepped forward, and embraced his former ship companion as if he had just discovered a lost soul.

♦ ♦ ♦

Carlos Soler had grown into a handsome young man, dark olive colored skinned, with light brown hair and matching ear length sideburns. Most of all he was gregarious, and a good listener. When asked about his background and heritage, he gave only sketchy details and changed the conversation politely. The details of his private life he would not share with anyone. Antonio Roche had adopted him and he considered him his true father. He'd always wondered who his real father was, but with the passage of time the importance of the question faded. He did remember the odd meeting with the priest who had later died, and how similar his features were to his own. His mother never answered his inquiries on how she had originally met Father Cervera. All he was able to get from her was that she knew the priest from long ago in Barcelona.

When Carlos returned to Puerto Rico from studying at the University of Salamanca, in 1896, he entered the family business because it was expected of him, not because he had the desire to make money. But he soon grew to appreciate its complexities. His specialty became the refining of aged rum. He had learned the process from other distillers at sugarcane mills and found the entire process of production immensely challenging. The thought of making the finest rum on the island gave him an incentive to work feverishly, and he thoroughly enjoyed the experience.

"*Papá*, I am certain that rum will be our ticket to saving Cambalache. Have you tasted what's currently available on the market? It all tastes like cough medicine and is rough, acidic, and burns your throat. All they produce are different variations of moonshine."

"I'm not much of a rum drinker, son, but I suppose you're right. It's especially true of the ones I have tasted. That's why I shy away from rum."

"It's the future, and we should take advantage of the opportunities while there is still room for competition."

"I see that rum will become your focus in the industry and you are right, this is the time." Antonio nodded approvingly to Carlos, who was delighted.

When the time came to help forge a business strategy for all of Cambalache's products, he assisted his father, and proved himself capable of recommending new approaches.

◆ ◆ ◆

As the date for the planned social banquet drew closer, he became involved in the details, including seating arrangements, the beverages, and the food to be served. Carlos wanted access to the scion of the Rodríguez family, Jacinto Rodríguez Durán, the family patriarch who owned and managed the rum producer, *Destileria Rodríguez*, in Ponce. Don Jacinto was well known on the island for his business savvy and Carlos thought it prudent to sit close to him and seek his advice.

To hide the obvious, he arranged the place cards to sit near Don Jacinto's daughter, three chairs away from her parents. In those three chairs he placed Paula, Antonio, and the local clergy, who would give the blessing. He had never laid eyes on Margarita Rodríguez, and had no expectations for the evening. He assumed he would be bored until the time when he was able to meet with Don Jacinto alone, and perhaps share a cognac. He would skip the cigar.

The evening of the dinner started inauspiciously as the 35 invitees arrived at the front portico of the newly decorated Soler-Roche mansion. Paula and Antonio met them at the front door, and greeted each of them with hugs and kisses. She had a servant escort the couples to a drawing room to partake of *Jeréz, Cava,* and light tapas before the formal meal. At the appointed hour, the Rodríguez family had not yet arrived.

Don Jacinto thrived in being late, in order to make a grand entrance with his boisterous personality and his loud voice, so that everyone knew he had finally come. He did so that evening. He escorted his wife, Doña Esperanza, into the room. His daughter, Margarita, followed a few steps behind in a flowing pink silk gown that was decorated with lace and little bows around elbow length sleeves. Her auburn hair was loose around her neck. She did not use the braids that were in style, which hinted at her manner. Her hair was her flag, one of a different country, a standard of her own personality. But she seemed to respect society's mores or what passed for proper behavior. She acted and spoke in delicate tones, albeit one could detect a subtle change in her when she spoke of a subject not to her liking. Carlos approached to introduce himself after contemplating her for a few minutes.

"*Bienvenida, Señorita,* I'm Carlos Roche Soler, the eldest son of the Roche family." His dark brown eyes sparkled when he looked directly at her.

"*Hola,* I'm Margarita." She addressed him, but quickly averted her glance.

"I believe we are seated next to each other at the dinner table, shall I escort you there?"

"Actually no, I want a glass of *Cava* first. Also, before I sit down, I want to greet some of my friends who are already here."

She said it with such resolve in her voice that there was no room for argument. Carlos liked her poise and style; it reminded him of his mother when they left Barcelona.

"As you please. Juan, please bring the *Señorita* some *Cava*," he said, calling the servant.

Carlos took the opportunity to examine her face. It was perfectly shaped, with slim cheeks, a petite nose, and dark green eyes. Her hair framed her pale white cheeks which bore a faint layer of rose blush powder.

After accepting the aperitif, Margarita drifted off in the direction of some invited guests who greeted her from afar. Carlos was puzzled that she had not excused herself and found it strange to be standing alone, so soon.

The *mayordomo* of the Soler residence rang the chimes indicating that dinner was served. The guests began to take their places around the huge polished wooden table. Carlos placed himself at the side of Margarita's chair and waited for her. There was a low hum of different conversations being held simultaneously. Many of the guests were following more than one conversation at a time, typical of these social occasions.

Carlos leaned over to Margarita as she took her place and sat down.

"How do you like San Juan? It's very different from Ponce, don't you think?"

"Yes, but at the same time it's just a larger, rougher version of Ponce without the familiarity and genteelness that I am accustomed to. If I have to choose, I prefer Ponce."

At that moment, Antonio gently tapped his wine glass with a knife in order to draw attention and ask for silence. He stood up and proposed a toast.

"To our respective families, may we all have health, love, and happiness, with the time to enjoy them."

It was an old familiar toast, but then he added, "And a toast to the new American friends, which I dearly hope will bring us all good fortune and many American dollars."

There was a light hearted laugh among the guests, a few of them clapped. It masked the arrival of uncertain times.

Carlos found the toast a bit pedestrian and almost out of place on this particular occasion, especially one where his family would be seeking financial investments in Cambalache. It was strange for his father to say that, given his rebellious past, but he realized that new times required new attitudes. His father had always sympathized with political groups seeking more liberties and self-governance. In essence, this toast was a tribute to the Americans and did not seem proper. Margarita didn't raise her glass and remained silent while Carlos observed her.

"What do you think the future holds for us," he asked her.

"You mean for you and me, or for all of us?" She grinned mischievously. He hesitated, he had been caught off guard.

She continued as if she had never asked the question. "I think that some good things will come out of this takeover by the Americans. It's not an encouraging sign, however, for the island's independence, or even for greater autonomy, not even for the limited one the Spaniards granted to us near the end of their reign.

"Do you want Puerto Rico to become a republic?" Carlos asked.

"Don't you?" she replied.

"I haven't really given it much thought, given the rapid turn of events."

"Well, you should. You belong, as I do, to the elite class of Puerto Rican society and you can do a lot of good with your family's money and influence, as I can with mine. We should be leaders in any movement for sovereignty." Carlos realized that she had no idea of the true purpose of the dinner.

"Do you have plans to go into politics?" he asked.

"Not at the moment," Margarita answered. She dropped the subject just as dinner was served.

Carlos was pleasantly surprised with his dinner companion; he expected a conversation full of superficial subjects, mostly about fashion, and shopping in Spain. She was not like that, as far as he could tell, yet he found her inscrutable. He tried to continue discussing the topic of politics, but she declined to expand on her views. She was high class indeed, but how closely she followed society's conventions was hard to tell. One thing he noticed was that while he was speaking to others, she would not take her eyes off him.

At the end of the evening, the guests moved in separate groups, by gender, to either the drawing room or the library. This was something Carlos did not appreciate, since he would have preferred to stay by her side. He had not expected this before he met her. After the men had retreated to smoke cigars and drink cognac, and the hour approached to end the dinner, Carlos went to Margarita, who was sitting in the drawing room.

"I would consider it a privilege to see you again at another time, perhaps at another gathering, smaller and more intimate than this one?" He said this but that had not been part of his plans. He couldn't stop himself from asking, since he was intrigued by her manner and feared he might never have another chance.

"Why would you want to see me?" she asked in a teasing manner. She didn't act surprised by the unexpected invitation. They had only spent a few hours together.

"I like how you speak your mind, and don't waste words on vain matters." He found his own excuse weak.

"I know practically nothing about you since you said so little, but you are a good listener, I'll give you that. And *guapo*." She smiled.

This last remark, unusual for a young lady of society, silenced him momentarily.

"Good, then can we make plans for me to listen to you some more?"

She laughed. It was infectious and he joined in the laughter.

"That was original. Yes, we can plan something, let me speak to my parents and I will send you a note by messenger," Margarita said.

Carlos kissed her gloved hand and watched her walk out the front entrance with her parents. She moved gracefully and before she left, looked back at him, smiled, and waved goodbye.

During the dinner, Antonio Roche had taken the opportunity to take Jacinto Rodríguez aside to discuss business. Don Jacinto was middle aged, portly, and almost bald, with a face that had huge lips that perennially held a small cigar. He walked like an aristocrat, although his posture had him bent somewhat at the waist.

He knew a good business opportunity when he saw one. The business of running a successful sugar mill was his only vocation. He had no other interests, except good food and entertainment, which he enjoyed often. When Antonio began discussing his interest in seeking an investor that would shore up Cambalache financially until the markets improved, he listened and weighed carefully to what Antonio had to say. He was not foolish enough to invest in lame projects or to give money to losers, but Antonio was not a failure and he liked him.

Antonio needed help, and Don Jacinto, who needed to expand his rum production and create brand recognition, could lend him money or purchase shares in the sugar mill.

He agreed to meet with Antonio in Ponce or Arecibo, to discuss the details of his proposal. Don Jacinto was partial to the idea, but wanted to first review the financial records of Cambalache and visit the Central at some point.

"Do you actually think that the American takeover will help our businesses?" He asked Antonio.

"It will help lower or eliminate the tariffs that our products pay when they are exported to the United States. That alone will lower our costs of production and increase profits. I see a bright future for our industry under American rule," Antonio said.

Don Jacinto paused and changed subjects.

"Would you favor the island becoming a state? I have heard that some political parties are advocating that, as opposed to what happened to Cuba and the Philippines."

"Not necessarily, besides the U.S. is not ready to grant statehood or anything that resembles it at this time, that I know for sure."

"What will they do with us? We are a poor country and have limited natural resources."

"We are a good market for their goods and they will be a good market for our agriculture, especially sugar," Antonio said.

"Until the time that we become a drain on their Treasury and they cut us loose."

"Is that what you are hoping for?"

"Isn't that better? A peaceful path to an independent nation, rather than a violent one?"

Antonio noticed a certain edge to Don Jacinto's voice and wondered what he meant by that expression. *Is he advocating support for separatists groups who preach outright rebellion? I never thought that the idea would come to repel me someday.*

The conversation ended and they agreed to meet the following month. An initial meeting in Ponce would be held, then a subsequent one in Arecibo.

When Antonio mentioned the Ponce meeting to Carlos, he immediately told his father he would attend. Antonio said that it was only a preliminary meeting which would be followed by many more, but Carlos was insistent. Antonio found that odd, but could only guess that it might have something to do with Don Jacinto's daughter. He had noticed the interaction between them at the dinner.

◆ ◆ ◆

A packet arrived from Spain the following week wrapped in a large burlap sack that bore the weather beaten signs of travel by sea. It was addressed to Antonio and had been sent from the Roche family residence in Barcelona. No other markings were evident except the costs of the postage. The package had been tied with a small rope that bore the same red wax seal used by his family when sending letters. He recognized it instantly. Antonio took out the contents, and found a large thick embossed leather folder with his father's initials engraved on the cover. Inside the folder was a wide dark wine colored ribbon placed diagonally from the upper left corner to lower right across the sole imprinted parchment page.

At the top of the page it read: *Indulto Oficial de la República Española* and was dated January 3, 1884. The document had taken more than 16 years to reach him. *The Official Pardon of the Spanish Republic? Why is my family sending me this?* Attached was a note from his mother.

> *My dearest son:*
>
> *Inside this leather folder you will find a document that exonerates you and grants you a pardon for the crime for which you were unjustly convicted and imprisoned many years ago. Your father used all of his good offices up to the day he became ill, to get this approved by Her Majesty's government after you left Barcelona, but he was met with little success. Ironically, it was after the First Spanish Republic was established that it was finally approved. Somehow, it got lost when the Republic fell and it was delivered to him just before he died. The document was discovered by your sister after we moved all of your father's belongings out of the study. It was inside a wooden box in a small drawer in his desk. I know this may be too late to provide you any real comfort, but our family lawyer said the unconditional pardon permanently expunges your criminal record in this country. This may prove beneficial to you someday.*
>
> *I do hope with all my heart that this arrives in your hands before your next birthday, so that it may provide some vindication to you on that very special occasion.*
>
> *Penélope sends her love and kisses. I have to say it was largely through her efforts that this discovery came to pass. Te quiero mucho, hijo mío,*
> *Tu madre, Manuela*

It had finally happened. Antonio could hardly read the entire note without tears.

All this time had passed with the conviction hanging over his head. It was one of the reasons that he had shied away from public office, and had even refused honorary posts in organizations that would place him in the public light. It was finally over, and yes, he was 50, an old man by many standards. The news made that a happy week for him, and once he informed Paula, they celebrated. A curse had finally been lifted from the family. Paula had always believed in his innocence, he knew that. The news would be kept secret, however, to be shared only with his children at the appropriate moment.

Part Three

Chapter Nine

The Ollers-1900

Pablo Oller was born in 1850 in Barcelona, Spain. When he reached the age of 18, he joined the Spanish Army and was assigned to a garrison in Santiago, Cuba. Once he finished his military service, he was transferred to San Juan, where he was discharged from the Army. He foresaw no future in his native country, and even though Puerto Rico did not possess the natural resources of Cuba, especially in agriculture, he chose a less crowded and less developed island in which to seek his fortune.

Shortly after his arrival on the island at age 22, he made his way south to Salinas, sought and found employment. He started working as a field hand on a cattle farm near the Central Aguirre, cleaning scrub timber from the land and preparing it for pasture. To the amazement of his employer, he did not want his salary to be paid in *pesos*. He preferred to be paid with livestock, and using his savings from his military pay he built a barn and purchased feed for the cattle that he acquired. By age 30, he was making a living selling livestock and leasing cattle to other farmers on the south coast. He was careful to maintain his own small herd to ensure the continued success of his enterprise.

In time, the profits from his labors enabled him to buy an ownership interest in a sugar mill in Bayamón, which he renamed Central Isabel, in honor of his first born daughter with his wife, Leonor Crúz.

He had met the original owner of the Central Isabel, Arnaldo Urrutia, through mutual friends. The sugar mill needed an infusion of capital, and Pablo Oller had the money to invest. When Don Arnaldo later offered him the chance to own the sugar mill outright, Don Pablo bought the majority stake without hesitation. It gave him ownership, but he would not be responsible for the day to day operations. Don Arnaldo would remain the onsite administrator since Central Isabel was on the north coast of the island.

Don Pablo was heavy-set, with a long jaw that made it seem as if he were always preoccupied. He had prematurely lost some of his salt and pepper hair and his brow seemed permanently furrowed. The exposure to the Caribbean sun, especially while working the fields at midday, had deepened the lines of his brow adding a leathery look and ten years to his countenance.

His manner was courteous and gentlemanly even with his limited schooling. He had acquired these social mores in the Spanish Army where he had to rub elbows with nobility, as well as the human dregs of society. His enormous ears made it possible to say, in jest, that he could identify anyone speaking nearby without looking at them.

One afternoon a few months earlier, at home for lunch, he had been lost in thought and after the meal ended had spoken to his wife.

"Leonor, do you see how many of our compatriots are leaving the island?" He'd said to her that summer day of 1897. He'd glanced at the pale blue afternoon sky through an open window, and paced the living room. Then he had stopped looking at the sky again, waiting for her reply.

"Pablo, it's the uncertainly of the growing tensions between *España* and *los Estados Unidos.*" He had turned to face her.

"The Spaniards here have begun selling their residences, and their investments. It may be an opportunity for us to increase our holdings. I was thinking that I might want to try another type of business, other than farming."

"That could benefit our family. What other business do you have in mind?"

"I was thinking of some *bodegas,* however, ones that will sell other things besides food."

"Where would you place these *bodegas*?"

"Most likely in the capital." He'd sat down.

"Aren't there enough *colmados* or dry goods stores already in San Juan?"

"Not enough, my dear. It's the only way to secure our future. I'm not satisfied with what we have." He'd instantly regretted those words.

"Pablo, you shouldn't say things like that, people will think that you are greedy."

"I know that, I'm sorry. Terrible words to use, but that's how I feel."

"Haven't you felt the desire to return to Spain and live, say in Madrid, with all that is happening there?"

"Not in the least, Spain is part of my past, and not my future. I'm happy to be here. Even if all my friends leave, I won't."

Thus, a dry goods store in Cataño became his third investment. The new company he created, Oller, S.A. would spawn branches in San Juan and he envisioned it eventually reaching the new suburbs of Santurce and Río Piedras, the latter being the future site of a new teachers' college.

His fourth purchase was a strip of vacant land on a narrow peninsula between a lagoon and the Atlantic Ocean close to *Puerta de Tierra* known as *El Condado de Santurce,* named for a Spanish count from a town in the Basque country. The land sold for half of its appraised value and was suitable enough to build a manor, a second home for the Ollers. It was in the same neighborhood where Antonio Roche and Paula Soler lived.

By the time Don Pablo was invited by Antonio Roche to invest in Cambalache, he was ready for a new venture. The invitation to the banquet, at the Soler-Roche mansion, came by private messenger. The enclosure stated that it was to be held on a Saturday evening in mid- December. With the Christmas season approaching, Don Pablo left Salinas earlier than usual for his vacation in the capital. There were more festivities during the holidays in San Juan, than in his home town adjoining Salinas. The village of Aguirre was a modest one with acres of flat lands surrounding it. Its main business activity was the Central Aguirre, a sugar plantation once owned by Spaniards, who had sold tho mill to a group of Americans after the invasion of 1898. The sugar mill and its residents had their own postal service and stores on a small main street, but during the holidays it was nearly deserted.

Don Pablo, quick to form opinions about events, changed them quickly when circumstances warranted. Contrary to his compatriots from Spain, he believed that the invasion by the Americans was the best thing that could happen to Puerto Rico, and he was among the first citizens to hoist the Stars and Stripes on a flagpole at his home, but only after he had been assured that the Spanish Army had surrendered. Some of his business associates and friends didn't share his feelings, and many of them had returned to Spain. He wasn't partial to that alternative.

When Antonio asked that question at the banquet for potential investors, he had answered without hesitation.

"As I told Leonor recently, I don't contemplate moving back to Spain now or in the near future. Why would I? Things have gone well for me here. Look at how I started and look at what I've accomplished." Don Pablo looked at Antonio smugly and smiled.

"The Americans have a different culture and invariably they will want to impose their traditions, language, and customs on us. Doesn't that bother you?" Antonio said.

Antonio was trying to ascertain if Don Pablo, a friend, would remain on the island and become a reliable investor.

"It does not, because we have a long tradition here of the Spanish language, its culture, and the arts. We will always in our hearts be Spaniards due to our heritage, and Puerto Ricans due to our choice. Perhaps someday we will become American citizens. The language issue is of no concern to me. And I do admire the American work ethic."

"I will never give up my Spanish citizenship. If the Americans make me choose, I know what I will do." Antonio said.

He said this with a fierce pride of being a Catalonian, but with the inner conflict that he felt being a *criollo*. Still a Spaniard at heart, he had evolved into a person that loved his adopted home.

"That's not going to happen soon, so don't worry. Let history take its course. Perhaps we can keep both citizenships, once tensions between the two countries die down and peace is secured," Don Pablo suggested.

"I take it then that you will stay for a significant period of time?"

"I can guarantee that."

Antonio smiled. Just what he wanted to hear. He had already approached Jacinto Rodríguez from Ponce, and solicited an investment from him. He was confident that a liaison would develop with Don Jacinto, but was uncertain whether he could count on Don Pablo, due to his sprawling interests. Another factor was that Don Jacinto's political leanings conflicted with Don Pablo's. This made for a strange partnership between the three men with their opposing views.

Antonio himself was not a separatist, and felt it would be premature to become one, since the United States had not announced its plans for the island. He thought it unlikely that the island would become an independent nation due to its particular political situation and to its lack of substantial natural resources. He could live with the status quo and remain an autonomist, just as he had under Spanish rule. The most important matter for him now was the future of Cambalache in the emerging political situation and its effect on the world market for sugar.

"I would like to sit down with you," Antonio said, "to discuss some plans I have for Cambalache." He skirted any further discussion of politics.

"I would be most willing to listen, just let me know the time and place. Maybe, before I return to Salinas, right after the Epiphany holiday."

"That would be splendid, Don Pablo."

"In any event, I could send Lorenzo, my son, or my daughter, Isabel, to visit the Arecibo plantation. Do you know that I named my sugar mill in Bayamón after her?"

"I did not."

"Both of them have good minds for business."

Later that same evening, Don Pablo confided to Leonor the substance of the conversation with Antonio. Leonor had no interest in the business dealings of her husband, as long as they provided the resources for her lifestyle and social standing. She had little advice to contribute. In contrast, Isabel, his only daughter, was interested in her father's commercial adventures now that she had finished her schooling. As first born, she relished the idea of becoming a successful business executive; if so, she would become one of the few women in Puerto Rico to achieve that. She had met Paula Soler and admired her strength of character, her mastery of the details of the Cambalache operation, and her outspokenness about the proper role of women in society. She was the one person that Isabel wanted to emulate.

Isabel Oller was younger than Paula, and had married early in life at the age of 20, later bearing two children in the process, Gabriela, and María Antonia. She had raised the girls in a protected environment and groomed them to appreciate the finer things in life, while providing for their every whim. Ambitious to her core, she laid the ground work for her daughters to realize her dreams, if she was unable to.

Lorenzo Oller, Don Pablo's son, had been sent to the United States to study engineering, but had to give up his studies and had returned to Puerto Rico when Don Pablo suddenly became ill. He was placed in charge of the Central Isabel and asked to manage the day to day business, since Arnaldo Urrutia had retired. Don Pablo also asked Lorenzo to include Isabel in all important decisions related to his investments. This would become essential he said, in the event that he was no longer able to work.

"Lorenzo, I'm counting on you to inherit the management of all my businesses, but I want you to share that management with your sister, who is also an heir," Don Pablo said. "Most importantly, you should always place your family first, before all other things, even business and country." His voice increased its volume and became stern to emphasize the importance of his advice.

"*Papá,* I always will be faithful to all the values you have taught us." Lorenzo sat silently thinking his sister would have to take instructions from him, not the other way around.

"And as for country, we are Americans now, remember that. The future is with them, it's the chosen destiny for us. The Spanish regime is gone; it's the past."

"Si, *Papá*."

♦ ♦ ♦

Carlos Roche had his own ideas about Puerto Rico's future. Except during family dinners, he didn't hide his opinions and had developed a strong sympathy towards the possibility of future independence for the island. This was one of the reasons for his initial attraction to Margarita Rodríguez.

A few weeks after the banquet at his home, he began to visit her in Ponce, whenever he could find an excuse to make the long journey. She was proud, but unconventional in an aristocratic way, and was constantly telling him about her plans. Unlike Carlos, who believed that autonomy of the island was a good political status for the present, Margarita held beliefs similar to her father, Don Jacinto, who had cultivated a fierce pride in being Puerto Rican.

"My father," she said, "belongs to the Autonomist Party, but most often sides with his colleagues in the Independence wing, when matters of political strategy are discussed. I believe as he does. We should actively strive to gain the island's independence."

"How will you achieve that? We won't get to vote on that issue for the foreseeable future," Carlos said. "The Americans won't relinquish this island without a fight."

"Then we will fight, or use any means necessary, to achieve our objectives. As an afterthought she added, "Peaceful means, of course.""

This kind of talk disturbed Carlos, but he regarded her remarks as political invective, and nothing else.

Most of the conversations between him and Margarita occurred on the porch of the Rodríguez home where they sat facing the street on Calle Atocha, in the center of Ponce.

Carlos was drawn to her beauty and the way she carried herself. He considered her to be a sophisticated high class rebel. She would make an ideal figure of a noble woman leading an army, a sort of Puerto Rican Joan of Arc.

They often walked around a quadrangle perimeter of the Ponce Plaza, and observed single women strolling in one direction around the plaza, with men strolling in the opposite direction to meet the women during each complete cycle. This was a custom from Spain imported to the island, Carlos mentioned this to her, and she nodded in agreement. The men wore straw hats, which they sometimes tipped; the women used parasols and twirled them. It was a mating ritual, a dance.

He had been courting Margarita for more than six months. The long trek to Ponce through the central *cordillera* in the center of the island was getting tiresome. The distance was challenging to traverse even though the Spanish government had built good roads from the north to the south coast which would last for generations.

They were discussing several mundane topics one day, when Margarita suddenly asked.

"Carlos, why don't you come to Ponce and work with my father? You could avoid the long trips to San Juan. I'm sure he could employ you in one of his plantations or businesses."

"Margarita, Don Jacinto is a competitor of mine. Don't you think that would be awkward?"

"Isn't my father going to invest in your Cambalache sugar mill soon?"

"It's an investment; the businesses will be separate and not merge. We would remain competitors, at least in practice."

"Still, if we were to have a future together, won't it be easier for us to plan if you live closer to me?"

Carlos had not expected these words from her, a former society debutante. He had never broached the subject. It was too soon. Still the exchange was typical of Margarita; she wasn't shy, demure or overly polite. She liked to take charge of any situation. *Had she even told her parents? How should I respond?*

"It seems like a good idea, but I want to think about it and share my thoughts with my parents. I value their opinion, even though it's my decision. I'm speaking about the engagement, not about working for your father. This is a big step for both of us and should not be decided without giving it more thought."

I have been courting her for less than a year, and no one has ever mentioned the topic. I think she may be right for me, but I need more time. I really don't want to get married right now, I'm not ready. Shouldn't I be the one who makes the first move? How can I say that without hurting her feelings or ending the relationship?

His last comment seemed to have unsettled Margarita, but she remained silent and looked away.

"If that's what you prefer. There's no real urgency, right?"

Her tone had changed, and as they said goodbye she did not return his kiss. He departed for San Juan without further comment.

On the way back to the capital, Carlos thought about the similarities Margarita shared with his own father. Both of them were rebels with aristocratic backgrounds, yet appreciated the finer things in life. He was more modest in his approach, he rarely felt comfortable in social gatherings held by the Puerto Rican elite. Margarita was from high society, and being a rebel was not consistent with her upbringing. Yes, she definitely reminded him of his father.

◆ ◆ ◆

The new partnership of Soler, Rodriguez, and Oller, now owners of Central Cambalache, became a profitable enterprise in its first years. The predicted rise of the price of sugar and the emergence of new markets had happened. But eight years later, one of the partners of the business succumbed to heart failure.

The death of Don Pablo Oller, at age 58, happened only one year after Lorenzo Oller had married a young woman from Cayey, and had a child with her.

Lorenzo assumed full control over Central Isabel and his father's business interests. It was 1908, and he reorganized and modernized all operations utilizing new and more reliable forms of transporting sugar from the mills to the markets. Lorenzo asked María Antonia, Isabel's daughter, that she travel to Arecibo- as the family representative- to check on the operations of Cambalache and help evaluate the value of the family's interest there. Contrary to his father's wishes, Lorenzo excluded Isabel from any major business decisions and consulted her only on ministerial tasks, using her more as a secretary, than a co-owner and shareholder of three sugar plantations, Central Isabel, Central Cambalache, and Central Aguirre, the last acquisition of her father.

One thing he made sure was that his niece be trained in all the aspects of the family businesses and their investments. She had finished most of her schooling in San Juan, at a private institution, and had been well tutored in financial matters. Lorenzo found her to be sharp, attentive, and willing to learn. She had a better grasp of the business details of a sugar central than her mother and became a perfect understudy. María Antonia relished her time with him, especially when they discussed politics and current events around the family dinner table.

Following her Uncle Lorenzo's wishes, she made plans to travel to Arecibo. The trip would be a long one, at least two days, the first day from Salinas to San Juan. The second day, she would travel by rail along the northern coast to Arecibo.

Her physical presence belied her young age. She had short curly brown hair that was a perfect match to her large brown eyes, and the smooth skin of her face. Her slight manner concealed her avid willingness to take on any challenge presented. A product of elite society, she did not behave like a child of privilege and dressed in a simple fashion. Doña Isabel had encouraged her to make decisions on matters that were supposed to belong only to the realm of men. María Antonia looked people straight in the eye when speaking, however, she avoided conflict. She displayed a willingness to state her opinions, but only if asked, and she did it with a certain charm. Her manner scared off many possible suitors. She also preferred to read books at home than attend society *fiestas.*

Her task at Cambalache was to review the financial books and records of the sugar mill and report her findings to her uncle. The Ollers, with subsequent purchases of stock, had significantly increased their ownership shares in that sugar mill.

On the second day of her visit, she met Carlos Roche. He had just come from San Juan on the new train, a recent and vastly improved method of travel. Carlos hadn't met her before, even though his mother had mentioned in passing, that she was the granddaughter of Don Pablo Oller and had recently finished her professional studies.

As he entered the mill offices, he observed her sitting at a desk reviewing financial reports and found her appearance to be unlike what he had expected. He approached and waited for a moment that wouldn't interrupt her work. She looked up at him and smiled.

"I assume that you are Carlos Roche, one of the owners?" She continued to look at the ledgers.

"You are correct, but I'm their son. May I ask who you are?"

"María Antonia Vivoni Oller. I'm Don Lorenzo Oller's niece."

"And to what do we owe the pleasure of your visit here?" Carlos said in a somewhat sarcastic tone. She looked up at him.

"I represent my family's interest in your company, and I've come to conduct the quarterly review of your operations, as it may concern our shares in Cambalache."

"I see. And how long will you be here?" Carlos liked the manner in which she addressed him in a firm but delicate voice, not the one he expected from an auditor. He had also anticipated dealing with a man, not a young woman.

"Two, maybe three days, or until I finish," she said. Again, she turned to her work and continued to write in her journal.

"Did you study accounting, if I may ask?" He tried not to sound condescending.

"I took business and commercial classes at a private school in San Juan, and was tutored by accountants, auditors, and employees of my grandfather, Don Pablo Oller, who died recently."

"I'm sorry about Don Pablo. I met him several times. He was quite respected." Carlos remained silent for a few moments.

"Perhaps when you finish your work today, we can have lunch, or dinner, and further discuss our operations?"

"*Gracias.* Dinner seems best, but it will have to be late. I want to complete the tasks I have planned for today."

"That's fine, you can decide at what time you would like to dine and just let me know."

Carlos was impressed by her officiousness and focus. He was not accustomed to working with a woman as his peer.

When the hour arrived, he met her at the front entrance of the warehouse where sugarcane was processed and stored. They walked around the surrounding grounds of the mill, Carlos studying her all the while. He guessed that she was much younger than him, in spite of the fact that she acted very mature. He pointed out the tall brick chimney of the Central and explained how it had been built with slave labor. It had now darkened with black soot and no longer reflected its original brown color.

María Antonia had put on some blush and changed clothes. She wore a cream colored summer dress with ruffles near the hem which moved slightly in the wind as she walked. Her perfume lingered in the air. Their conversation quickly shifted from sugarcane operations to the history of each of their families. She mentioned, not in great detail, how her own parents had met and married.

It was Carlos' turn to speak and he struggled on how to explain his childhood and his parents.

"My mother came from Barcelona, as did my father. Actually Antonio Roche adopted me; I never met my natural father." Carlos swallowed hard, regretting his revelation. *What a poor choice of words.*

He continued. "My parents met in Barcelona when they were both young, but didn't really come together until after each of them had immigrated to America. I was a young boy at the time and came with my mother."

María Antonia was puzzled at the sudden intimacy of the conversation, but remained silent and listened.

"Antonio Roche was a rebel in his youth and even spent some time in prison, falsely accused by the government of----------," Carlos said. *Another family secret, what is wrong with me?"*

She interrupted Carlos.

"My grandfather was also a Catalán, but he moved to Palma de Majorca, and then served in the Spanish Army in Cuba before he came to Puerto Rico. At first, he traded his salary in his job for cattle, in order to plan a future of his own."

"That's quite a different story."

"Do you ever wish your parents hadn't come here?" she said.

"Not really, I love Puerto Rico and its culture, especially its people; humble, hospitable, and generous. I do hope that someday, however, we can govern ourselves, or at least remain as separate as possible from the *Yanquis.* That would give us a better chance to bring progress, relying on the good will that we *criollos* possess."

This statement struck María Antonia, coming from a born Spaniard.

"What is your opinion on that?" He then asked.

"I don't believe that is the solution," she blurted out, " I think that if we join the United States as a state, we can have a future without limits, without the handcuffs that Spain put on our society and on our development. They plundered Puerto Rico and enslaved Africans, after they murdered the *Taíno* Indians." She sounded shrill, but she couldn't help it.

"I'm not surprised you believe that, since your grandfather was a firm believer of the island's annexation to the United States."

"Yes, but we don't like to use that word, it's a negative way to refer to the statehood movement. I find it demeaning," she said. Her response reminded him of Margarita.

As they approached the main house, the conversation shifted to other topics. They ate silently for a while, then Carlos said,

"Forgive me for asking, but you're a very attractive young woman. Do you have a suitor?"

María Antonia took her time before answering.

"Why do you ask? Aren't you married?"

"Not yet. But I do plan to get engaged sometime this summer, there is no firm date."

"Does your *novia* know this?" She asked in a mildly sarcastic tone, but he didn't notice.

"I think that she has a pretty good idea of what may happen, since she herself suggested it."

"She suggested it? I find that odd," María Antonia said.

"In a certain way, so do I. Times change, don't they? Isn't this is the Twentieth Century?"

"Certain customs should never change. I believe a man should ask first, not the other way around. I'm very traditional in that sense. I can't imagine asking a man to marry me." Carlos found the words quaint. He laughed.

As they finished their meal, Carlos eyed her carefully and observed her refined dinner manners when using utensils and napkins, and handling her wine glass. She was well bred and enticing. He found in her some odd traits, having modern manners and ideas, yet conservative social customs. *Polite yet direct. Yes, a bit contradictory.*

During the next three days both María Antonia and Carlos often found time to be together for their evening meals. But one day, in mid-afternoon, he took her horseback riding in the nearby fields surrounding Cambalache. The hot sun made the ride an effort, but she didn't complain and later they sat in the shade, to give their horses a respite. The sky was peacock blue, the air was crystal; the sea viewed from the hill where they rested served as a backdrop of emerald and sapphire water. The day was golden, the color of Puerto Rico.

After a period of silence, she spoke about her imminent return to Salinas.

"I never answered your question, Carlos," she added suddenly. "No, I don't have a *novio*. I have never met anyone whom I was really attracted to, or who wasn't just interested in my family's wealth."

"No doubt it will happen to you before you even realize it. You have all the attributes to deserve someone worthy, believe me," he said.

At that moment he took her hand to reaffirm what he had just said and she didn't resist. She gazed silently at him, then averted her eyes and slowly rose to her feet. He kept her hand in his.

On her last night at Cambalache, she followed her usual routine. She wore simple work clothes in the day, and in the evening wore one of the nicer dresses. That night she used a bright yellow dress that contrasted sharply with her light olive skin and her dark hair. She became a sunflower.

Huge round candles decorated the dinner table, while smaller ones were placed on nearby cocktail tables. The aroma of gardenias filled the air. The light reflected softly on her as if she embodied the approaching sunset. A soft warm feeling came over him as she entered the room and he felt goose bumps for a few seconds. He wondered if what he was feeling was more than just a passing attraction that would dissipate soon after she left.

She smiled gracefully, sat down, and carefully placed the folds of her dress beneath her on the chair. Carlos was watching her every move. How different she was in the day and what a transformation occurred in the evening. Women had a way of doing that.

Margarita Rodríguez, his future fiancée was, in a certain sense, more beautiful than María Antonia, perhaps more worldly. He considered Margarita a self-styled revolutionary, a rich one, of course, and María Antonia, who was part of the same social class, yet so different. Her manner was unspoiled, much like that of a humble person. There was also a gentle kindness in her eyes, so different from his bride to be. He tried to stop comparing them.

Carlos had hired two guitarists that would serenade them on this her last night in Arecibo. The music flowed varying its tempo for each piece. The duo played old Spanish songs, some of them set to Caribbean rhythms, and they played popular *boleros*. The night was perfect. The *coquís* chimed in like a backup chorus during pauses in the music.

"María Antonia, I truly enjoyed your stay here. It was totally different from what I expected. Forgive me, I thought your uncle would send an older boring male employee to examine the books and that the visit would not have had any social element at all. I'm so glad it was you."

"And you are an interesting and charming person, not at all what I expected, and much younger as well. I enjoyed your company and appreciate all the courtesies that you have extended while I was here. I do hope that our paths cross again and I wish you happiness with your future fiancée." Carlos cringed at her last words, but smiled anyway.

For the moment it seemed that the goodbyes were beginning too soon and it spoiled the general mood they felt. He almost regretted mentioning his future engagement to Margarita, but it was too late.

"So tell me about your future plans."

"Well now that you ask, my father has asked me to help reorganize the Republican Party here in Puerto Rico, and make it a real contender in the next election. The platform will include attacking the problem of extreme poverty and advancing statehood for the island. I, myself, have no political ambitions. I can't even vote yet, but a push for women's suffrage is on the agenda. I know it will take time to obtain that vote, but I am confident it will happen someday, before I'm too old to exercise it. My plans shouldn't stop me from coming back to Cambalache."

"I'm sorry I asked, but I do hope you will return," Carlos said with a chuckle. She also laughed.

The *coquís* were serenading them again after the musicians departed, and as the night grew longer, he wished that it wouldn't end. This woman had magic in her spirit, and shared many of his beliefs on improving the living conditions that afflicted the poor. She was on the opposite side of the political spectrum of his beliefs, but somehow that didn't matter. If he were younger, he could easily imagine falling in love with her, but banished the thought.

Before they parted, he kissed her on both cheeks, as he said goodnight. He lingered momentarily in her fragrance. She touched him gently on the arm and returned both kisses, and was in no hurry to let go.

Chapter Ten

The Elite, the Criollos

Vicente Ferrer had settled into a quiet life in Arecibo; he had worked hard at Cambalache for years and had been mostly successful supervising the workers there and keeping the mill productive.

His dream of owning a coffee plantation had never faded and his hard work and savings had finally made it possible. When he announced his departure from Cambalache, Antonio had congratulated him and wished him the best. Belén, now his wife, had agreed with the decision to move to Sábana Grande, especially since it would take her close to her family and it would remove Vicente from temptation, as she was prone to say every time the subject was discussed.

He started his coffee farm and made every effort possible to have it succeed. His laborers were few, but loyal to him and glad to have work. Vicente had always treated his underlings fairly, a practice he continued on his own farm. The job of picking coffee beans was strenuous and when in season, accompanied by long hours and hot sun. The years had slipped by and it was now 1914. As he approached 50, he was tired of farming. It was a routine and less exciting than before.

As he grew older, he believed he had become more tolerant. No longer were there frequent wild rages for some unintended slight, and he tried his best to curb his temper. The volatile Vicente of yesteryear had all but disappeared. Belén had borne three children, all now fully grown. His oldest son, Gregorio, had made him a grandfather before it became too late for him to enjoy toddlers. He doted on the first born grandson, Juan, and let the little one dominate his free time. The time spent with his grandchild resulted in him visiting Rosalina less often. The weekly sojourns with her had been reduced to infrequent visits to provide money for her necessities. The passion he once felt had all but dissipated. His sense of duty, however, would not let him abandon her. She was his mistress for life, or at least so he thought. In the time between his visits, she had found new friends, both male and female. Rosalina, just past her prime was still attractive, and men were drawn to her.

Vicente had noticed a change in her demeanor during his last few visits; she couldn't hide the fact that she was anxious for him to leave quickly. He thought nothing of it until one evening; he spotted a man's shirt partially hidden behind the bedroom door. It wasn't his.

He waited for her to come into the room.

"*Mija*. Who does that shirt belong to?"

"What shirt?"

Vicente, with a rising level of anger provoked by her halfhearted denial, took the shirt, rolled it up into a ball, and threw it on the bed.

"This one!"

"I don't know. Perhaps it's an old shirt of yours?"

"Lie." Vicente retrieved the shirt and ripped it apart. He approached Rosalina and grabbed her by the throat.

"If you've been seeing someone, at your age it would be disgraceful." He let go of her.

"No more disgraceful than being your *querida* for the last twenty years. I want someone to be with me day and night, not just for a few stolen moments of time. I want a companion for when I get older, before I become too weak to take care of myself. My life is a sad, lonely one, always waiting for your leftovers. I have never gotten used to you leaving me to be with your miserable wife."

Vicente slapped her hard at this last remark, and she collapsed on the bed. He opened the door, turning back to look at her.

"I don't want to die alone." She said in an anguished plea. Vicente hesitated, but then said,

"If I catch you with someone else, I will kill you!"

He could hear her sobbing all the way to his wagon. His loss of control ate at him as did his remorse at hitting her. His temple was throbbing, signs of the headache to come. *I will never leave Belén, she knows that by now. Nothing will change. How foolish of her, like I wouldn't find out. She's getting old, but she knew that I was going to stay married from the very beginning. Yet maybe I am selfish, maybe all I care about is myself.*

In the days to come, the more he thought about her, the guiltier he felt. He returned to her home two weeks later at night, in an attempt to apologize. Rosalina wasn't expecting him. As he approached her house, he heard voices within and instead of knocking at the front door; he circled around the back to reach her bedroom window. The voices inside were of Rosalina and someone else. Without hesitation, he went back to the unlocked front door and entered the house. He headed to the bedroom, and after kicking the bedroom door open, found his mistress in bed with a much older man.

Vicente exploded and started smashing objects in the bedroom while shouting obscenities. He headed towards Alberto Miranda, a farm hand he recognized, since the man had once worked for him.

"*Puta*, I caught you. This is how you pay me back for all of my help? You cheated on me and you'll regret it. And as for you *cabrón*, it's the end of the line."

Rosalina tried to come between Miranda and Vicente.

"Leave him alone, he's here because I asked him to come."

The man had been hiding under the bedspread. Vicente pushed her away with such force that she fell on the floor. He then grabbed the man by the throat and started hitting him.

"I said, leave him alone!" Rosalina screamed.

She picked herself up, lifted a vase off a nightstand and hit Vicente on the back of the head. The vase split and chunks of it fell to the floor.

The blow caused him to temporarily lose his balance and fall on one knee, while holding on to the bed.

"Oh God, what have I done?" Rosalina screamed. "Vicente *estas bien*?"

Vicente got up and resumed his attack on Miranda, while bleeding profusely from the gash on the back of his head. He grabbed the man by the shirt and dragged him outside where he began kicking his stomach.

"Come with me you bastard," Vicente was yelling.

"Stop, please stop, Vicente, you'll kill him," Rosalina cried out. Her pulse was pounding in her ears and she struggled to run after them.

Notwithstanding Rosalina's screams, who was calling for a neighbor to stop the assault, Vicente in a rage, strode over to his wagon and pulled out a machete. He returned to the poor wretch and swung the blade. It came down on the man's clavicle and in one swift deadly stroke, Vicente almost decapitated him. Miranda went limp and stopped breathing.

By then, a group of neighbors who heard the commotion ran over from cluster of nearby *bohíos*, quickly restraining and disarming Vicente. He did not resist and fell to his knees heaving and sobbing.

It had all happened in less than ten minutes. One neighbor mounted a horse and went to fetch the authorities. Rosalina was kneeling on the ground near her lover, not wanting to rise and mumbling incoherent words. Another woman neighbor tried to pull her away from the corpse and made a futile effort to calm her.

"I hope you rot in hell, Vicente. You are evil, and God will not forgive you for taking this man from me. I had very little to live for, and now I have nothing." Rosalina cried. "You will pay dearly for this, believe me."

"Please try to calm down, *cállate*," the neighbor urged.

When the authorities arrived, Vicente was still there, sitting on the ground under the watchful eyes of two of Rosalina's neighbors. After speaking to her, the police took Vicente into custody, placed him in handcuffs, and headed back to the town's police station. He was put into a small cell in the jailhouse to await his arraignment. Vicente refused all food and drank only water in small amounts. Each night, unable to sleep, he relived the fatal encounter in all its bloody details, fighting his demons. His life in the New World, the main focus of his dreams, had suddenly come to an abrupt halt.

◆ ◆ ◆

Two days later, the Municipal Magistrate summoned Vicente to his court-room and read him the charges of which he was accused.

"You are accused of murder, *Señor* Ferrer," the Magistrate said.

Vicente did not speak.

"Do you understand what is happening here today?"

Vicente nodded.

"How do you plead to these charges filed against you?"

Vicente was nonresponsive; he stood there in a trance.

"You must speak up. Again I ask, how do you plead?"

At the Magistrate's insistence he said. "*Lo siento, perdón.*"

He neither admitted nor denied the facts, and in view of his answer, the Magistrate entered a plea of not guilty, set bail, and had Vicente re-manded to the municipal jail pending further proceedings.

Later that day, Vicente sent word to Belén through a messenger, sum-marizing in a few lines the past events. She had not heard from him during all this time.

Belén, in turn, sent a telegram to the only person whom she thought might help. Seeking assistance from her family was not possible; they had no money or assets other than their farm, and she could never ask them to pledge it as bail. She wrote to the address Félix had given her husband when they last met.

> **URGENT**
> **Vicente Ferrer arrested for murder. In jail, need funds**
> **for bail.**
> **Tribunal requesting $5,000.   Please help.**
> **STOP Belén Ferrer**

She was uncertain if any response would be received, however, Félix answered immediately saying he would travel to Sábana Grande, using the newly established rail link through Aguadilla. When he finally arrived at Belén's home the next day, after 9 hours of travel, he found her surrounded by friends and family.

"Thank you so much for coming," Belén said in a raspy voice, barely more than a whisper. Events had taken their toll on her.

"It is my duty to help Vicente, he's my lifelong friend. I owe him that much."

Belén recounted the events that had led to Vicente's arrest and his incarceration.

"I will go today to the court and post bail for him. Under the law, he has that right, regardless of the charges. I know this for a fact."

"It will require a large sum of money," Belén said.

"I 'm prepared to meet any conditions imposed for bail, and secure his release. I'll also get him a lawyer."

"You truly are a good friend, many thanks."

"I promise you, I will have him here soon."

Félix hugged Belén, bid his farewell and left for the courthouse. He arrived an hour later and entered the pink one story building that had once housed the Spanish mayor's administrative offices, now a decrepit reminder of that era. It had a dilapidated exterior with a large wooden door that badly needed a fresh coat of varnish. The hallways reeked of smoke and stale coffee, and the stench of rot reminded Félix of his days aboard the *Regina* when he and Vicente were young and full of desire for adventure.

Once he reached the front desk, he inquired about Vicente and asked if he could place a bond for him. The clerk looked at him warily and asked if he had sufficient money. The sum had been set at 5,000 U.S. dollars in cash, or the equivalent value of unencumbered real estate property.

Félix didn't answer the question. He just produced a bag full of gold coins and U.S. dollars and handed it to the clerk. The clerk took the bag to an assistant in the back room to have the money counted. He told

Félix to sit on a nearby bench while he prepared the necessary papers and sought an appointment with the Magistrate. The bag bore the initials *IM*, which Félix had forgotten to remove. The money was part of the embezzlement stash from the *Mundillo* store that had never been spent.

◆ ◆ ◆

That same year of 1914, a downward spiral in the price of sugar threatened the collapse of the market for that agricultural product. The coffee markets had already failed for similar reasons, only sugar had survived. Tobacco was barely hanging on.

Antonio Roche had been appointed to the Executive Council that ran the territorial government in Puerto Rico. He was at the forefront of trying to save the sugarcane industry from high tariffs and the competition that stemmed from the marketing of beets, sugarcane's main rival on the U.S. mainland.

When the price of sugar finally stabilized, at the insistence of Carlos, he began trying to garner enough technical expertise to produce high-quality rum in Cambalache, one he had named *Ron Borinquén*. He was convinced that his new formula for distilling rum would lead to a resurgence of the product and produce good profits for his sugar mill. There was plenty of competition in the island's rum industry but he anticipated room for a better product, especially in aged rums. His partner, Jacinto Rodríguez, had succeeded in marketing and selling a blended rum named *Ron Caribe*. Antonio was confident that he could produce one of better quality, and hoped Carlos would help him realize that goal.

Carlos was struggling with his own ambitions, however, and wanted to leave Cambalache. After dating Margarita Rodríguez for more than a year, he was being pressured to marry her, even though they had been formally engaged for only a few months. His parents had insisted that their union would be good for both families and their respective businesses. One night having dinner with them in San Juan, the subject came up again.

"Mother, you know that I have always wanted to be a writer, a journalist. There is a possibility that I could work for *La Democracia*, the newspaper founded by Luis Muñoz Rivera. The paper is supporting a campaign against making English the principal language in the public schools, as the American government would like to do. I would like to be part of the effort to resist the change."

"That's a noble thought, son, but who would run Cambalache in Arecibo? You are the general manager, now that your father is on the Executive Council and spends most of his time in San Juan," Paula said.

"I am also thinking of postponing my marriage to Margarita. It's not that she isn't a lovely person; it's that I want to make it on my own, before I marry her. I don't want to rely on anyone for support-----------." That really wasn't his primary reason, but he wasn't ready to share it.

Antonio stopped eating and interrupted him.

"You don't need to rely on us, but if you leave Cambalache you will have no other means of income. I doubt the newspaper will pay you enough to maintain a family, and you should consider that most of their news business is here in San Juan. I thought you were going to live with Margarita in Ponce, or in Arecibo at the Central," he said.

"Don't you want to marry Margarita? I assume you love her, right? Paula asked. Then she added, "Or is there someone else?"

Carlos didn't answer and looked as his food warily. His throat tightened, and he made an effort to eat, but had little appetite.

"My son, what exactly do you think that the newspaper will be able to do with the American mandate on the English language?" Antonio asked, "We have been debating the issue at the Council and it is supported by some, but opposed by the others. Some people think that it's a first step in granting Puerto Ricans, U.S. citizenship which a few don't want; others see it as a welcome move. There is no consensus to oppose the law, so it will pass. We are powerless. Don't waste your time writing about it. You're needed in Arecibo. Marry your fiancée, don't hesitate." At the moment, Antonio had briefly forgotten his own experiences with his father in Barcelona and the difficult meals they'd had together. Those scenes were repeated in his mind, how Don Agustín had instructed him to lay off politics and find a job. He sounded his father.

Carlos ignored those last words. They were harder to digest than the food.

"*Papá,* I don't think the Americans will do anything to reverse the trend until the public opposition is made evident through news reports. The publicity will create wide opposition to this change. If Americans truly believe in a real democracy, as they say they do, the public outcry will make Washington rescind the directive. Right now, those damn bureaucrats are blind to our reality."

"I find that a difficult mountain to climb, my son, even though I'm sympathetic to your views. I believe it's an outrage that the U.S. would try to impose the English language on a Spanish speaking nation, but it's the language of the occupier. That's exactly what the British have been known for."

"I feel that the fight is worth it. I might not earn a good living for a while, so what? To me, being associated with the newspaper and its editor, Muñoz Rivera, is worth any economic risk I may take," Carlos said. "I want to postpone the marriage." His words were blunt.

"You will come to regret it," Paula said. "And you, Antonio, don't let the others in the Council hear what you just said, or you will be asked to resign. Did you hear yourself talking?"

"It might be for the best, I don't believe our opinions really matter to the Governor. The Executive Council has no real power. There will come a day when policies will be adopted which will go against my core beliefs. I will then take a stand and resign my post, if necessary. Look at the arguments for making all residents of Puerto Rico, U.S. citizens. Is it to better our lot as Puerto Ricans, or is it to supply the necessary soldiers in case the United States enters the European War that has begun?" Antonio got up from the table and left the room.

After a short silence, Carlos spoke.

"What is happening to him? I thought that he was getting more conservative as he grew older, but what he just said is what I have been thinking for months now. He's not consistent."

"Your father has many opinions on various political and economic issues and tends to change his mind frequently. Don't pay any attention to what he just said. He's just upset that you might leave Cambalache."

"*Mamá*, I think that if Margarita knows I want to quit Cambalache, she will receive the news gladly. She wants me to live in Ponce with her, but my loss of a steady salary will affect us. I don't know how she will react."

Carlos didn't tell his mother about María Antonia. He often thought of her and how much she had impacted his feelings for his fiancée. Her laugh, her gentle voice, her eyes and her spirit were ever present with him.

"Then wait until you have made a final decision on your future, before you decide to marry. I think your marriage would be good for the family business, but not if you are going to be miserable, especially if Margarita is going link her happiness to your income." Paula said.

"By the way you never answered my question about your feelings towards Margarita, or if you have found someone else."

"It's complicated, *Mamá*."

◆ ◆ ◆

Vicente pled guilty to involuntary manslaughter, and was sentenced to 10 years in prison. The district attorney wanted to avoid a trial and accepted the plea, as did the Judge. The sentence could have been harsher, but his guilty plea based on temporary insanity, plus his age, permitted the Judge to impose a lighter sentence. Many friends and neighbors testified as to his character, which helped Vicente. Being an act of passion, not unusual In those parts of the island, and only his first crime, the Judge found it easier to be lenient.

Before Vicente was incarcerated, he spoke to Félix and asked him to take charge of the coffee farm. No mention was made of Rosalina or of his child with her. Félix had never imagined that he would become the administrator of a coffee farm, but he couldn't refuse Vicente, not after what he had done for him.

"Félix, I'm also depending on you to watch over my family. I realize you don't have to, but I beg you as a special favor."

"It's a privilege and an honor for me to help. It's the least I can do for you. All of the profits obtained from the farm will be used to sustain Belén, and the children. You can trust me. Remember the promises we made to each other on the ship?"

"I do, and I trust you." He looked at Félix and bowed his head.

The guards led Vicente away. Félix saw him board the wagon to the prison, and reminisced how they both had come to Borinquén together, almost like brothers, and how their lives had taken different paths. Félix had always hoped that he might have a second chance to begin a new life, but he never like this.

The prison wagon traveled its slow journey to Ponce and after half a day they arrived at the prison. At least Vicente's imprisonment there would make visits by Belén and Gregorio easier than if he had been incarcerated in the main prison in San Juan. He could only guess what his future might have been if he had let Rosalina live her own life, as she had pleaded with him so many times. He had ignored her pleas and would now pay the price.

◆ ◆ ◆

Antonio was reading in the *San Juan Gazeta* news, that the United States Congress had added an amendment to the Jones Act of 1917, stating that all persons born in Puerto Rico from the effective date of the Act would be considered natural born citizens of the United States. The remaining residents could choose, within a given timeframe, the citizenship they preferred the Spanish, or the U.S. one. The news article further explained that the bill's passage had been received with great delight by many islanders, yet had been denounced in a Resolution by the Puerto Rican House of Delegates, but ignored by Congress. Antonio grabbed the newspaper and flung it to the other side of the room. *So much for democracy, when our voice was never heard.*

The Puerto Rican Republican Party, which had among its founders Pablo Oller, was currently led by his son, Lorenzo. They celebrated the passage of the legislation as the beginning of a successful effort to make the island a permanent part of the United States. The Ollers were thrilled; the Roche family and the Rodríguez family were not.

Jacinto Rodríguez saw it as a setback for the political movement towards greater autonomy and eventual independence for Puerto Rico. Antonio Roche refused to accept or apply for the new U. S. citizenship although Paula disagreed with him. They all had the options of remaining Spaniards, becoming citizens of Puerto Rico- a special status with limited benefits- or becoming naturalized U.S. citizens. Some Spaniards, however, made plans to leave Puerto Rico given those choices.

Pablo Oller had become a U.S. citizen before he died, by applying before the legislation was even enacted. After its passage, his son Lorenzo Oller, immediately renounced his Spanish citizenship, and embraced the new one. So did the rest of his family, including María Antonia, his niece.

After a few months, Antonio was beginning to question the wisdom of his initial decision of not accepting U.S. citizenship, and its effect on his business. After mounting pressure from Paula and his business advisors, who felt that the sugar mill business would suffer losses, he relented.

"This goes against my very nature, I will never become a *gringo,*" he said, when asked by Paula. "Once Spanish citizenship becomes available again, I will restore my status as a Spaniard, if dual citizenship is eventually permitted." He had left Spain due to a wrongful conviction, but could not fathom losing his Spanish identity and was torn between the two.

"It's the right decision for our business and for our family," she said. "Forget Spain and the past, we are here now. Didn't you so desperately want to leave Barcelona after what happened to you?"

"Yes, I did, but I have always felt like a Spaniard and never had to choose between countries."

"You chose countries the day you boarded the ship that brought you to Puerto Rico."

The island's elite class was mostly in favor of the U.S. legislation. The citizens who formed the new middle class, the few that comprised it, were divided in their opinions. The *criollos* in the interior, and the poor, just wanted to live with decent wages and weren't focused on which option they had to choose.

For Félix, the new law didn't matter; all he wanted was to survive and was more interested in the economic reality he faced every day. In his mind, the Spaniard's had exploited the island and the lower classes. The poor expected they would fare better under U.S. rule, but he wasn't convinced that their living conditions would improve in any way. His fake title of nobility had become worthless, a relic of the past.

Antonio's newly preferred political organization and one of the most influential parties in the island, the Union Party, had a new platform including self- rule for the island. This suited the Roches fine, they marginally belonged to that party. Their main concern was the continued viability of the sugarcane plantation given the changes that had erupted in the world markets with the U.S. takeover. Antonio, concerned that his choice of U.S. citizenship would cause a rupture with Jacinto Rodríguez, wrote him a note.

My dear Jacinto: 7th day of December 1917

How could we have predicted that the topic of our conversations that evening at the banquet not so long ago, would come to pass sooner than expected? You are right. The U.S. has taken over and has ambiguous plans for the island. I know you favor independence, as would I, if the circumstances on the island were different, but the economic reality doesn't make this option viable for now, in my humble opinion.

Due to this, I have decided to apply for U.S. citizenship hoping that someday I can reacquire the Spanish one, or even better, acquire one that would be based on the island's own citizenship as a sovereign nation. I am changing my political affiliation as you will soon find out. I think it's better for our business interests that I remain on the Executive Council to monitor the island government, although I realize the Council has no real power. I thought I would express my intentions to you before they become public, since I value your opinion and your partnership in Cambalache.

Saludos,
Antonio

Antonio received a cryptic reply from Don Jacinto which said:

Do what you have to do.
Jacinto

♦ ♦ ♦

Carlos thought of his options if he chose to leave Cambalache and begin working for *La Democracia*. Rumors had that its founder, Luis Muñoz Rivera, was ill and would soon retire. Luis Muñoz Marín, his son, had taken over the newspaper to become its new Editor. The prospect of a change in management could affect Carlos's tenure with the paper, so he opted to become a freelance reporter and continue for the time being at Cambalache, delegating some of his duties to an assistant.

Another reason to not quit was that if he stopped working at the sugar mill, he wouldn't see María Antonia again. His periodic meetings with her had become the favorite part of his duties. She now was fully in charge of the quarterly audits of Cambalache on behalf of the Oller enterprises, and had finally become a company director. She reported only to Lorenzo Oller.

The incessant health and family problems that had begun with one of his children consumed most of Lorenzo's time. In essence, she was practically her own boss.

Carlos kept putting off the wedding date, but deemed his marriage to Margarita inevitable regardless of his growing affections for María Antonia, who was reluctant to respond to his advances or accept any of his social invitations.

"Carlos, it isn't that I don't like you, you're promised to another, and I have to respect that."

"María, we can be friends and go out occasionally, can't we?" His tone was unconvincing and every time he mentioned the subject his voice weakened. "I'm still a free man."

"You have made a choice, so honor it."

"It's not a final choice yet. At least not totally final." His voice wavered, he really didn't believe that.

"Why are you still debating the wisdom of your choice, it's going to happen anyway, isn't it?"

She too, felt an irresistible attraction to Carlos, but also found it hard to believe, that a bachelor like him, over 40, would commit to anyone after breaking an engagement.

"I have to move to Ponce if I get married, and the social circles that Margarita moves in, contrary to her rebellious nature, are filled with superficial people. I find that many in her family along with their friends are insincere. And I don't think her mother likes me."

"Have you mentioned this to Margarita?"

"Not as much as I would have liked to. Another thing, she loves speaking about the workers, the rights they don't have, and how an independent Puerto Rico would fix the island's social ills, but I don't think she really believes it. I can tell when her eyes harden as she speaks of sacrificing her lifestyle. She doesn't mean it. She talks like a rebel, but behaves like an aristocrat."

"That's a strange thing to say, coming from you," María Antonia said.

"I know. I do have feelings for her, but it means moving to Ponce and changing my life. She would never live here in Arecibo, or in San Juan, and would never consider any major changes to her lifestyle." His tone became irritable and he began sweating, using a handkerchief to wipe his brow.

"Why not? In San Juan there is so much more to do than in Ponce, and remember I'm a girl from *el campo*, who finds Ponce sophisticated and elegant."

"I think it has to do with the fact that in Ponce, her family is one of the most prestigious families there, and they belong to Ponce's high society. In San Juan, she would be just another rich young woman. One of many."

"Do you really think that matters? If you love her, you should want to be with her all the time."

Carlos let the conversation end with María Antonia's last remark, but stared at her as if she was his salvation, his only way out. She looked down at her hands.

They never kissed, except in a perfunctory manner, although both of them felt the desire. After finishing his coffee, Carlos stood up and went back to his office. He left her on the veranda of the plantation house while she followed him with her eyes.

♦ ♦ ♦

Carlos Roche married Margarita Rodríguez late one summer day in June 1918. He had misgivings, and on their wedding day spent part of the early dawn hours on a dock near the Ponce waterfront, thinking about the upcoming nuptials later that day. He saw a small dinghy struggling to make its way out of the port, the tide was coming in and the sea was choppy. It seemed that for every few yards that the sailboat advanced, it was battered back by the ocean. The boat's struggle mirrored his, in what he wished for, as opposed to his reality.

Margarita was sometimes interesting and vivacious, but despite her leftist leanings she at heart was really a conservative, social and otherwise. To Carlos, her defiant attitude in defending all things Puerto Rican, and her sympathies for the underprivileged were just a cover. He knew she loved the finer things in life, just like her mother, although she concealed it better. His own father, Antonio, had been a high class anarchist in his youth, and the woman he was about to marry was a high class separatist. *How ironic. They were built in the same mold. His father had changed, but would she?*

He also tried to visualize what it might have been like to marry María Antonia. On his last meeting with her, he informed her of his wedding. *Entre ella y tu,* he thought, over and over.

A week before, he had worked the whole day at Cambalache and didn't want it to end. It was early evening and he was preparing to meet María Antonia for their final dinner together. Carlos could smell the pork tenderloin being roasted, rice and beans, and the scent of yucca and other vegetables permeated the air. While he waited, he drank a couple of glasses of Spanish wine. Candles had been lit at the dinner table as was the custom when they dined together. A light wind made the candles flicker.

He hesitated when he welcomed her to the table. After she was seated they both drank the wine. He took a deep first gulp trying to delay the inevitable.

"I am going to marry Margarita next week." He couldn't predict how she would react, so he said it softly and very slowly. A short silence followed.

"I read about it in the social columns and never doubted that you would, so why tell me now? It's the same date the papers said, right?" She had tried to mask her surprise that the dinner had commenced with this topic.

"I may have chosen the wrong moment to say it, but it's better that you know now. We moved the date up."

The mood of the dinner changed. This was a real goodbye, not just a temporary parting.

Tonight there was no trio playing music, just the sound of *coquís* and palm trees rustling in the wind. María Antonia fidgeted with her glass and drank only small sips.

They ate slowly and barely spoke. As the meal came to an end, he rose, went over to her and took her hand. She rose from the table, not expecting him continue to hold onto her.

"There is one last favor that I ask of you before I leave."

"Of course, what do you need?"

"I have never kissed you, and I want to have a memory of what that would be like, to have you in my arms one time, if only once--------." His voice trailed off.

His request left María Antonia speechless; she started blushing before she could answer.

"Why would you want to do that? It wouldn't help you, or me, in any way. It would only complicate our relationship. A kiss doesn't last long anyway and is soon forgotten."

"I think I love you, even though I'm much older than you, and I could never harbor any hopes that you would feel the same."

"You love me? She was incredulous and took her hand away.

"I do." Antonio could tell that she was confused.

"When did that happen? And you never thought of telling me?"

"I didn't want to scare or push you away. It happened soon after I met you the first time. I came to realize it after one of the many dinners we had alone. Something special happened on one of those nights. The feeling grew with time."

"You say this to me just before you are going to marry another woman? And now you want to kiss me?" She stepped away from him.

"It doesn't make sense, I know it's a strange request, but it would mean so much to me, and it would be the only time that I would ever ask you to do this." He began to regret his request.

"What if I don't feel the same way?" María Antonia said. "I have my own feelings, and I don't go around kissing my male friends."

A gust of wind blew out a few of the candles and near darkness enveloped them. Only the full moon was left.

He began to apologize, but suddenly she approached him, looked at him, put her arm around his neck and kissed him full on the mouth, at first tentatively, then later with passion. She did not let go of him immediately. When she finally pulled back she looked directly into his eyes. Her emotions were captured in her glance, and as her eyes moistened, he could tell that she loved him too.

"Carlos, I do have feelings for you, but at the moment they must remain just that. You have given your word to Margarita, and I won't be responsible for breaking up an engagement, no matter how I feel. I just can't do that. And when you marry her, please forget me. I will try to do the same." She barely whispered these last words.

Carlos nodded that he understood. She watched him as he walked away and did not call him back. He packed his bags and drove back to Ponce that same night to avoid prolonging his pain. Carlos had forgotten that he had left a note on his desk addressed to María Antonia. His secretary found it the following Monday and delivered it.

María Antonia:

Since the day I met you, I have been torn between you, a woman I never imagined I would ever fall in love with, and my fiancée. I have thought about this for a long time and realize that I will never stop loving you regardless of whom I marry. I am committed to helping my family with the survival of Cambalache, but this will never happen if I don't marry Margarita. I do care for her.

You may have noticed that we are facing hard times in the sugarcane industry. People will say that mine is a marriage of convenience, I can't really dispute that. But what I truly feel inside is the most important thing for me.

I have to set that apart, however, and not think of my own happiness, but also that of my family.

I know that you would never become my mistress. Even if I wanted you to be my lover-selfish as that might sound- it would not be fair to you and I would never ask.

María Antonia, you are young, charming, and lovely, and have your whole life ahead of you. You deserve to marry someone who will provide you with a future, and your very own family. Please find in your heart a way to forgive me for making this decision, it's the most difficult thing I've ever done.

By making this choice of leaving you alone, I hope it will prove how much I really do love you. I will never forget you.

Te recordaré hasta el día en que me muera.
Te amo,
Carlos

Chapter Eleven

The Descendants

The U.S. Congress enacted the Prohibition Act in 1919, which became effective in 1920. With its passage, the sale of alcoholic beverages in the U.S. was banned. The mandate extended to Puerto Rico, where the law prohibited the manufacture, sale, transportation, and the exportation of rum to the U.S. The only difference in its application to the island was that first a referendum would be held to determine if the general population supported the new law.

A ballot was created for that purpose with the symbol of a coconut representing a vote for Prohibition, and the symbol of a liquor bottle signifying a vote against the new measure. To Antonio Roche, the new U.S. law was a death knell for the manufacture of rum at Cambalache. Further development of *Ron Borinquén* (dark rum) and *Ron Taíno* (light rum) would be impossible, if Cambalache was going to obey the law. Prohibition was a not well understood concept; throughout history Puerto Rican social customs had always included drinking spirits like wine, brandy, and rum.

Antonio, from his position on the Executive Council, campaigned against having the Prohibition Act apply to the island, but his arguments fell on deaf ears. The governor at the time, Arthur Yeager, was not sympathetic to trying to get Puerto Rico exempted from the legislation and did not lend his support to Antonio. Once the referendum was held, and the votes counted, the coconut votes prevailed and the law was extended to Puerto Rico. He predicted that in a large measure the law would be ignored.

The rum industry fizzled, although some was produced on the black market. Underground distribution made it possible to obtain *Ron Cañita* *or* Moonshine, if one really wanted it.

Cambalache, already taking a hit from the drop of sugar prices in the market, was in perilous financial straits. Carlos Roche had to lay off employees, many of whom had no other source of income for their families, and had to cut operational costs as well. Some shareholders, like the Ollers, were threatening to withdraw their investments. He was able to convince María Antonia, however, that if her uncle removed his capital the paper losses would become actual losses, since the shares of the sugar mill had fallen in value.

María Antonia was able to persuade her Uncle Lorenzo to stay the course and not bail out of Cambalache. At the time he had other more profitable investments, and did not feel the economic pinch; more importantly, he trusted her. He could focus on another investment he had developed, constructing a plant for a new product in home building, cement. Most of the conversations between Carlos and María Antonia were now limited to strictly business and he avoided sharing the dinners that they'd once had.

His visits to Ponce to be with his own family became less frequent with the economic crises. The relationship with his family suffered and his time away from home increased with each passing year.

Two years after they were married, Carlos and Margarita had their first son, Toñito. Soon after his first birthday, they had a daughter, and named her Ana.

When he was in Ponce, the typical dinner hour at home would end with a conversation not suitable for a family meal.

"Carlos, why are you spending so much time in Arecibo? Your family obligations are here, you know that." Margarita said.

Carlos was trying to finish his dinner and leave the table.

"Don't you read the newspapers? Don't you realize that the sugar industry is in peril, as are your own father's fortunes?"

"That will pass, what will not pass is the time you spend away from our children who are growing up quickly and don't have a father present on a daily basis."

"That's not fair. I come home as often as I can. You are the lucky one who doesn't work and can be with them all day."

The tone shifted.

"Are you sure that all you do at Cambalache is work? No time for a little entertainment of the female kind or some other interests?"

"What are you insinuating?"

"I see how you look at the Oller woman when we are at social gatherings and she is present."

"Now you are talking nonsense."

"Can you tell me honestly that you have no feelings for her? Both of you spend a lot of time together."

Carlos put his knife and fork down and resisted an urge to slam his fist on the table. The children were staring at them.

"You're crazy," He got up and left the table as his face changed shades, pink to red.

It was always like this, he came to the dinner table for the children's sake and no other reason. At work, his moments alone with María Antonia were pure torture. Her perfume lingered with him for days, as did her face. When she wasn't in Arecibo, he thought about her day and night. Margarita was right; he had never stopped yearning for her.

♦ ♦ ♦

María Antonia had experienced many suitors and even been engaged to one that had all the qualities that her mother, Isabel, would have desired. He was a physician from a well-known family in Caguas, but he had postponed the wedding at the last minute, for no apparent valid reason. After waiting a reasonable time for a new wedding date and not getting one, she had broken off the engagement. While she had genuine affection for the man, it wasn't the same feeling she had for Carlos.

Her subsequent liaisons did not last, since she was fearful of another broken promise. Her mother had warned her that she was not getting any younger and would wind up an old maid if she didn't marry soon.

She was not fearful, since after having first lost Carlos, then the physician, it had prepared her for disappointments in romance.

"*Hija,* what was wrong with that last young man who recently came calling? He will graduate from law school next year, and isn't bad looking. He's from a good family that is well known in San Germán. They are quite wealthy, you know."

"Do you like him that much, *Mamá?*"

"Yes, I do, *cariño,*" Isabel said, not realizing she was walking into a trap.

"Then why don't you marry him?" María Antonia yelled as she left the room. These exchanges had become the norm, and that was her typical reaction. She felt that her mother who had always taught her to be independent, like she had tried to be, was betraying her own beliefs.

"You are taking yourself out of the market for available men, and you will regret it," Isabel shouted back.

María Antonia was on the porch preparing to leave and couldn't hear her. She was still in love with Carlos Roche and other men simply did not measure up to him.

◆ ◆ ◆

Vicente was released from prison in late summer 1922, after completing seven years of his prison sentence. He returned to Sábana Grande to see that his son, Gregorio, appeared to be well in charge of the coffee farm. On the day of his release, he came home and embraced Belén, who remained stiff in his arms and kissed him in a perfunctory manner. She had prepared a separate bedroom for him to readjust to home life. When Vicente realized that he would not be sharing the marital bed, he was disappointed but remained silent. He then asked Gregorio questions about the farm.

"How have you been? I haven't seen you since the end of last year. I thought you might return for a prison visit in February, but it's now summer."

"We were very busy Papá, trying to plant new crops and cultivate other staples. Coffee has lost much of its value on the market. We planted tobacco plants and avocado trees to make up for our losses on coffee, but it's too soon to tell if that will help. We will know more by next year's harvest."

"Where is Félix? He was supposed to help you and be here for my release," Vicente asked.

"He no longer works here. We caught him stealing some of the profits from the sale of coffee beans, and asked him to leave or we would report him to the authorities."

"What?"

"Papá, he was helpful the first two years that you were away, but then he moved back to San Juan and returned less and less, and only at the end of the month for the inventory. When I examined the books, they didn't reflect the sums of money we had received in prior coffee auctions."

"How did you come to discover this?"

Gregorio didn't answer, but Belén did.

"I kept a secret log of expenses and income which Félix never saw," she said. "We suspected something was wrong after he had been here a little over a year. I held off facing him since it could have been a book error, but it wasn't."

Vicente pounded the table and could barely control his temper. He couldn't believe that Félix had betrayed him once again. He had never really believed Félix's version of the missing wedding gift monies. Right now, however, he tried to focus on not succumbing to one of his outbursts so soon after arriving home.

"Someday I will settle accounts with him, even if I have to kill him."

"Do you want to spend the rest of your days in prison?" Belén asked.

That wasn't the worst of the fortunes that befell the coffee farm. Nature had in store a terrible setback for the island's agriculture. In early 1928, Hurricane *San Felipe II* caught the island by surprise and hit Sábana Grande especially hard. The entire coffee crop was lost, as were the new plantings of avocado and tobacco. If that weren't enough, the following year the Great Depression in the economy of the U.S. spread to the island. Both events left Vicente and his family destitute. The only recourse he had was to go to Arecibo to see if Carlos Roche, whom he had known since Carlos was a child, could lend him funds to replant and restore his farm. His main relationship had been with the elder Antonio, but the latter hardly ever went to Arecibo anymore. Antonio was 65, and traveled as little as possible, not even using the trains that reached the center of town.

Vicente arrived one afternoon at Cambalache after having contacted Carlos by telegram. *San Felipe* had destroyed much of the infrastructure that the telephone system depended on, leaving the island with no phone service for several months after the storm hit. He arrived at noon, and Carlos welcomed him warmly and immediately invited him to stay for lunch.

"How good of you to come see us again," Carlos said, not being able to say anything else once he saw Vicente's demeanor. He appeared pale grey and thin, with eyes protruding from his sockets as if he were a marionette. Carlos stepped forward and hugged him.

"It is nice to see you again; it has been too many years." Vicente said and assumed that Carlos knew of his time in jail, but didn't mention it. He sat down and fidgeted in the chair, uncertain of where to place his hands.

"I haven't forgotten, my father always spoke highly of you," Carlos said. He told him how he remembered when Vicente worked at the sugar mill and how much his father had relied on him to manage Cambalache.

"What brings you to Arecibo?"

Vicente hesitated in responding. He struggled to find the right words.

"I need your help. As you know, the times have been hard on all of us with *San Felipe* and the Depression. My coffee plantation was destroyed and I need money. I'm not coming here for a handout, however, I must tell you first that I cannot guarantee the repayment of any loan with collateral."

"Didn't you have emergency funds?" Carlos asked.

"Yes, a small amount, but they were exhausted while I was away from the farm for a period of time. I also had some money losses." Carlos assumed he was referring to his prison time, and didn't pursue the topic. Vicente didn't elaborate.

"I don't know if I'm the person to help you, but I can think of someone who might be able to. The Oller family has survived the onslaught of the Depression and they invested wisely before the *San Felipe* storm. Lorenzo Oller is the patriarch of the family, and his niece, María Antonia Vivoni, is the one who oversees his investments here and in other towns. She will be coming by tomorrow, if you wish to spend the night and wait for her."

Vicente pondered the suggestion, and having no other place to go, or money to afford an inn, accepted Carlos's offer.

"*Gracias,* I'll stay."

As Carlos thought about her, Vicente sat silently and watched him. Carlos broke the silence.

"She is the right person speak to. María Antonia has influence over her uncle, who has sufficient capital and may be able to assist you. And I say this for your sake; she doesn't need to know your entire personal history. I will vouch for your reliability," Carlos said, in a softer tone to not offend him.

"Lorenzo Oller may want a guarantor," Vicente said.

"I'm sure that my father can provide you with his signature."

"I wouldn't dare ask that of him."

"You don't have to, I will."

Carlos had lately avoided coming to Cambalache, if María was there. He would plan his trips for the weeks when he knew that she would be away. It was easy, since she went to Arecibo only during the first week of the month. This practice had lasted several years, and although he had seen her accompanied by other gentlemen at social gatherings, he simply greeted her warmly and found excuses to keep their conversations short. Margarita had been right, María Antonia would look at him from afar and at times they would lock their eyes on each other. They found few chances to be alone, as his wife always accompanied him to those events.

María Antonia, as expected, arrived the next afternoon from San Juan. When she reached Cambalache by livery coach, she went directly to the main house to place her luggage in her room. She found Carlos in the hallway, smiled and greeted him politely, not expecting anything else.

"I am surprised that you are here this week, Carlos."

He looked at her intently, and observed that she had cut her hair, gained some weight, but had not lost her alluring look. He had known her for many years, yet she had not aged much. She had not married, from what he had heard, but he had never broached the subject. María Antonia knew nothing of his troubles with Margarita or that his marriage was on the verge of collapse. He continued to stare beyond her without saying anything.

"What is it, Carlos?" His eyes had glazed over when she first greeted him.

"Nothing. I was thinking about our first meeting here so many years ago."

He was actually thinking about the last kiss she gave him.

"And what were your thoughts?"

"That's not important right now. I have a visitor that wants to meet you for a business matter. Once you settle in, I will take him to your office. By the way, has telephone service been restored in San Juan?"

"No, not yet. There are rumors that the whole system will be revamped and modernized since the infrastructure on the south coast was completely destroyed by the storm. The telephone company says it plans to build an entirely new and better system."

Carlos smiled, pecked her on the cheek and said, "I will tell Vicente Ferrer that you are here, and I will try to see you before I leave. We need to talk." He hadn't done that in a very long time. María Antonia felt her cheek with two fingers as he departed, and didn't reply.

Vicente expected to see a mature matron. He was surprised when he first saw María Antonia. It unsettled him that she was so youthful looking and attractive. He would be asking for a business loan from a woman, something he was not used to. His first thought was that he wished he was 30 years younger and had met her then, but soon realized that she was the type of woman who would never have noticed him. The world was changing and he had to accept it.

When he entered her office, he held a respectful silence while she finished reviewing some documents. When she paused, he told her of his reason for coming to Arecibo.

"Carlos recommended that I speak to you concerning my coffee farm which was destroyed by *San Felipe*."

"So were many others. Please sit down and tell me what happened."

Vicente's uneasiness increased, he broke into a sweat and his throat tightened. He struggled to articulate a reply.

"I had a good productive farm. My coffee beans were the best in the southwest mountains."

"But that's all gone now. What makes you think that you can rebuild your farm?"

"The land is still good, and fertile. The coffee trees will grow again in a few years and we will be back in production. I need some financing now to prepare the fields and rebuild the warehouses, as well as my own home."

"And what can you offer as collateral?"

"Nothing, except my reputation for producing a good crop every year and for being honest and responsible."

María Antonia stood up indicating that the meeting had ended. He also rose.

"Don Antonio Roche will guarantee any loan you give me."

She paused, sat down again and he followed suit.

"When did you last speak to him?"

"I haven't yet, but Don Carlos assured me that he will recommend to his father that he become a guarantor of the loan."

"Do you think that Carlos can persuade Don Antonio to take that risk?"

"I cannot guarantee it, but Don Carlos assured me that he will ask his father and support my request."

"Then let's wait for confirmation of that. Carlos is good for his word, so I'm not concerned. Once I receive it in writing from Don Antonio, I will then have my attorney draw up the papers for your loan. How much will you need?"

The following day, Vicente headed back to his farm confident that he would receive the funds to save it. María Antonia seemed to understand the details of what it would take to restore his coffee production and had promised to create a timetable for him to repay the agricultural loan, should it be granted. All he needed now was the confirmation from Don Antonio on the guarantee.

Carlos asked to speak to María Antonia on the morning of his departure to Ponce. She agreed to meet him for breakfast in the dining room. While he was waiting for her, he reminisced on the many moments they'd had together those years when he lived at Cambalache.

It's too late now; I had my chance and failed to embrace it. I still have feelings for her, but I dare not mention them or even suggest that by anything I say. Does María Antonia even have feelings for me after all this time? I just wish I could kiss her and hold her again and tell her how much I love her. How terribly wrong I was in choosing Margarita. Do I have the will to divorce her? What would happen to Toñito and Ana?

As she walked in, he stood up. Instead of the usual kiss on the cheek, he greeted her and sat down, after she had taken her place.

"Did you take care of Vicente? He's a good man."

"Yes. I spoke to him and he says your father will guarantee the loan on the coffee farm."

"I believe so, and Vicente will not fail you. I'm sure of that."

"Isn't he the same man who went to prison for killing the lover of his mistress?"

Carlos almost choked on a piece of bread he was eating.

"I'm not sure," Carlos lied.

"It doesn't matter to me, by the way. I believe in redemption."

"You are a real liberal, María."

"What is on your mind, Carlos? You seem distant, and even though I haven't seen you for a long time, I remember your moods."

Carlos put down his fork.

"My marriage is broken and I probably deserve it. I was really fond of Margarita when we were engaged, but never really fell in love with her, and now both of us are miserable. She's not the same woman I met when I was single, and I'm not the same man. The abyss between us grows by the month, and it seems that nothing can save our marriage."

María Antonia's face reddened; she shifted uneasily in her seat, put down her utensils, and said, "I am sorry to hear that you are unhappy. You deserve better." It may have been the polite thing to say, but the conversation made her stop eating.

"I can't divorce her right now, not with two young children. We have separated our living quarters and since no one asks, we don't mention the subject. There is no physical relationship between us anymore and there hasn't been one for years."

"And do you plan to live that way, indefinitely?"

Carlos looked at her and shook his head. It was not a polite question, but he didn't care.

She focused on him. "I remember you once said you had feelings for me, but it was so long ago that I had almost forgotten. I still have the letter you wrote the day you left. I also remember that last kiss." Tears welled up in her eyes, and she wiped them with a small handkerchief.

"María, those were my feelings then and now. For me, nothing has changed since that day."

"Are you saying what I think you are saying?"

"You mean, do I still love you? Yes, I do. But that means little to you right now."

"And if it did mean something, where do those terrible words leave us? I can't become your mistress. I won't live that way."

"I would never ask you to, and I don't like the way it sounds. I just want to be with you for the rest of my life. That, I can assure you, is how I have felt all of these past years. I will leave her and see if she will agree to a divorce. My marriage is over, regardless." His voice broke.

She seemed confused by what he said and looked down. He rose and started to leave. As he passed by, she grabbed his arm.

"Carlos, I have always loved you. I still do after all this time, even if it's against my better judgment. I never married any of the men who actually proposed to me. It was a simple decision; I didn't love them enough. That has been my life until now."

Carlos bent down and kissed her and held her close for a few minutes. His eyes moistened and his pulse was racing after finally hearing her say what he had always longed for. This was truly his last chance to be with her, and he wouldn't waste it.

"I will return with a plan for our situation. My marriage to Margarita has to end."

◆ ◆ ◆

Margarita Rodríguez, despite her wealth, had become deeply involved with the independence movement and had been radicalized by the ideas promulgated by many splinter groups. She took her son, Toñito, to all of the meetings of the independence parties, and started going with him to several public gatherings to hear a new leader speak, Pedro Albizu Campos. He was a rising star in a new political movement, the Nationalist Party. She was swayed by his fiery speeches and collected all the literature and pamphlets that were handed out to spectators at each gathering. The party had begun as a fringe movement advocating immediate independence for the island, and was quickly adding followers and growing increasingly radical. For her, there was a romantic aura surrounding the founders of the Nationalist Party and she admired their idealized dreams of a free Puerto Rico.

Toñito Roche, 14 years old, was already attracted to the movement through the influence of his mother and his grandfather, Jacinto Rodríguez, who was a financial supporter of the Independence Now Party. Don Jacinto did not support the Nationalist Party initially, but had adopted a wait and see attitude, stopping short of openly backing them. He admired Pedro Albizu Campos, who was a Harvard educated lawyer, and U.S. Army veteran of mixed race. According to news reports, he had suffered indignities and discrimination in the Army, where he had served as an officer in a racially segregated company battalion. Due to that experience, and others influencing his life, like being denied attendance at his Harvard University graduation, Albizu Campos became a fierce advocate of independence for Puerto Rico. After heavy surveillance by the authorities, and his claimed harassment by the Puerto Rican police force and the FBI, his separatist views had hardened.

It was a good time for that movement to prosper. The economy had stalled and the final crashing blow came with Hurricane *San Ciprián,* which struck the island in 1932, leaving 255 people dead, 3,000 people wounded, and 100,000 homeless, according to the island newspapers. The news accounts of the destruction were widespread and many became concerned with the future of the island they so dearly loved. Among those most concerned was the Roche Soler family.

Contrary to Margarita and Don Jacinto, Carlos had developed a more conservative view of the methods needed to cure the island's ills. He was worried, as well, with the improper path his son would take if he listened only to his mother. He observed that she had undergone a dramatic shift in her attitudes, now shunning the same people in society who she once wanted to be a part of. It was inexplicable. She refused to attend parties, galas, *quinceañeros* and other celebrations. She changed her wardrobe to simple dresses, used a bandana, wore almost no makeup, and sold her jewelry to donate the proceeds to the separatist movement. She dressed in a simple white blouse and black skirt, the colors of the Nationalist Party, when she went to their rallies.

Carlos had joined the Liberal Party and was especially impressed with one its leaders, the former reporter for *La Democracia*, Luis Muñoz Marín, son of Luis Muñoz Rivera. After the death of Muñoz Rivera, Carlos had worked directly for Muñoz Marín in researching various news articles for the newspaper.

The newspaper didn't embrace the politics of the Nationalists; it was a paper that was moderate in its editorials, yet sympathetic to independence. Carlos strongly opposed the political platform adopted by that party. While they were not yet advocating violence, he suspected that it was only a matter of time.

Carlos and Margarita were at the house on Atocha Street on his last visit. They had just finished a light lunch together, a rarity for them. Afterwards, he went into the garden, and she followed him.

A flash of lightning made them race back to the house.to escape an afternoon thundershower. At that point, he couldn't postpone the difficult conversation any longer. They were both dripping wet and he was drying himself. Without looking up he said.

"Why do you insist on taking Toñito to those meetings? He's too young to properly understand what is happening."

"How old was your father when he started his activism as an anarchist in Barcelona?" Margarita answered angrily.

"That was a different time and a different country. We have not been oppressed here like the Spaniards did to *Cataluña*."

"That's not true, look how the United States is treating us like a colony, with no voice or vote on our political future."

"I believe in independence as well, but not with the leaders you believe in. Luis Muñoz Marín sympathizes with the eventual independence of the island, as did his father before him, but he differs on the right path used to achieve that goal. He has vision and courage and more than that, he's practical, and faces reality when dealing with a giant like the United States."

"Muñoz is a demagogue, Carlos, and you can't see that." Her voice became shrill.

"And what will you do when Albizu starts advocating violence to fight the Americans and overthrow the local government?"

"He hasn't said that."

"Just give him time. Meanwhile, keep Toñito out of those meetings; it can only lead to bad results. If you choose to ignore my warnings, so be it, but I won't let you ruin his life. If I'm forced to, I will take him with me to Arecibo."

"The hell you will. We shall see who it is that will ruin his life. I know about your *puta* girlfriend," she said, as she left him standing on the porch.

It took him a moment to recover from her last remark, but when he thought about it, he really didn't care. He had already made his decision to be with María Antonia.

◆ ◆ ◆

Paula and Antonio were entertaining friends when Carlos showed up unannounced. He motioned to his mother that she should meet him in the kitchen. When she approached, he blurted out, "*Mamá,* I need to talk."

"What's wrong, son?"

Paula and Antonio had aged gracefully, she was now 75, but didn't reflect her true age.

The family had gained some wealth, surviving hard times on the island, and was settling into a comfortable retirement with no worries. So Carlos' agitated state unsettled her.

"I'm going to leave Margarita. Our marriage is over," he said.

"This isn't the first time you have said that, what makes this time different?"

"I finally have the courage to say it openly, I'm in love with another woman and have been so for years."

'Men do that sometimes, the answer is usually 'Don't leave your wife. No one will know'."

"This is not a sexual liaison. I want to marry María Antonia, you know that."

"Why now? You said you've had this feeling for years."

"Yes, but I won't live a lie for the rest of my days."

"Your father will be shocked and upset."

"Let me deal with that. Didn't he love you from afar for many years, before he finally proposed?"

Paula nodded and said, "Prepare yourself for a different reaction than mine".

Antonio spoke to Carlos after his guests had left, but his father remained silent at the news. He was 78 and retired, giving business advice to his son only when he needed it. He had no interest in politics anymore, or in other controversies, and would shy away from any possible scandal.

After Carlos left the mansion, he spoke to Paula. He had avoided a situation similar to one he would have had with Don Agustín in earlier times, but was still at a loss to understand his son's decision.

"He seems to have made up his mind on breaking up his family. How can he do that, especially at his age?"

"His family has been broken for many years, Antonio, but you ignored it."

"I don't understand why he would do that and create such conflict. Can't he have her as a mistress, like other men do?"

"She's not that kind of woman. Have you forgotten that chaos was your middle name when you were young? He's older than you were at the time, but life changes, and so do people."

♦ ♦ ♦

As if it were a gift from Washington D.C., in 1933 Congress ended Prohibition with the passage of the 21st Amendment to the Constitution,

Although it would take time to restart the production of rum in the Central, and get it to the markets, the repeal of that law provided a jolt to the local economy and to the sugarcane industry, in particular. The newspapers on the island ran the headline:

PROHIBITION ENDS TODAY, RUM IS KING ONCE MORE

Carlos returned to Arecibo to oversee the effort to restore production and return Cambalache to profitability. He would now spend even more time in Arecibo and San Juan, than in Ponce.

Earlier that year, Luis Muñoz Marín had been elected to the Puerto Rican Senate representing the Liberal Party. Also helpful to the island was the fact that Theodore Roosevelt, Jr., nephew of then President Franklin Delano Roosevelt, as appointed governor, brought fresh progressive ideas to running the colonial government. While Theodore Roosevelt was governor for only 18 months, he caught the ear of President Roosevelt and his wife, Eleanor, and suggested ways on how the U.S. could help improve the island's economy. The governor became friends with Luis Muñoz Marín and together they proposed ideas on legislation, which if approved by Congress, would help lift the island out of its desperate poverty.

Muñoz Marín consulted with both Antonio and Carlos Roche, and asked for their opinions on forthcoming legislation. They all had met the new governor at the welcoming reception for him at La Fortaleza, the mansion of the chief executive.

Clouds, however, were on the horizon. Labor troubles became inevitable with the near economic collapse of the island. A general strike was called in 1934, when food staples had doubled in price. By now, the Nationalist Party had adopted a plank in its platform calling for any means necessary, including armed insurrection, to rid the island of its colonial powers, something Carlos had predicted correctly. The violence started a year later.

Notwithstanding those problems, Carlos worked diligently to have his *Ron Borinquén* make a comeback, and the first year of production showed signs that his efforts might bear fruit, and that the industry would recover albeit slowly.

However, when he was called by Muñoz Marín to help organize a new political movement, he responded, though his days were full of activity at the sugar mill. Carlos went to the first meeting of the new party which would adopt as its name, the Popular Democratic Party, and featured in its white flag a red profile of a country peasant wearing a wide straw hat, with the slogan *Pan, Tierra, y Libertad* in red lettering surrounding the silhouette.

"I love the flag and the slogan of the new party," Carlos said to María Antonia, "It's inspirational and progressive, "Bread, Land, and Liberty!" He punched the air with his fist.

"To me, it sounds socialistic, like a Russian slogan," she answered.

Carlos groaned, not sure if she was teasing him. "I hope you are joking."

It was the same week that Carlos moved out of his home in Ponce and established permanent living quarters in Arecibo.

Chapter Twelve

Endings and Beginnings

Paula Soler dreamt of Barcelona in the spring, the grand boulevards, the *Passeig de Gracia,* and the strolls down *La Rambla de Cataluñya.* All was perfect in the world, she had Antonio and Carlos at her side. They were all young and beautiful, people smiled as they passed by and men tipped their hats. It was lovely to witness.

She envisioned the grand salons where couples danced to the rhythms of a *danza* and to local romantic ballads sung by a famous tenor. It all seemed so close and real; she could almost touch the singer and request another song. Antonio and her danced seamlessly through the night, never changing partners and never tiring.

Paula awoke to a strange odor from the medicines that the physician had given her to help break the fever. She then realized that her dream was caused by her delirious state. The doctor had used the word *dengue,* a mosquito- driven disease that could prove fatal if not treated by rest and proper medicine. She was 84, and had lived to see her grandchild, Toñito, grow up to be a handsome lad. A boy, who at 17, exhibited the best of his inherited genes, a wiry firm athletic frame, light reddish blond curly hair, and striking sky blue eyes.

She was proud of her young prince, and as her illness deepened and wouldn't release her from its grip, she kept on dreaming of Barcelona, and Toñito. Her stupor sometimes ended with the sound of a rifle shot that never failed to awaken her.

◆ ◆ ◆

Toñito managed to travel with the family chauffer to San Juan to see his grandmother, as often as his mother permitted. He would not stay long due to his studies and extracurricular activities, all managed by Margarita. Those activities often centered on the political events of the time. As such, he never had much quality time to spend with his grandparents, in particular Antonio, whom he worshipped.

His other grandfather, Don Jacinto Rodriguez, supported his mother's political militancy up to a certain point, but was smart enough to know that his financial backing of the Nationalist Party could negatively affect his business. Don Jacinto started disengaging himself from all of that party's activities. Upon the advice of friends, and the not so friendly advice of business associates and representatives of the government, he withdrew his entire financial support of the Nationalists. He resigned from its Board of Advisors and all organizations that had any ties to radical leftist movements including the Independence Now Party. He gave no reason for doing so.

Margarita didn't follow her father's example and continued her political activities, taking Toñito to all of the meetings of her favorite separatist groups. She joined the women's group known as the *Mujeres Para Independencia Ahora*, which wasn't formally affiliated with the Nationalist Party, but supported its goals of achieving independence.

Toñito admired his mother, but had a less of an emotional connection with his father who constantly warned him about her activities. Carlos had warned him of irreparable damage to his reputation if he wasn't careful. He didn't hide his displeasure from his son.

"Toñito, you are very young and the world seems ideal to you right now, but watch what you do. What you sow is what you'll reap; any criminal record that you create now will follow you as long as you live.

You have to recognize that once you are branded a radical, or a leftist, people won't forget. They will judge you by that label, not by whom you really are.

"*Papá,* I know what I'm doing. I want to live to see this island free from chains, and not give up as you and *abuelo* did."

"Who said I have given up? I'm just a realist. Given our current economic situation, this island cannot prosper, if we become a republic. And you must remember that *abuelo* paid a dear price for his beliefs when he was a young radical, much like you want to be. What you do now will close many doors in your future."

"Are you becoming a statehooder, or worse, a Republican like María Antonia?" Toñito said with disdain. He looked away from his father.

"No, the fact that I'm now with her has nothing to do with my politics. I believe that what Don Luis Muñoz Marín is trying to do for the island's future is the best practical solution, and--------"

"*Papá,* he has betrayed the cause of independence after supporting it for so long."

"That is not true," Carlos said. "Also, you should make an effort to get to know María Antonia, she will eventually be my wife and your stepmother." Toñito frowned at these last words. He had formed a negative opinion of María Antonia, based mostly on his mother's opinions.

These discussions left Carlos distraught; he could sense that he was losing his son. Toñito wouldn't listen to reason and he was trying his best not to lecture him, but rather to persuade him to follow a different path.

It was worse with Margarita. He had finally filed for divorce and she had accepted the end of their marriage with one condition. She had asked for full custody of Toñito. Carlos had refused. Their meetings, when he visited his family in Ponce, were full of acrimony.

"You have left the family home to be with that whore of a woman. She's one of those who would sell this country to the *gringos* for a few *pesos,* like Judas. She has no morals, dating a married man. "

"Margarita, you must stop talking like that. I fell in love with her before we were even married. I patiently waited for years to see if we could salvage our relationship. But you have changed into someone else."

An awkward silence followed.

"I want you to stop taking Toñito to all of your political gatherings. You can't force him to become like you, or have him adopt your ideals," Carlos said. "You are causing him harm. I beg of you to cease, not for my sake, but for his."

"I'm not forcing him to do anything, he can think for himself. He's a man now, and can make his own choices. Is that what your *puta* girlfriend wants for our son? To become like you, or even worse, betray his ideals?"

"You must not speak like that of María Antonia, she has nothing to do with this, and she has never done anything to you." Carlos raised his voice.

"Like hell, she hasn't. She stole you from us, your real family."

It would always end like this, whenever the subject was Toñito and his involvement in his mother's politics.

◆ ◆ ◆

María Antonia had accepted the fact that her future seemed tied to Carlos whether he was still legally married or not. His separation from his wife had helped her cope, but the divorce would take a long time, since Margarita would seek to prolong it with all the tools at her disposal. She had accused María Antonia of adultery and of engineering the breakup of her marriage. She had also sent her nasty letters. When referring to her in public, she used all sorts of unkind words and adjectives laced with explicitly foul language.

María Antonia took all of this in stride, trying her best to ignore her. She focused on her multiple responsibilities with the Oller companies and had encouraged Carlos to invest in other projects when the sugarcane industry was on its deathbed. Although the end of Prohibition had opened a new source of income for Cambalache, the industry of the future seemed to be cement production. Her Uncle Lorenzo was pivotal in convincing Carlos to invest in the new business.

Don Lorenzo Oller had learned from his colleagues. They had a vision that the construction of homes and buildings in a modern Puerto Rico would have to be made of reinforced cement, to withstand the fury of the hurricanes that often battered the island's shores. He had established a small cement plant on the outskirts of Salinas and named it, Cemento Oller and Cía. It proved to be a successful experiment. In less than a year, profits from this new industry duplicated Carlos's initial investment in the plant.

Carlos entered into direct competition with Don Jacinto in Ponce, who had begun plans to convert his entire company to cement production. As this conflict with the Rodríguez family increased, the family had already pulled out their money from Cambalache when Carlos separated from Margarita. Their business interests were no longer aligned. Adversarial actions were unavoidable.

♦ ♦ ♦

Paula was dreaming again, but this time the dream ended with death, and she cried out for her grandson. She saw him covered with blood and screamed his name repeatedly. No, this wasn't possible; it was a nightmare from the past, from the street battles of Barcelona, not from the present. *Please God, make this go away* she prayed, and hoped He would listen. There was only tragedy in her visions, no music, and no gaiety.

The nurse that had been hired to care for Paula ran to her bedside and found her in extreme distress. Paula mumbled a few words in her delirious state.

"Where am I?"

"Doña Paula, you are at home, you are sick, Please try to sleep," the nurse said.

"Who are you?"

"You are in your home in San Juan, *Señora*."

"But I was in Barcelona, why am I still here?" She tried to rise from the bed.

"You are very sick, please lie down."

The nurse was concerned and went to seek Antonio, who was frail but still had mobility. He was sleeping in another bedroom.

Antonio awoke, put on a robe and went to Paula's side. Her hair was grayish brown, with some speckles of white, but her pride in her appearance kept it well groomed. Her face, though wrinkled, reflected a light shade of blush on her cheeks. The lips had pink gloss on them; even while sick she made sure she had on sufficient makeup. Her countenance was the one he remembered from their first encounter at the Soler mansion in Barcelona. He put his hand on her forehead and felt the warmness of her brow. He bent over her and kissed her, touching the bun that was tied with tresses of her long hair. Antonio looked at her strained efforts at breathing and realized the end was near. The Catalonian beauty, the flirt, the debutante, the lover, the wife, the mother, and grandmother was letting go of life with each passing breath. Their days together were coming to a close and Antonio was prepared.

They had married, and while he may not have been deeply in love with her at the beginning, his affection for her had transformed itself over the years. She had borne a son out of wedlock, two children of their own, and had truly become the love of his life.

Earlier that day, Antonio had gone to his library and in an old wooden chest had retrieved his diary from his prison days at Montjuic. In it, he had written that all he desired in life was to find true happiness, regardless of whether he became rich or not. The entry was written in late 1871, and now over 60 years later, he reread it and realized that his dreams had come true. He had found his soul mate in Paula.

"Paula, try to rest, I'm sure you will feel better tomorrow," he said, holding her left hand and kissing it. She didn't answer, and turned her head on the pillow and smiled at him. She then emitted a soft sigh, as her arm went limp in Antonio's hands. He kissed her lips for the very last time.

After few minutes alone with her, Antonio called his valet and asked him to contact Cambalache, and inform Carlos of his mother's death. As he stood up from her side, he noticed a small envelope tucked beneath her pillow. It was addressed to Carlos. He opened it.

> *Carlitos:*
>
> *By the time you read this, I may be gone. You were my first child and my love for you knew no limits. And it is that love that brings me to write you this last note about the truth of your birth. The priest you met so many years ago, Father Cervera, was your natural father. I'm deeply sorry that I waited so long to tell you, but I was embarrassed and didn't know whether you would ever understand or if the truth would ever help you. Antonio loves you as much as I do, and he raised you as his own son. He is your real father as I'm sure you know. Please find it in your heart to forgive me.*
> *Te amo, hijo querido*
> *Mamá*

Paula's funeral was a simple affair, as she had requested. She was cremated and half her ashes were buried at the Municipal cemetery in old San Juan. The other half was shipped to Barcelona to be buried in the Soler family plot. A small cameo of her at age 17 was placed on each of the tombstones. Inscribed was the word Barcelona, followed by the date of her birth, and next the word Borinquén, next to her date of death. She had loved those two places immensely.

◆ ◆ ◆

The Nationalist Party sponsored a student strike at the University of Puerto Rico in 1935, in which various student groups united to protest the policies of the University administration. The marches and protests had a definitive political tone to them, since most of the protesters were sympathetic to the independence movement on the island, and many were members of one political movement or another that shared those ideals. There were news items of the strike in the local papers on a daily basis.

In one incident, several protesters traveling in a vehicle on the avenue in front of the University of Puerto Rico were stopped by the police and an argument erupted. Shots were fired and four of the occupants of the vehicle were killed. When the news spread, there were more angry protests, and the marchers claimed that the students in the car had been assassinated.

The police claimed self -defense and based their version on oral statements by participants, which said that the occupants of the car were armed. No evidence of this fact ever surfaced. Those policemen involved in the killing were never arrested or brought to trial to face charges. Both major newspapers *El Imparcial* and *El Mundo* were relentless in their coverage of the events.

Margarita called the incident a massacre of innocent students and rallied with her fellow independence sympathizers in marches against the government and the police. Margarita spoke to her son privately.

"Do you see what has begun, my son? They are out to kill us, and will not stop until we are all in jail or dead."

"But *Mamá,* why are they doing this?"

"Because they see us as a threat to the established order. They want to crush our yearning for freedom."

"What are we going to do?" Toñito asked.

"Our time will come, and the population will rise up and join our cause. Never fear, Toñito. You are part of the next generation that will fight to set us free."

Toñito could detect the desperation in his mother and wondered what his father would say about the events.

Speculation was rampant, with some government sources claiming that the Independence Party, and the Nationalists, had staged the entire incident. Both these organizations denied any involvement. Carlos after reading the newspaper accounts didn't know what to think.

In the aftermath of the killings of the university students, one evening two men ambushed the Chief of Police, Colonel Riggs, and murdered him. Once word got out, the police initiated a manhunt and quickly found and arrested two suspects, who they claimed had murdered Riggs. Their guilt was never proven, since the two men were shot to death in a police station in Old San Juan days later, as reported in the press. None of these events were ever subject to any official investigation or to court proceedings.

Deep anxiety enveloped the Roche family since they could not foresee a peaceful resolution of the conflict between the Nationalist Party and the Puerto Rican government. The latter was now led by Gov. Blanton Winship, a former U.S. Army General and a Washington appointee.

Don Antonio said to Carlos, "Expect more violence, more tragedy. I have given my notice of resignation from the Executive Council."

"I'm sorry father that it has come to this; you were a voice of reason there."

"My resignation means nothing to them. I've been told that the situation will deteriorate badly and that the government is out to crush the Nationalists and their sympathizers, by whatever means necessary. That means more bloodshed."

Carlos could feel the hairs rise on his neck and a shiver ran throughout his body as he thought of Toñito.

This conversation precipitated another visit by Carlos to Ponce. He went there and when he saw his son, he implored him to stop his political activities. His mother, now a member of the Daughters of Liberty, a women's offshoot of the Nationalist Party, had Toñito sign up to join the Cadets of the Republic, its youth wing.

"Hijo mío, please listen to me. One thing is to sympathize with the ideal of independence, which I still do, and another is to militate in a movement that preaches armed revolution. It's a dangerous game your mother is playing and once you are marked, you will have the government spying on all of your movements. Just ask *Abuelo* Antonio what it was like for him when he lived in Barcelona."

"*Papá*, it's not like that. I would never harm anyone. Think of it more like a Boy Scout movement, *Boricua* style."

"That's not humorous, and you're playing with fire. You'll get burned."

"No one in the Cadets is armed. We're just a youth club supporting the adults. We even have our own uniform, a black shirt with white pants and a medieval cross symbol sewn on our sleeves. No one is taught to fire weapons or make bombs. Those are all lies that the police spreads. We use only fake wooden rifles when we march."

At this moment, Margarita entered the room and overheard the last part of the conversation. She walked over to Toñito and put her arm around his shoulders.

"What is going on, what you are saying to our son?" she said, facing Carlos with a defiant glare.

"I'm saying that this little game of yours is going to extract a dear price on this family. We will become outcasts in Puerto Rican society, the same society you so dearly wanted to be part of."

"That's all in the past. I see now how foolish I was then, and don't want Toñito or Ana to follow the same path."

"If anything happens to our son, you will be the only one to blame. I will never forgive you or let you forget it."

"So be it," she said. She put her arm around Toñito and led him from the room, not giving him a chance to say goodbye.

◆ ◆ ◆

The governor's palace of La Fortaleza received word of a march to be held by the Nationalists in Ponce on March 21, 1937. Gov.Winship instructed the new Chief of Police in San Juan to stop the march at all costs. He said that the event would not be a celebration of the Emancipation of Slavery

as the Nationalists claimed, but a paramilitary march, thus making it il-
legal. These instructions were forwarded to the mayor and police chief in
Ponce. That Sunday also happened to be Palm Sunday on the Christian
calendar.

The Nationalist leadership told the mayor that they did not have to request a permit to hold the march since it was not a political one, however,
they applied for a permit anyway. The mayor of Ponce was on vacation at
the time, and they were told that the permit couldn't be granted until he
returned. At that point, the authorities believed that they had avoided the
challenge presented by the Nationalists. Each step of the process was
published in the newspapers.

When the mayor returned to Ponce, however, he granted the permit.
Once Governor Winship was notified, he instructed an emissary to go to
Ponce and tell the mayor to revoke it. This was just a few days before the
scheduled march and the emissary was told that it was too late, but that
the mayor might try to convince the party leaders to suspend the march.
There was also pressure from the Catholic Church to revoke the permit
due to Holy Week. The mayor finally relented.

El Mundo, the newspaper, reported the revocation and it increased
the tension among the population of the Ponce community and local authorities. No tension was greater than the one felt by Carlos when he read
the news. He made a special trip to Ponce, three days before the scheduled march, hoping to bring Toñito back to Arecibo.

"I'm saying to you that you must not march on Sunday," Carlos said
to Toñito in the presence of Margarita.

"He's already committed to the group and pulling him out would show
a sign of cowardice and lack of will." Margarita interjected.

"There could be violence, have you thought about that?" He was facing his son.

"I'm not afraid," Toñito said, "They would never shoot children."

"He's right, who would give the order to shoot unarmed peaceful
marchers, especially those of his age," Margarita said in agreement, but
she hesitated before continuing. "Nothing will happen, *nada*."

Carlos tried again, but was unable to persuade Margarita to have Toñito withdraw from the Cadet march. He even attempted to convince Toñito to go back home with him for a short holiday, but he refused. Carlos blamed himself for not having more influence over his son, a direct result of his absences. He considered staying until Sunday, but pressing business in Arecibo made it impractical. He had to rely on Margarita, who said at the last minute, that she would go to the parade as well.

Carlos couldn't make Margarita doubt the wisdom of letting Toñito march in the event. There was a calculated risk to all the participants since the police had said they were going to try to stop the parade at any cost. He explained this to her to no avail.

♦ ♦ ♦

Sunday morning was a bright day under the tropical spring sun. A light breeze carried the scent of bougainvilleas and gardenias planted in the flower boxes of homes along the streets of Ponce. March happened to be one of the coolest months on the island. Margarita tried to feel optimistic about the events of the day. *We will show them that the people are united against police brutality and the despotic regime.*

People gathered near the main office of the Nationalist Party just off the corner of Aurora and Marína Street, in the center of town. They waited for the march to begin. More than 10,000 spectators were present on the streets of Ponce that morning.

What Margarita and Toñito didn't know was that a force of 150 policemen and soldiers, many of whom had come from San Juan at the request of the Governor and would reinforce the local policemen who were standing alongside the spectators. Dressed in khaki uniforms, they aligned themselves in rows along the parade route, armed with semi-automatic rifles and Thompson submachine guns.

Toñito joined the Cadets of the Republic, all 80 of them, who took their positions in a formation that would march down Aurora Street. He placed himself in the third row of marchers directly behind the flag bearer.

The mayor's efforts to stop the march had failed. Toñito observed that one of the municipal officials tried one last time to persuade them to abandon the protest. The official was unsuccessful, and then a police ieutenant, following orders given by his superiors, strode to the front line of marchers and ordered them to disband. He was met with angry stares and verbal protests from the cadets. At that point, there was a standoff and a deafening silence. No one knew what would happen next. The national anthem of Puerto Rico was played by the cadet band and a few moments later, the march began upon the orders of the lead cadet. A police sergeant, in an unwise and hasty attempt to scare the cadets, fired his pistol into the air. Mayhem erupted.

As Toñito watched, the policemen and soldiers that lined both sides of the street opened fire on the unarmed marchers, in a wild and disorganized manner, each policeman shooting at will. He ducked, fell down and stayed on his knees for a few minutes, then felt a sharp sting in his neck.

On the ground he laid, a stray bullet had severed his carotid artery and he was bleeding profusely. Attempts to arrest the remaining cadets were futile at first, since many of them scattered in different directions. Some wounded marchers, who made the mistake of returning to their home base soon after the shooting, were arrested by the police in pursuit,and a few of them were killed. Those that tried to find shelter in nearby homes were pulled out of those houses by police and executed on the spot. Bystanders, who played no part in the march, had also been shot in the back while fleeing the scene. Blood covered the sidewalks and street gutters. By the time the order to stop firing was given, 15 minutes later, 19 cadets had been killed by gunfire and more than 100 people had been wounded, including cadets, bystanders, and small children. Two policemen were killed in the crossfire by their own comrades. A massacre had occurred.

Margarita Rodríguez had not gone to the march with her son. She had demurred saying she didn't feel well. Later, fearing she would be branded a coward for sending her son alone, she left her home and walked quickly to the parade route. She heard the gunshots and started running in their direction. When she arrived at the scene, the stench of burning flesh and gunpowder overwhelmed her. She couldn't find Toñito at first, but finally she saw him as he lay crumpled on the ground beside a wall which bordered the sidewalk. His reddish blond hair was stained with blood, as were his white pants. Just as a soldier was approaching Toñito to apparently finish him off, she ran to her son, threw her body over his, and turned upwards to face the man.

"You will have to shoot me first, you coward. I'm Margarita Rodríguez, a close friend of the mayor," she screamed, "And this is my son, *Asesino!*"

The man stopped, looked at her, raised his rifle and then turned away. She rolled Toñito over, and saw him drenched in blood, barely breathing. She looked up. The words *"Libertad"* had been placed on the wall by his own hand. They were written in blood.

"Toñito, what have they done to you?" Margarita cried. The stricken cadet tried to answer, but his mouth was full of liquid and the only sound she heard was a gurgle. He could not form words to speak to her.

"Please stay still; I will seek medical help." She shouted at some passers-by to get a doctor, but no one responded. At this point, Toñito was losing consciousness and she could not leave him. As she tried to stem the blood flow with her white cotton shawl, which had turned a deep red color, Margarita realized that her son was dying and could not be saved.

What have I done? I fought for an ideal and at the last minute I weakened. I placed Toñito in mortal danger and I have reaped the consequences. How stupid could I be? Carlos had warned me that something bad might happen. Now I have lost the one person whom I truly loved. I should have been shot, not him. She trembled and cried as her grief overcame her, and buried her head in his chest.

Toñito expired in her arms, but just before dying he whispered in a weak voice,

"Mami. le dices a Papá que me perdone."

*   *   *

Enlargements of black and white photographs of the massacre appeared the next day on the front pages of all the island newspapers.

Massacre in Ponce, Police kill Cadets and Spectators

News photographers had captured the gruesome aftermath of the shootings. One photograph depicted a policeman firing into the back of a fleeing spectator, who wasn't even a participant. Coverage of the slaughter was extensive; the news reached the mainland.

Both Congress and President Roosevelt launched investigations into the massacre. As for Governor Winship, he never apologized for his acts notwithstanding that the responsibility for the Ponce Massacre laid squarely on him, even though there was plenty of blame to share. One result of the investigation was Governor Winship's eventual dismissal as Governor of Puerto Rico, albeit two years later. The supervisors in the Puerto Rican Police Department, who were responsible for the use of force against the cadets and spectators, were fired. But not one single person was arrested or prosecuted for manslaughter. .

Pedro Albizu Campos, the Nationalist leader, had previously been convicted of sedition by the local U.S. District Court, well before these events happened and could not logically be blamed for provoking the massacre, since he was in a stateside prison. That didn't stop his political opponents from accusing him of planning the march and the resulting consequences. In essence, the local authorities argued that the cadets were responsible for their own deaths.

Carlos read the edition of *El Imparcial* that next morning. His initial shock at reading the name of his son among those listed as fatalities gave way to anger. Had he been in the presence of Margarita at that same moment, he might have done something he would have regretted for the rest of his life. He took his vehicle and without informing anyone drove to Ponce. After the long drive, he arrived at the corner of Aurora Street, not far from the site of the massacre.

He found many roadways still blocked by police and was able to reach his house only after persuading a police officer that he lived on the same street and that his family needed him. He showed his press pass of *La Democracia*. His name was known in the community and the officer finally let him pass. Blood stains were still on the walls of houses, fences, and on the street pavement as he drove by.

At his home he found most of the windows shuttered and the front door locked. He had no key with him but managed to go to the back of the residence and entered through the kitchen door reserved for the help. No one was in the parlor. He went to the main bedroom and saw Margarita prostrated on the bed, sobbing. His desire to scream at her and blame her for Toñito's death was suppressed by the sight of her deep despair. Her dress was drenched in Carlitos' blood.

"Margarita, it's me," he said softly.

"I suppose you came to tell me that you were right, and that it's my fault this happened. You blame me for Toñito's death, and you're right."

He remained silent. He had no doubt that Margarita loved Toñito as much as he did, however, this was not the moment to accuse her of blind, stupid, and misguided conduct.

"I came to be with you, and help you through this. I know you loved him. "After a pause he said, "I want Ana to come with me to Arecibo for a period of time, until the impact of this tragedy has subsided."

"You want me to be alone?"

"It will be better for all concerned, Margarita. You have your parents."

"I'm so sorry Carlos, I acted stupidly, and I'll never be able to forgive myself," she said, as she broke down again. He eyes welled up.

Carlos could never forgive her. He would try to keep his daughter in Arecibo even if it meant having to sue for custody. But that could wait.

He noticed that Don Jacinto and Dona Adelaida had not come to the house yet, and he anticipated an awkward reunion with them and wanted to avoid a confrontation. They would find no fault in their daughter, even though they had also warned her of the dire consequences of enrolling Toñito in the Cadets. Carlos left the house and checked himself into at a small hotel in front of the main square in Ponce, while he awaited preparations for the funeral of his only son.

◆ ◆ ◆

Vicente read the newspaper coverage and felt the urge to visit Don Antonio in San Juan to give his condolences, and later would try to see Carlos in Arecibo. His telephone calls to each of them were unsuccessful; no one answered. The last time they had talked was when his coffee farm loan had been approved.

As he was thinking of his options, his son, Gregorio, offered to take him to either city if he chose to go. Vicente thanked him and said he would think it over. A tragedy such as this one called for a personal visit. A letter would not suffice. Don Antonio, his benefactor, was in his late eighties. Vicente imagined that the news of the violent death of his grandchild might be enough to cause him to have a stroke.

He planned to travel by train to San Juan. On his return trip he would make a layover in Arecibo, once he had confirmed that Carlos Roche was back at Cambalache. His relationship with Belén was on the mend, and when she saw the grief in his face, she encouraged him to go. Vicente had made many mistakes in his life, but one of his enduring virtues was of loyalty to those that had helped him. His poor judgment in Rosalina's affair had cost him seven years of his life, but the Solers had not held that against him, and had helped him when he needed it most.

Vicente arrived in San Juan three days after the massacre and went directly to *El Condado* where Don Antonio lived. In the foyer as he entered the mansion, he saw Antonio's collection of swords and artwork from famous Spanish painters, including a Picasso that hung on one wall. An oil painting of Paula, which dated from her 21st birthday, hung on another wall in a prominent place. Its lifelike effect made him imagine that the young woman depicted in the canvass would step out of the frame and greet him.

He contemplated the artwork and waited.

"Don Antonio," he said, as his friend approached, "I'm here to give you my deepest condolences on the loss of Toñito, and of course, on the death of Doña Paula."

Antonio walked in with a cane and measured steps, embraced Vicente and wouldn't let go. He had tears in his eyes when he looked at his former plant manager of long ago.

"I can't tell you that I know how you feel, because I don't, and hope I never will," Vicente said.

"The death of a young man like Toñito doesn't make sense. He was just beginning his life, there was so much ahead for him. Now, it's suddenly cut off,"

Antonio replied. "First, the passing of Paula, and now this." They both sat down.

"I hope that you believe in a superior being, it may give you some consolation and help you with your pain."

"Now I do, not when I was young. The sad thing is that I didn't spend enough time with Toñito. The distance didn't help, and his mother always had plans for her son that interfered with him coming to visit us."

"I would like to be of some assistance to you. I place myself at your service." He saw Antonio choking up.

"*Gracias*, Vicente, but your presence here is enough. I would like you to stay for a couple of days. Can you accompany me to Toñito's funeral in Ponce?"

"I would consider it an honor, Don Antonio."

After a while, and after some coffee had been served to them, Vicente said,

"By the way, do you have a copy of yesterday's *El Mundo*? I have been told that a notice appeared concerning the death of a former friend of mine."

"I do. I was going to ask you about it." Antonio looked for the newspaper and when he found it, handed it to him.

"Yes. Here is the obituary of Félix Hidalgo Prats," Vicente said.

El Mundo, Tuesday, 23rd of March 1937
Sr. Félix Hidalgo Prats, Marqués de Arecibo, died yesterday at Nuestra Señora de la Providencia Asylum in Puerta de Tierra, at age 74. No funeral arrangements have been announced.

"Did you know this Hidalgo Prats? Carlos mentioned his death and that he once worked for you at Cambalache."

"Yes, he did. At one time we were very close. We both came over from Barcelona on the same ship; he was a friend from my home town of Tossa del Mar. He chose a different path for himself. I tried to help him, but once he strayed, he never really recovered enough to lead an honest life. He became a thief yet I was the one who went to prison. Isn't that ironic?"

"That notice in *El Mundo*, announced his death in a pauper's asylum. It's managed by nuns."

"He must have paid to have his death published so he could use his title, Marqués of Arecibo. Was he really a Marqués?" Antonio asked.

"That title was a fake; he paid a large sum of *pesetas* for title documents which were forged to make it appear he was of noble birth. He then added Arecibo to his title. Félix was in fact a *desgraciado*."

Vicente wondered if the monies Félix had paid for the news obituary came from the stolen funds of his coffee farm.

"After I spoke to Carlos, I happened to call the shelter to inquire about him, and a nun there, a Sister Priscilla, told me that during the last months of his life, an elderly woman spent many days by his side, several times a week. She didn't remember the full name of the woman, but she remembered the man him calling her.......... Natalia."

◆ ◆ ◆

Toñito Roche's funeral was attended by people of all political persuasions. While Carlos forbade the showing of any symbols or flags of the

Nationalist party, or the wearing of their uniforms, he allowed members and families of the slain cadets to witness the burial. The only music played was classical and at the conclusion, the *Borinqueña*, the anthem of Puerto Rico. While the rainy season was common in March, the deluge that fell on the ceremony was unexpected and forced the funeral to be a brief one, due to the scarcity of shelter from the pouring rains. It was an appropriate setting for the internment. Carlos, with María Antonia at his side, gave the eulogy. Margarita stood with her parents on the opposite side of the casket, which was draped with the Puerto Rican flag. The priest gave the closing benediction and thanked all for coming.

Carlos and María Antonia, who were now planning to get married after his divorce was final, walked away from the burial site, without bidding farewell to the Rodriquez family. Ana Roche, now an adolescent, left with her father after kissing her mother goodbye.

The loss of Toñito only intensified in María Antonia the feeling that life was short and precious. She had met him on a few occasions, but he had been cool and distant with her, speaking only a few words in her presence. She knew that it wasn't his fault; he was probably complying with his mother's wishes.

After the funeral, she had labored to help Carlos deal with his trauma. He had some good moments, recalling how smart Toñito had been, but had many sorrowful memories regarding the manner in which his son had met his maker.

♦ ♦ ♦

Carlos and María Antonia had no children of their own since they had gotten married when she was past the normal age for childbirth. She wished she could have been a mother, but was happy to have married the only man she had ever loved.

The years passed and María Antonia Vivoni Oller achieved many of her goals. She occupied an important position in the Republican Party, and was in charge of the women's wing of that organization. She fought for the women's right to vote and several years earlier, in 1929, she had helped the movement achieve that significant first step. Women's Suffrage had been approved by the local legislature, but it was limited only to women who could read and write. This oversight was corrected by subsequent legislation in 1935, when suffrage was granted to all women in Puerto Rico, regardless of literacy.

A year after his son's death, Carlos flung himself headfirst into making sure that the new Popular Democratic Party would succeed at the polls, and perhaps unite the politically divided island for the good its people. This gave new purpose to his life.

When the PDP adopted its slogan, *Pan, Tierra, y Libertad*, it was accused of being a socialist party in disguise, just as María had predicted in a joking fashion. Its support for land reform scared the oligarchy of the island, the landholders who owned thousands of acres of farmland. Many of these acres lay fallow and unproductive, at a time when hunger was widespread. The Popular Democrats took advantage of prevailing winds in Washington, where President Roosevelt facilitated an economic recovery for the island by sponsoring legislation. It provided for rural electrification, housing, schools, and construction of new buildings made to withstand the force of hurricanes. The law also provided a bonanza for the cement factories in Puerto Rico and that spurred renewed growth.

Carlos had profited from the legislation with his business growing in importance and size. In this, he had the support of María Antonia, who was also a reformer, a bit out of sync with her fellow Republicans. She took charge of Oller Enterprises and became one of the most prominent business women on the island. The dreams of her mother, Isabel Oller, lived on, as she vicariously viewed the achievements of her daughter as her own. Isabel had lived long enough to cast her first vote.

♦ ♦ ♦

Antonio Roche died in his sleep at the age of 89. He had requested that he be buried in the cemetery in Old San Juan, next to Paula, in the family crypt. The obituary in the San Juan newspapers featured an article on all his contributions to Puerto Rican society from the turn of the century until 1940. In his honor, the mayor of Arecibo named a plaza in that town, Plaza Antonio Roche, and commissioned a bust to be placed in its center. Carlos donated the funds to have this bust include twin plaques of the flags of Cataluña and Puerto Rico. At the dedication in Arecibo, Carlos gave a short eulogy.

"My father was a good and decent man, a wonderful father and devoted husband. He lived a life of challenges, triumphs and disappointments, but he never gave up. Do not be sad for him, he lived a rich full life and died peacefully in bed, surrounded by his loved ones. As those plaques reflect, **Barcelona-Borinquén** were the two lands he truly loved, just like Paula, my mother."

"While all the news articles and obituaries of Don Antonio have contained facts relative to his immigration to the island from Barcelona," Carlos added, "None of them have stated that he gave up his Spanish citizenship in order to serve on the Executive Council of the insular government. It was a personal sacrifice he made in order to serve his fellow Puerto Ricans."

The ceremony ended with the playing of the island's national anthem and with a "*sardana*" a popular folk dance from Cataluña.

Carlos had in his pocket the note left by Paula on her death bed. He had read it and felt now, as he had then, that it really didn't matter. In reality, Antonio had always been his father.

♦ ♦ ♦

Carlos finally saw his political dreams realized. The Popular Democratic Party (PDP), the one he had helped found, along with many other Puerto Rican leaders, won its first island wide election in 1940, and had promised a new beginning for the island with a charted path to economic recovery. Luis Muñoz Marín had become a leader with a vision, a man who gave up his ideal of an Independent Puerto Rico, a topic which had consumed much debate and created so much division in island politics. He had now adopted the idea of a Commonwealth relationship with the United States, and emphasized that the status of the island was not an issue of overriding importance, as was poverty and economic recovery.

The PDP won a majority of the municipalities in the island, and a majority in the Senate as part of its electoral victory. It was a mandate for change, one that could not be diluted. The party had earned the support of voters of most political persuasions.

Carlos was jubilant. He was a senior member of the newly victorious political entity but personally did not harbor any political aspirations. He was content to see a peaceful revolution, one that would change the island's future for many generations to come.

"We did it, it's the dawn of a new era, and I only wish that *Papá* and *Mamá* could have lived a little longer to see this. I'm sure they would have been joyous."

"They both are happy in heaven, watching us," María Antonia said.

She joined with him in celebration. Their time had come.

Sources

1- Barcelona, Robert Hughes, 1993, Vintage Books, a division of Random House

2- Museo de la Historia de Catalunya, Barcelona, Spain, 3rd Floor. On different occasions I spent hours at this magnificent museum, where the history of the country is organized by separate floors

3- Puerto Rico, A Political and Cultural History, Arturo Morales Carrión and Others, 1983, W.W. Norton and Company, Inc.

4- Puerto Rico, Cinco Siglos de Historia, 2nds Edición, Francisco A. Scarano, 2000, McGraw-Hill Companies, Inc.

5- Puerto Rico en el Siglo Americano desde 1898, Cesar Ayala y Rafael Bernabe, 2011, Libros El Navegante, Inc., Ediciones Callejón

6- Borinquen is the Taino Indian word for Puerto Rico

Acknowledgments

I am forever grateful to all the persons that helped me achieve this life-long goal, to write a historical fiction book about the contributions of the Catalonians, other Spaniards, Criollos (Native born Puerto Ricans), and Americans to the transformation of the island of Puerto Rico from a poor agrarian society to a modern industrialized country.

Foremost among these persons were my two editors, Gabriella Lessa from Brazil, and Mary Carroll Moore, from Massachusetts, a teacher at Grubb Street in Boston and an author herself. To all my other instructors at Grubb Street, and at the Muse and the Marketplace Writers' Conferences in Boston, my undying thanks. My appreciation as well to all the fellow writers at the Writers' Loft in Sherborn Massachusetts, who put up with my questions and gave me the valuable feedback I needed for getting my story published.

My close friends and family served as Beta Readers to help make this a better narrative during the many years it took to finalize. I'm indebted to Ana Luz, my wife, critic, and personal editor who was relentless and to Rafy Cortes, Carol Lach, Carlos Marin, David Morales, and Jorge Velez, each of whom contributed wise advice for revisions. I cannot imagine how I will ever repay all their efforts to help make this book more interesting. My deepest thanks to my lifelong friend, Antonio Monroig, who shared stories with me of persons he has known which inspired a few of my fictional characters.